NO PROMISES

A BAD BOY BILLIONAIRE ROMANCE

MICHELLE LOVE

HOT AND STEAMY ROMANCE

CONTENTS

About the Author — vii
Sign Up to Receive Free Books — ix

Blurb — 1
1. Chapter One — 3
2. Chapter Two — 14
3. Chapter Three — 20
4. Chapter Four — 28
5. Chapter Five — 33
6. Chapter Six — 40
7. Chapter Seven — 46
8. Chapter Eight — 53
9. Chapter Nine — 61
10. Chapter Ten — 68
11. Chapter Eleven — 78
12. Chapter Twelve — 88
13. Chapter Thirteen — 92
14. Chapter Fourteen — 100
15. Chapter Fifteen — 104
16. Chapter Sixteen — 111
17. Chapter Seventeen — 119
18. Chapter Eighteen — 130
19. Chapter Nineteen — 134
20. Chapter Twenty — 140
21. Chapter Twenty-One — 147
22. Chapter Twenty-Two — 153
23. Chapter Twenty-Three — 159
24. Chapter Twenty-Four — 163
25. Chapter Twenty-Five — 168
26. Chapter Twenty-Six — 175
27. Chapter Twenty-Seven — 181
28. Chapter Twenty-Eight — 184
29. Chapter Twenty-Nine — 191

30. Chapter Thirty		197
Sign Up to Receive Free Books		201
Preview of Please Me		202
Chapter One		204
Chapter Two		216
Chapter Three		225
Chapter Four		235
Chapter Five		242
Other Books By This Author		253
About the Author		257
Copyright		259

Made in "The United States by:

Michelle Love

© Copyright 2020 – Michelle Love

ISBN: 978-1-64808-088-3

ALL RIGHTS RESERVED. No part of this publication may be reproduced or transmitted in any form whatsoever, electronic, or mechanical, including photocopying, recording, or by any informational storage or retrieval system without express written, dated and signed permission from the author

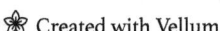 Created with Vellum

ABOUT THE AUTHOR

Mrs. Love writes about smart, sexy women and the hot alpha billionaires who love them. She has found her own happily ever after with her dream husband and adorable 6 and 2 year old kids.

Currently, Michelle is hard at work on the next book in the series, and trying to stay off the Internet.

"Thank you for supporting an indie author. Anything you can do, whether it be writing a review, or even simply telling a fellow reader that you enjoyed this. Thanks

Facebook
   facebook.com/HotAndSteamyRomance

SIGN UP TO RECEIVE FREE BOOKS

Sign Up to Receive Free E-Books and Audiobook Codes.

Would you like to read **The Unexpected Nanny, Dirty Little Virgin** and **other romance books for free**?

You can sign up to receive these free e-books and audiobooks by typing this link into your browser:

https://www.steamyromance.info/free-books-and-audiobooks-hot-and-steamy/

Or this one:

https://www.steamyromance.info/the-unexpected-nanny-free/

BLURB

English grad student Anoushka 'Noosh' Taylor is working as a junior reporter for a successful New York City radio network under the mentorship of her heroine, Allison Monroe. On the cusp of producing her first big story, an exposé of New York's BDSM club scene, Noosh is issued a challenge to go the extra mile and attend a club to see for herself. Summoning her courage, she finds herself caught up in a moment she can't escape with a devastatingly handsome man, and after being humiliated by him, she leaves in tears, vowing never to return.

Angry and hurt, Noosh drops the piece but cannot stop thinking about her almost lover.

When they decide to do a piece on the most eligible bachelor in New York, Noosh is thrown into the path of Christofalo Montecito, playboy and son of organized crime boss, Fogliano Montecito. Christo is gorgeous, brooding, sensual – and the man who humiliated her at the BDSM club.

Noosh reacts badly, but when Christo apologizes, she begins to see a different side of him. Soon, their mutual attraction grows, and Noosh finds herself falling for Christo – but can a son of a crime boss ever be reliable, trustworthy?

When dark secrets from both of their pasts reveal themselves, Noosh and Christo have to decide whether their attraction is more than just a casual thing, and discover just how far they will go to save it.

Can Noosh give him the trust he has yet to earn? Or will Christo reveal himself to be his father's son?

CHAPTER ONE

Long Island, New York

CHRISTOFALO MONTECITO STARED at his father in astonishment. He *couldn't* be taking Christo's news this easily. *Nuh-uh, no way.* "Dad, you understand what I'm telling you?"

Fogliano Montecito gazed back at his son with the same brilliant green eyes he had bestowed on his only child. "Christo, do I look like an idiot? You want out of my business, that's the crux of the matter, right?"

Christo hesitated. "Right. Look, Dad, it's not as if I haven't mentioned this before, and I'm almost forty now, and it's time. I've given you the last seventeen years, all my time after college."

"College that my business paid for."

Here we go. "Yes, Dad, and I'm grateful for it, don't get me wrong. But I need to make my own way...and some aspects of the family business don't sit easily with me."

Fogliano held up his hands. "Enough. Christo, you must do

what you think is right, what is appropriate." He sighed and pushed back from his desk, standing and clapping his son on the back. "Now, you'll still be coming to the meal tonight?"

Christo, still stunned, nodded. "Sure, Dad."

"Good. Now, I have to get back to work. You can see yourself out?"

"Of course. See you later."

CHRISTO NODDED to his father's personal assistant, Mandy, who simpered at him. Christo tried not to roll his eyes and instead gave her a polite smile. At thirty-eight, with his father's Italian good looks and devastating smile, Christofalo Montecito had turned heads since he was a teenager. Wild dark curls, long, long legs and a body to die for meant that Christo had the pick of any women he wanted. And he took full advantage.

Lately, though, the constant stream of ready women was tiresome. *Where was the challenge, where was the fight?* Christo was feeling jaded by his entire lifestyle. Rich beyond imagination, he had begun to crave a simpler life, with a partner he could settle down with. Someone who would challenge him hold her own against the shattering weight of his family's reputation.

The Montecitos were well known in New York as one of the biggest family businesses – and that business was crime. Corruption, drugs, murder – Fogliano Montecito's reputation was feared by everyone, even his son. Christo had lost his mother to Fogliano's devotion to his corporation. Ornella Montecito had leaped to her death from the roof of the family's eighteen million dollar home in Sands Point, Long Island when Christo was seven years old, leaving her only son bewildered and broken. Christo had become an expert at shutting off his feelings after that, and after graduating *summa cum laude* from

Harvard Law, he had passively gone straight to work for his father.

Over the years, Christo had told himself that at least he, personally, was on the right side of the law, that he himself never oversaw anything that was *technically* illegal...but as he'd reached his late thirties, his conscience began to nag at him.

And there was something else. Christo, like his mother, had an artist's soul, and the more mired he got into practicing law, the more that side of him – and therefore his connection to his mother – faded. For the last couple of years he had been living a double life, and now that *other* life was the one he wanted to live. Hence the conversation with his father this morning.

Christo took the glass elevator from the top of his father's building down to the basement parking garage, and then slid into his Mercedes. He sighed, blowing out his cheeks, and dialed his best friend's number.

Bertie Franklin-Hart answered on the first ring. "Hey, dude, how'd it go?"

"It went...well." Christo knew Bertie would hear the astonishment in his voice, and by Bertie's silence, he knew Bertie was feeling it too.

"*Well?*" Total disbelief. Christo's mouth hitched up in a smile.

"Yup. Can you believe it?"

Bertie let out a long breath. "Well, no, to be honest. What's his game?"

Bertie, who had been Christo's roommate at Harvard, had no time for Christo's father or his associates, and was the only one of Christo's friends to say as much to his face. Bertie came from old money, older and even more powerful than the infamous Five Families and their successors. Bertie's money dated all the way back to the signing of the Declaration of Independence – and no one fucked with Bertie's family. *No one.*

Bertie sighed. "Well, I guess you're clear. Just, for me, take

Fogliano's word at face value for now, but don't trust him, Christo."

"I know. But it's the first step."

"I know you, Christo. You've got a glimpse of freedom, and you'll run at it full tilt. I love that about you, brother, but as your best friend...well...I got your back."

"Don't trust to hope." Christo's smile faded, although he knew Bertie was right. Fogliano wasn't someone people left behind without consequence, not even his own son.

"That's what I'm saying, but at the same time, go for it."

Christo mulled over his words. "Okay. Look, the dinner tonight?"

"I'll come, of course I'll come. I don't suppose there will be any chance of some beautiful women to distract us?"

Christo laughed. "No, it's one of Dad's sausage parties. But after...drinks at *La Forge*?"

"Deal."

NEW YORK CITY

ANOUSHKA 'NOOSH' Taylor shifted in her chair nervously as her boss, Allison, read through her proposal. Yes, it was her first big story, and yes, it was out there – even for a late-night radio talk show known for tackling dangerous subjects – but in her bones, Noosh knew Ally would go for it. It was the kind of story Allison Monroe had built her fearsome reputation on; a look into the BDSM clubs of New York's subculture. Noosh had spent months researching and talking to people who worked the clubs, and now she had put together a fifteen-minute segment for the show – her first chance to be on air.

Noosh had come to New York from London a year ago,

straight from a doctorate in creative writing, and now she had cultivated an honest and friendly working relationship with one of New York's major radio stars.

Allison Monroe was known for her exacting methods, razor-sharp intellect, and her ability to convey her natural warmth and vivacity with her interviewees. She set the proposal down now and looked at Noosh over her spectacles. Noosh's heart was pounding hard against her ribs; she couldn't read her boss's expression.

Allison studied her young friend for a minute then took her spectacles off, laying them gently down on her desk. "Noosh... how old are you again?"

Noosh felt her face redden. "Twenty-four."

"And I'm assuming you're not a virgin?"

The blush deepened. "No."

Allison sighed. "Sweetheart, while this proposal is well-written, obviously researched, and full of good intentions, it sounds like it was written by a virgin."

Noosh felt a lump settle on her chest. "Oh."

Allison smiled kindly at her. "I don't mean to be rude, darling, but here's my thing – there's a sense of 'Gosh, golly' about it. And by that, I mean you're painting this world as some kind of otherworldly experience that ordinary people don't subscribe to. The people you've interviewed here – hookers, security guards, club owners...what about the clientele? And I have one more major question which overrides all that."

"Which is?" Noosh tried to stop her voice from croaking with distress but failed, and Allison got up and came to sit on the desk in front of her.

"Noosh...did you actually *go* to the clubs?"

"Yes, of course," Noosh said defiantly. *Don't sulk, you're not a teenager.*

Allison smiled. "I mean, at night, as a client?"

Noosh was horrified. "No, of course not."

"See? How on earth can you expect to convince our listeners you're an expert on this subject if you yourself have no experience with the places? And Noosh, just so you know, BDSM is no longer a dirty little secret. With safety in mind, it can be a thrilling experience if that's where your particular peccadillos find their home." She sat back down behind her desk. "I'm not saying you have to go out and fuck a ton of men or get spanked by them, I'm just saying you should go, sit at the bar, have a drink and see what happens. Watch the interactions between people, talk to them. But don't tell them you're a journalist, for fuck's sake. Pretend you're the clientele for the night. You might surprise yourself."

Noosh's face was burning. "So..."

"So...keep working on it. There's promise, but it's not quite there yet." Allison handed the proposal back to Noosh. "Darling, it's coming along. I just think you need to go the extra mile. I'm pushing you because I believe in you. I believe you could be a rising star. I just want your debut to be as perfect as it should be."

NOOSH WAS STILL THINKING about Allison's words as she took the train home to her studio apartment in Queens. The 7 train was crowded and sweaty, and by the time she opened the door and dropped her bag on her floor, Noosh was exhausted. Coming from London, she was used to the hassle and annoyance of the Tube, so the actual train journey didn't bother her, just the amount of people. *Then why did you move to one of the most crowded cities in the world?*

To disappear...

Noosh pushed the thought away and stripped off her clothes. She thanked God she didn't have to wear a suit to work, that her usual uniform of blue jeans, t-shirt and Chuck Taylor's was accepted office attire. She didn't own anything that could be described as formal wear, except for the ruby-red dress she had worn for her graduation. She loved that dress. It had been a gift from her parents – her parents who had loved and supported her throughout her education, cheered her on, and scraped together their money to buy the designer dress for her. Noosh had worked and paid for her degrees with loans and grants – her parents would never have been able to afford to pay for it themselves.

Noosh had been born into a working-class family and had been brought up without wanting anything other than the food they provided and the love that they shared. In a modest two-up, two-down house out in the suburbs, both her parents worked as bank clerks and made sure that, even without the material things some of her classmates had, Noosh wanted for nothing.

To their credit, she had grown up with a strong work ethic, and their pride in their daughter knew no bounds as they watched her graduate with top honors from one of London's most prestigious universities.

Then it had all come crashing down. Noosh had been targeted by a powerful man who had set out to make her his – whether she wanted him or not. It had almost destroyed her. Now, she could hardly stand to think his name.

Noosh stepped into the shower and turned on the hot water, enjoying the feel of the spray cleansing her tired skin. Her whole life now was work. Maybe Allison was right – maybe she should get out there, experience a little more of what this beautiful, vibrant city had to offer.

Supper was a bowl of cereal and then she fell asleep on the couch, not bothering to pull a blanket over herself. It was early fall in New York, still stifling hot on some days and Noosh wriggled uncomfortably in her sleep until she awoke at three a.m., sitting bolt upright. The thin drape at her window was billowing in. She'd left the window open. God, she never did that...*ever*. Not since...

Noosh skittered over to the window and slammed it shut, forgetting about the hour. She sent a silent apology to her neighbors upstairs. If only this studio weren't on the first floor, but the rent had been perfect for her budget and beggars couldn't be choosers. And baking in the heat of the non-air-conditioned apartment was a small price to pay for her safety.

After moving to her bed she found she couldn't sleep. She tried to read but by four had given up on that and was cleaning the apartment – again. She called it her 'Monica time' after the character from *Friends* – cleaning relaxed her, gave her time to think, to try and order her life a little better.

She thought back to what Allison had said. She *should* check out one of those clubs. The thought both scared and excited her. *Next week,* she told herself. *Next week, I'll go and see what gives in those places.* She blew out her cheeks. Yep, it would take a week to get her courage up, but she was determined to do it now. Finally, as the city began to wake, she fell asleep again and slept in until mid-morning.

SENATOR DESTRY PAPPS always woke at 5 a.m. sharp to begin his day. A six-mile run was followed by a shower then a breakfast of oatmeal and a protein shake, and then he was down in his office by 7.30 a.m. It had been his routine for at least a decade now, waking up in his Georgetown townhouse, a block from his office.

At fifty-three, Destry, a native of New York, had lived his entire life in politics. Following in his father's footsteps, he had become the senator for the District at thirty-eight and had remained in office for nearly two decades. He'd carefully planned his ascension through the party ranks and now he was, at last, going for the big job.

There was nothing Destry wanted more than to become President of the United States, and for the last couple of years he had been clearing house, ironing out anything that could stop him from realizing his goal. People were paid off, offered roles in his cabinet. His lovers, of which there had been many, had been vetted, and even his ex-wife, Telly, had been paid off to keep their dirty laundry private. Destry had no doubt that one day Telly would come to him with something more that she wanted from him, and it would be understood that whatever it was, Destry would provide it. But that was fine with him.

He checked his reflection out now. Tall, stately, with dark hair shot through with silver at the temples, he knew his handsome face was his ticket to getting what he wanted and had always used it. His patented 'aw-shucks' charm worked on the voting public as well as it did with his bed partners.

There was only one part of his life – as yet, a private part – that he reflected on with anger and resentment. The time in London, the time he'd seen *her* and felt his whole world shift. That dark, thick wavy hair, those large chocolate-brown eyes, that full mouth. Destry Papps had pursued Anoushka Taylor with the subtlety of a wrecking ball, and even his closest advisors had been scared by his passion for the girl. She was thirty years the Senator's junior, a grad student, and an unknown quantity.

What Destry knew and no one else did was that Anoushka – his Noosh – had resisted his charms at first, had expressed doubts over their relationship. At least, she did until he wore her down, first by love-bombing her, promising her that he would give it all up for her, and then when she showed signs of independence from him, he'd shown her in an entirely different way that had nothing to do with love.

She'd escaped him, finally, disappearing from London entirely. He'd tracked her down, though, to a cottage in the north of England. Destry had made sure Noosh knew how angry he was.

He thought of her now, how she'd cringed away from his rage, and he smiled. He could still feel her skin under his fingertips, her mouth on his as he took her. He'd told her then, "If you ever leave me again, I'll kill you." And he had meant it.

Then Noosh did the unthinkable and tried to commit suicide. Her parents, those seemingly weak fools, had spirited her away from the hospital in the middle of the night, and Noosh had disappeared – for real, this time. But she was there, out in the world somewhere and ready to use his behavior against him at the most critical moment. That couldn't be happen, obviously.

Which is why he had sent his best men out to scour the globe for her. There had been sightings – in London, in Mumbai, where her mother hailed from, in Sydney. Destry's gut instinct told him that she was somewhere in plain sight, but it frustrated him that she was so well hidden.

"Come out, come out, wherever you are." Destry closed the door to his office and flicked on his computer. He ignored the hundreds of emails and instead clicked on his private folder. Photo after photo of her, always with that haunted look in her eyes. Broken. Beautiful. He traced the outline of her face and sighed. "I can't let you live, my darling. Not without me. Never without me." He closed his eyes, imagining his hands around her throat, squeezing, or driving a knife deep into her gut as she begged for her life. His dick hardened, and he wondered if he could risk jerking off before his assistant got into the office. He heard someone moving in the outer office and sighed, closing the folder. "Another time, my love."

He picked up the phone and called his Head of Security. "Any news?"

"No, Destry. We haven't found anything on where she might be,"

"Jesus...she's just one woman, for fuck's sake. How hard can it be?"

His employee apologized. "I promise we'll find her, it just may take some time."

"I'm announcing my candidacy in two weeks. I don't want anything spoiling that moment. Find her. That's all I ask of you. When you do, I'll take care of her."

"Boss, if I find her, I'll end her. There's no need for you..."

"No," Destry said, interrupting him. "I'll be the one to kill Anoushka. *Me*. Just tell me where to find her."

He hung up the phone and smiled to himself. He could hardly wait.

CHAPTER TWO

Christo pushed his food around his plate, not hungry. He was all too aware of the brooding figure of his father at the end of the dining table. His father's business associates, some of Christo's uncles and cousins, and Bertie too, were all there as well, but Christo could feel his father's scrutiny. He met his father's gaze with a question in his eyes. Fogliano had been quiet all throughout the meal, but now he tapped his fork on his glass, asking for their attention.

"Friends, family, thank you for coming this evening, on what, to my surprise, is quite an auspicious night."

Christo's back stiffened, and Bertie shot him a warning look. *Let your father say his piece.* Christo sighed. He had no idea what his father would tell the others and so had no defense prepared.

Fogliano smiled, but there was no warmth in it. "My son, my only child, came to me today and told me he didn't want my business."

"And here we go," breathed Bertie under his breath. Christo's gaze never left his father's.

"Now," Fogliano continued, "I have always been proud of my son, proud of what he has achieved, of how much he has given me, and so the fact he wants to make his own way in the world is pleasing to me."

Christo's eyes widened slightly, and he relaxed a little. Fogliano smiled a little. "And do you know what my son, my Harvard-educated lawyer son, wants to do with his life now that he no longer wishes to be part of our working life?"

Christo's hope faded. Nope, this wasn't going to be a rousing speech singing his praises. He knew the look in his father's eyes – he was about to be roasted, broiled alive, mocked mercilessly. *Well, bring it, Pa. I can handle it.*

"He wants to make *furniture!*" Fogliano spat triumphantly. "Furniture! Like some damn hipster fool in the Village, can you believe it? I'm so glad I spent hundreds of thousands of dollars on your education, son, so that you can prance around with your bespoke hand-crafted side tables and rocking chairs. Such a privilege to be able to say that my son, who I raised as my heir to the business I have given my life to create...wants *nothing* to do with it. How is it I have raised such an ungrateful child?"

The room was silent, the atmosphere thick and unsettling as Fogliano got up and moved down the table to his son. Christo gritted his teeth. This was going to be one of Fogliano's rants, clearly. *I should have known,* Christo thought, *I should have known he wouldn't take it well, that he was waiting to humiliate me in front of everyone.* He caught Bertie's eyes. Bertie's expression was angry but watchful. Christo shook his head – he knew Bertie would stand up to his father in defense of his friend, but Christo felt numb. *So be it,* he thought, *bring it on, Dad. Do your worst.*

The anger that had been building inside him for years now was almost at its peak. As Fogliano bore down on his son, Christo got to his feet. "What's up, Dad? Can't bear the thought of someone making an honest buck for a change?"

Fogliano stopped. "An *honest* buck? I've had just about enough of your moralizing, boy. My money was good enough to feed you, clothe you, put you through college and now you're too good for it?"

Christo squared up to his father. "No, Pa. I'm not good. I'll never be good, but I can try to redress the balance. For Mom, as well as myself."

He knew mentioning Ornella would set his father off, but Christo didn't care. He wanted to push Fogliano, wanted that fight to happen so he could feel good about making the break. He didn't have to wait long. Fogliano cold-cocked him, and he slammed into the table, crashing against the plates and cutlery. The men around the table shot to their feet as Fogliano hauled his son up and hit him again. Bertie lunged forward, but Christo shouted for him to stop. Fogliano beat his son again until Christo's nose poured with blood. The room was silent as Fogliano let Christo go, his own breath ragged.

"Get out of my house," he growled, his face a mask of pure rage. Christo got unsteadily to his feet and looked his father in the eyes.

"My fucking *pleasure*."

He let Bertie steer him out of the mansion and into Bertie's car. Christo gazed up at the house as Bertie drove him away from it, knowing he would never see it again. He was free.

"Dude, let's get to the club," he said, wiping the blood from his face. "I need a drink...or seven."

It wasn't until, very drunk, he went home to his apartment that night, that Christo let himself break.

Two weeks later and Noosh still hadn't summoned the courage to go to the sex club. She had quietly pushed her story aside and helped out with Allison's punishing schedule, hoping her boss would simply forget about it, but then, one Thursday night as they shared pizza late in the evening, Allison studied her. "So?"

Noosh feigned ignorance. "So, what?"

Allison rolled her eyes. "Noosh."

Noosh sighed. "So…it's on hold."

"Until?"

"Until I can persuade myself to go to the club. I mean, you're right. I need to experience it, it's just…I'm not sure BDSM is my thing."

"Do you suppose journalists who go to war-torn countries like what they have to see? The story's the thing, not your personal preferences. Besides, I never said you had to try out any of that stuff." Allison shoved a piece of pizza into her mouth and studied Noosh. "When was the last time you got laid, anyway?"

Noosh laughed, half-shocked, although it was exactly the kind of thing Allison would come out with. "A while," Noosh answered honestly, then grinned at her boss. "And you?"

"Last night. A delectable lawyer from mid-town. Nice guy. Big cock."

Noosh almost spat her soda out, laughing. She shook her head at her boss. "You're incorrigible."

"And satisfied. God, Noosh, have you looked in the mirror? You could have any man you wanted, you know that, right?"

Noosh felt the cold hand close over her heart – the way it had ever since *him*. "I don't want a man. I'm fine the way I am."

Allison harrumphed, unconvinced, but was distracted by her phone beeping. "Oh, here we go. Senator Papps has announced. Thought that might be coming."

Noosh wondered if her shock was visible on her face. "Destry Papps?"

"Yup. Mr. Smooth is running for President, and the way I hear it, he has a pretty good shot."

Noosh felt sick but covered her distress by tidying up their dinner things. "That's not something we'll cover though, right? I mean, politics isn't really in our remit."

Allison brushed crumbs off her pants. "Not directly, but Papps is popular with women. Good-looking guy."

Noosh felt her face burn. "Not my type."

Allison, missing Noosh's red face, chuckled. "Well, he's a bit too polished for my taste too, but each to their own. Hey, are you okay?"

Finally, she had noticed that Noosh was looking sick. Noosh nodded. "Just tired."

"Well, let's get you a cab – god, it's way past eleven, Noosh, why didn't you say? You must think me a real taskmaster." She smiled at her young friend. "Sweetheart, take tomorrow off, and Monday. Have a long weekend, and get some rest. Don't think I haven't noticed how much work you put in here – it is very much appreciated. I don't often say this, but these last few months you really have made me excited about this job again."

As she sat in the backseat of her cab on the way to her apartment, Noosh concentrated on Allison's compliments. It felt so good to hear her heroine, her idol, her mentor say those things to her, but still, the evening had been tarnished by the thought of Destry.

God...

Noosh felt like throwing up, imagining him as President. Of course, if anyone could stop that, it would be her. She could tell a thousand stories of his hateful, vicious personality. His violence...his threats to kill her.

But even if anyone actually believed her, going to the press or the police would be as good as signing her own death warrant.

As she trudged into her apartment, making sure the deadbolt was on, she realized a hard truth. If Destry ever found her... she had no doubt she would be dead. Why the hell had she come to America? To *his* home? Was it spite? Was it to hide in plain sight?

No. *Fuck him.* It was to pursue her dream of being a radio journalist – to work with Allison – to have something for herself. She had already lost so much because of him... Seeing her parents, for one. She missed them so much and lived for the phone calls to the burner phones she replaced every week. Her friends back in London, her extended family in Mumbai. All of them were out of bounds now, because of the chance Destry might use them to find her. Even at work she used a pseudonym for her writing credits – Sarah Marsh. Something completely unconnected with her real name.

Noosh lay on her bed, staring sleeplessly at the ceiling. To live under a death threat was still unreal and yet all too real to her. It made her angry, and full of sorrow.

She rolled onto her side. *You know what? I will go the club, and maybe I will fuck some random guy there...because I can Destry. It'll be my choice. Screw you and your political ambitions. If I hear one – just one story – of you treating another woman like me, I'll go public, and hang the consequences.*

I will bring your house of cards down, even if it costs me my own life.

CHAPTER THREE

Bertie glanced over at his friend. Christo was drinking steadily now, his handsome face set in anger. He had been like this ever since that terrible night at his father's house, and Bertie was worried. Christo had never been a big drinker, and to see him throw back expensive whiskey as if it were soda was wrong somehow. Between the two of them, Christo was usually the down-to-earth one, the one who would prop up Bertie after a night out, the one who would stop drinking before the hangover set in.

Now, though, his friend was on a knife's edge, and Bertie didn't know how the hell to pull him back from it. He sat up as Christo lurched from the bar stool and staggered towards the door. "Dude, where the hell are you going?"

"To get laid." Christo shot back darkly, and Bertie sighed. That was the other thing. Endless women – a different one every night for the last few weeks. Christo waking up in a stranger's house every time, from which Bertie had to pick him up.

"Christo, I'm flying to LA in the morning. I won't be there to pick you up."

Christo stopped at the door, turning to gave his friend a sad smile. "You've been picking me up too many times, my friend. It's time you let me fall where I need to, even if it's the gutter."

Bertie was surprised at how lucid, if depressed, his friend sounded. He got up and went to him. "Come on, Christo, let me take you home instead. Get some rest."

Christo considered but then shook his head. "It's okay, Bertie. I'll go to my club...they know how to put me in a cab. I need to fuck, Bertie. I need to get this rage out somehow, and fucking is the least destructive way I can think of."

Bertie sighed. "The women are okay with that?"

"They just want to fuck too." Christo, his green eyes sad, looked away from his friend's scrutiny. "Let me go, Bert. I need to do this my way. I'll come out of it, I promise."

Bertie watched helplessly as Christo walked out of the bar and hailed a cab. Christo was right – the only person who could pull him out of this slump was himself. Bertie almost couldn't believe this was the result of Christo finally freeing himself from his father. He was so sure that his friend would be celebratory, not depressed. He'd gotten what he wanted, right? So why was he so self-destructive? Had his father's beating really fucked with his head that much?

Bertie shook his head and went back to collect his jacket. One thing he knew for sure was this: Christo was right – Bertie had to let him fall before he could begin to help him get back on his feet.

He just hoped it wouldn't be too late.

NOOSH WAS DEBATING whether to walk into the club confidently, or to simply just throw up. She shivered in the night air despite it being very warm, and then smoothed her dress down for the fourteenth time. "Option one," she told herself, and lifted her chin, stepping into the club's entrance. The security man at the door nodded politely to her and opened the door. Noosh thanked him, making sure her voice didn't shake before walking in.

A wash of music came over her, and as she walked into the bar area, a thousand different thoughts invaded her mind. Her vision was bombarded by the sights to her left, where a small stage showed people writhing and dancing, all naked and sweaty.

Okay, she told herself, *you expected this. Don't freak out. Don't look like a rookie.*

She walked steadily to the bar and sat down. The bartender greeted her – everyone was so polite – and she ordered a cosmopolitan. Sipping her drink, she took her time to look around.

At a table in the corner, a woman dressed entirely in latex was blindfolding a man, who was stripped down to his jeans. When he couldn't see, the woman picked up a candle and dripped hot wax onto his chest – slowly – smiling as he groaned. Other people watched them, but the connection between the two of them was so palpable that Noosh couldn't look away. The dominatrix caught her eye and smiled. Noosh smiled back.

The atmosphere of the club surprised her. Unlike the sweaty, handsy feel of the usual Friday night clubs, here was a relaxed, open atmosphere that astonished her. After an hour, she was even enjoying watching what was going, which seemed to be okay by everyone, even if she didn't join in.

Noosh had to admit that the overtly open atmosphere was erotic, and when a beautiful woman came up to order a drink at the bar and turned to her, surprising her with a soft kiss on the mouth, Noosh went with it.

"You're beautiful," the woman said, stroking her hands up Noosh's thighs, "but overdressed. First time?"

Noosh nodded shyly. The woman, a gorgeous, voluptuous

blonde, nodded her head towards the opposite side of the bar, grinning. "There's a man who has been gazing at you and you alone for an hour. He's sensational. Go, enjoy."

Noosh looked over to where the blonde nodded, and her stomach gave a strange lurch of pure desire. 'Sensational' didn't begin to cover it.

The man met her gaze. His eyes were bright green, contrasting to great effect with his dark hair and beard, and they burned into Noosh's. Her body reacted to him immediately; her nipples hardened almost painfully, and her cunt flooded with arousal.

She couldn't catch her breath. The man slid from his seat and walked towards her, and Noosh couldn't move. He was tall, at least a foot taller than her five-five, and as he reached her, he stared down at her, not speaking. For a moment they just gazed at each other, then he bent his head, and his mouth met hers.

The kiss was soft at first, but as Noosh gave into it, his lips became hungry against hers. Finally, breaking away only because she ran out of oxygen, Noosh felt her entire body tremble uncontrollably. Who *was* this man?

She opened her mouth to speak, but he shook his head, taking her hand and leading her deeper into the club. Noosh went with him because not doing so was unthinkable. They walked for what seemed like miles, until they reached a locked door. Her companion unlocked it and drew her inside. He didn't pause as he locked the door before sliding his hands around her waist, kissing her again, pressing his body against hers.

Noosh tangled her hands in his hair, pulling on the dark curls as she kissed him back, her mind swirling with delirious pleasure. She could feel the hot length of his cock through his pants, pressing against her belly. She moaned slightly at the thought of what they were about to do.

Her moan seemed to set something off in him, and he

tugged down the straps of her dress, exposing her breasts to his mouth. His lips fixed themselves on her nipple, making her gasp. She could feel an orgasm already beginning to build, but she wanted to prolong this pleasure as long as she could.

Tentatively, she snaked her hand down to his fly, unzipping his pants and sliding her hand in, feeling his cock harden against her hand. God, he was *huge*...

He was pushing up her skirt then tearing at her underwear, and Noosh felt a desperate need to have him inside her. Her lover rolled a condom quickly down the length of his ram-rod hard cock and then, with a confident thrust, he entered her.

Noosh gave a shaky gasp as they began to fuck, clawing at each other, kissing as if they wanted to devour each other. He pressed her up against the wall and took her, his arms easily holding her up, his cock driving deeper and deeper into her with every stroke. His eyes never left hers.

Noosh moaned as he thrust harder, deeper, and for the first time she saw in his eyes anger, rage, and something else...pain. She kissed him fiercely, wanting to take that pain – whatever it was – away.

But then her eyes were rolling back in her head, and she cried out as her orgasm hit her hard. His free hand was stroking her clit, his mouth on hers...he knew exactly what he was doing.

With a groan he came too, and they tumbled to the floor. Noosh caught her breath, enjoying the feel of his weight on her. After a moment he sat up, breathing hard. Noosh pulled her dress up and sat by him.

After a long moment, when she thought he would never say anything, he turned to her. God, he was so beautiful... As he opened his mouth to speak, Noosh couldn't help but touch his face. It seemed to take him by surprise. She cupped his cheek in her hand, stroking her thumb gently over his skin, taking in every detail of his face. If she never saw him again, she wanted to remember everything.

The atmosphere changed between them then. No longer did he look like a glowering, dangerously sexual man, but someone vulnerable, tired...sad. He closed his eyes as she stroked his face, leaning into her touch.

Then he pulled away, pain creasing his handsome face. "Don't."

Stung, Noosh withdrew her hand. "I'm sorry, it's just..."

"We're here to fuck. Fucking is all I do now."

His voice was hard, and he no longer looked at her.

"Did I do something wrong?"

"*Jesus.*" He hissed out the word. "Look, I'm not into schooling newbies. I come here to fuck and be fucked, not to deal with some virgin."

He got up and Noosh scrambled to her feet, her heart pounding. How had things turned so quickly? "I'm no virgin," she managed to say, her voice only slightly shaking.

She glanced around the room and saw a cabinet of paddles, ropes, leather crops, and other toys. She swallowed hard and looked back at him. He was watching her again, glowering from beneath his long, thick lashes. She lifted her chin and deliberately dropped the shoulder straps of her dress, exposing her breasts. "Fuck me again and I'll show you just how far from a virgin I really am."

"No."

God, that hurt. She wouldn't beg this man, this glorious man, whose pain she could see etched across his gorgeous face. But she didn't want the memory of their coupling sullied by this... whatever *this* was. What had she done wrong? She pulled the straps of her dress up, taking a deep breath in. She stepped towards him, saw he didn't back away. "What is it?" She asked him gently. "Why are you in so much pain?"

"I think you should go. You don't belong here."

"Neither do you."

He gave a short, humorless laugh. "Sweetheart, you have no idea what you're talking about. Please, just go."

With her thighs still aching from the fucking her gave her, Noosh stood her ground. *No.* She would not walk away. There had been something here, something worth exploring. She knew he felt it too.

Her lover shook his head. "Get out. Please, just go, I can't bear this."

Her heart gave a sickening lurch. "No. I won't go."

"Please."

She stepped forward and reached out to him, but he backed away, his hands curling into tight fists by his side. "Get out...now. While you still can."

A thrill of danger went through her. "No."

A silence, then he stalked across the room and dragged her to the door. Noosh laid her hands on his chest as she put her back against the door. "No, you don't get to throw me away like that. Not after that... That was incredible..."

He closed his eyes. "Please, I'm begging you. Go. *Go*."

"But..."

"*Go!*"

The ferocity of the roar coming from this man, this dangerous man who towered above her, finally broke her resolve. Noosh fumbled for the door handle and opened the door, skittering down the hallway, hearing him slam the door behind her. She raced through the club, not bothering to look at anything else as she took the stairs to the doorway.

It was only when she stepped – barefoot – out onto the streets of New York City that she realized she was crying.

. . .

THE MAN SAT in the car parked opposite the club and smiled to himself. He wondered if he should go over, say hello, help her get home...but that wasn't why he was here. He had been tasked with finding Anoushka Taylor, and after a tip, he had finally found where she lived. He had to confirm the address was right before he contacted the boss, however, and after seeing her at the club, he'd followed her here. Who knew the girl was into kink? It made his dick hard to think of her like that, but now, seeing her in tears, he realized she must be new to the scene.

He snickered to himself and pulled out his cell phone. Destry Papps answered on the first ring.

The man in the car watched Anoushka Taylor hail a cab and smiled into the phone. "Yeah, it's me. I found her."

CHAPTER FOUR

After she'd gone, Christo slumped to the floor, breathing deeply. God, what had he become? Screaming at that girl, that sweet, kind, beautiful girl? And yet, it was her sweetness that had made him react like that. He didn't deserve her. The way she had touched his face, the way she had *seen* him…

"Fuck. *Fuck.*" He cursed quietly, his head in his hands. *Go after her, apologize, beg her to come back.* But he knew he couldn't. The moment he saw her earlier, something had twisted inside him. She was so lovely, her big brown eyes warm and kind, and she looked so lost. He'd wanted to take her in his arms, protect her from the seediness around them, but as soon as he kissed her, something animal had taken over. Making love to her was exhilarating – her voluptuous body curving against his, his cock driving deep into her velvety cunt…it had been an awakening to him. He'd never felt that way with any woman…and it terrified him.

He tried to stop the sobs that were constricting his chest, but they burst out anyway. What the fuck was happening to him?

Bertie was right; he'd gotten what he wanted – away from his father. So why was he so goddamn miserable?

He let himself cry it out then snagged his phone from his pocket and dialed Bertie. When his friend answered, he just said "Rock bottom."

Bertie understood immediately. "Where are you?"

Christo told him, and Bertie told him to stay there. "I'm coming to get you."

In an hour, Christo was on a plane to Arizona where Bertie booked him into rehab.

Noosh buried herself in her work after that strange, wonderful, terrible night. She'd told Allison she was dropping the story about the BDSM clubs, and although Allison had questioned her about what had happened, Noosh kept it to herself. She felt wrecked by the experience, but at the same time, she couldn't stop thinking about her mercurial lover. Who was he? In moments of weakness, she closed her eyes and remembered the feel of his hands on her body, his mouth against hers, his cock thrusting deep inside her. She shivered, the pleasure all still too real for her. But then afterward...

Stop thinking about him, she told herself now. *It's been a month. You'll never see him again.* She dragged her attention back to the meeting. They were brainstorming ideas for the next year's stories and so far, Noosh hadn't heard a thing.

She blinked and focused on what Allison was saying. "Something I was thinking about was the next generation of New York's crime families. A lot of them are eschewing the old life and branching out on their own with legitimate businesses. I've heard the reaction from the old timers has been...mixed, to say the least. I'd like to focus in on three or four of the heirs who have broken free."

"Any ideas on who and how?" Seth, one of the station's head honchos, looked interested.

Allison nodded, her grey eyes serious. "A four-part series. I interview each of them, ask them the hard questions about how they feel about their family mob connections and why they chose to break free. Hang on, I have a list here." She dug around in her notebook. "Richard Viera, Dominick Octavo, Christofalo Montecito, and Helena De Vito. Those are the names I came up with through very basic research."

Seth nodded, and Noosh wrote down the names, glad of something else to concentrate on. "I like your thinking, Ally," Seth said and nodded at Noosh. "You'll work together with Allison on this?"

Noosh smiled gratefully. "Love to."

Allison winked at her. "And then, we can't ignore that it's election year next year. With any luck, we'll get the candidates in for an interview."

"Will they want to be associated with such a cutting-edge show as yours?" Felix, a snide show runner who loathed Allison and her talent, interjected, but Seth waved his hand.

"We'll get the ones who have enough guts, the ones who willingly go on Colbert. They're the ones we want. Harper, Seagram, Papps – they're the ones we want – or don't want, in the case of some of them."

"Destry Papps would be a get." Allison conceded, and Noosh's heart sank. *God, no.* She knew instantly she'd be calling in sick the day Destry came into the station. She found that her fingernails were digging into her palm, leaving deep welts, and flexed her fingers.

After the meeting, she hunkered back down in her cubicle and worked her way through the paperwork, immersing herself in admin work. It was only when Allison came by her desk that she looked at the clock and realized it was past eight p.m.

"Hey, kiddo, time you went home. But before you do, I've been thinking. You know, this mob-heir thing – this could be the thing you take the lead on, and I'll tell you why it could be interesting. You're not from New York or even the States. Your perspective as an outsider could be the thing that makes them open up to you. What do you say?"

Noosh gaped at her boss. To be asked to lead such a huge story was incredible. "I don't know what to say."

"Say yes," Allison grinned, then her smile faded. "Noosh, you deserve this, and there's something else... I don't know what happened to you at that club, but I know something did, and I feel bad. I encouraged you to go, and whatever happened – "

"Whatever happened, happened," Noosh interrupted her. "It's not your fault."

There was a long silence. "Who was he?"

Noosh struggled for a moment to find the words, and decided the truth was the only way to go. "The most incredible man I've ever met. And the most damaged. Not a good combination."

Allison patted her shoulder. "I'm sorry, honey. I've known men like that. They're instantly addictive, like sugar or heroin, but so, so bad for you."

Noosh nodded but looked away from her boss's gaze. "I agree."

"Anyway, sweetheart, go home and we'll talk more about this in the morning. The mob stories, I mean, although you know you can talk to me about anything."

Noosh smiled at her. "I know. Thanks, I'll see you tomorrow."

On the subway home, Noosh indulged in another fantasy about her mysterious lover, imagining him turning up at her apartment door, begging for her forgiveness. Would she make him beg? Noosh smirked to herself. Probably not – one look at those green eyes of his and she would cave. *Pathetic,* she told herself, but still visualized pulling him into her apartment, tearing off his clothes and fucking him until they were both exhausted.

At home, she took a long soak in the bathtub, indulging the fantasy some more, her hand between her legs, caressing her clit, imagining it was his tongue on her. She shivered through a mellow orgasm before pushing thoughts of him away.

Maybe some people were just meant to be experienced once in a lifetime, she told herself, as she pulled the comforter over her shoulders and settled down to watch the television.

Noosh never knew what woke her. Whether it was the sound of the television, which was still on, or the sense of someone being in the room with her. Noosh opened her eyes and froze. A dark figure was standing next to her sofa bed. She barely had time to try and make out his or her features before whoever it was shot her, the flash of the muzzle lighting up the room as he pumped three bullets into Noosh's belly, the sound muffled by a silencer.

Noosh gasped, stunned. The pain hit her full force she knew one thing for sure as she lay bleeding out.

Destry had found her.

CHAPTER FIVE

Six months later...

THE PHYSIOTHERAPIST GAVE her a long stare. "Noosh, you're pushing yourself too hard. I told you this would take time."

Noosh, balancing herself between the bars, shook her head. "Doc, it's been *too* long. I'm going stir-crazy in this hospital. I want to go back to work."

The doctor, a tired-looking woman in her thirties named Beth, rolled her eyes. "And don't think I don't know you've been working from your room. Rest is anathema to you, isn't it?"

"I had plenty of rest when I was brought in." Noosh propelled herself painfully along the treadmill. One good thing about having a bullet in the spine, it sure helped your upper body strength when you tried to learn to walk again, she thought, as she puffed her way along the walkway.

"For the record, a coma isn't rest, Noosh. Come on, that's it for today." Beth helped Noosh back into her chair. Noosh gave a frustrated sigh.

"Come on, Beth, do a girl a solid and let me out of here."

Beth couldn't help but grin. "Just so you know, that expression coming from your English mouth sounds weird. And, okay then."

Noosh was already geared up for an argument, so Beth's agreement took her by surprise. "Really?"

"Really." Beth nevertheless insisted on wheeling Noosh back to her room. "Tomorrow, and I mean it. Get some sleep tonight, and if your stats are good in the morning, you can go home. I'm not happy about you being alone, though."

"I won't be alone, for the most part."

Noosh's parents had been flown over by the radio station after Noosh had been shot, but when it had been clear their daughter would survive, they'd had to return to their lives in London, albeit Skyping Noosh every day. Allison, shaken to her core by the attempted murder, had sworn to them that she would take care of Noosh, and had insisted Noosh move in with her in her Upper East Side apartment.

"With *security*," she'd emphasized when Noosh protested, and Noosh couldn't argue. The man – she presumed it was a man – who had shot her was still out there, and the police had no leads. Noosh hadn't told them of her suspicions – that Senator Destry Papps, candidate for the office of the President of the United States, was the one who had shot her mercilessly. Who the hell would believe that? Her mother and father had looked at her with pain in their eyes, and she knew they guessed the same. Would Destry try again?

Noosh hoped against hope that by not revealing him now, he would understand she wouldn't go the press about him at all, but she knew that was a naïve hope. So the promise of being secure, at least at home, was appealing.

Allison had been to see her every day, and Noosh knew from the topics of conversation on her radio show that the shooting had affected her usually unflappable boss to the core. Allison had persuaded the station to run an anti-firearms campaign, and by sharing Noosh's – or rather, 'Sarah's' – story with her listeners, Allison had managed to both bring awareness to the subject and, Noosh hoped, to broadcast to the assailant that she was now going to be protected.

Noosh knew Destry had heard the program because the day after, a huge bouquet of red roses had arrived for her with the card just saying "*Sarah...*" on it. Funny how threatening just that one word could be, she mused as she'd dumped the flowers into the trash can.

ALLISON INSISTED on coming personally to pick her up from the hospital after Noosh was discharged, and she settled Noosh into the back seat of the limousine, fussing around her, making Noosh grin. "You really have gone full-on Momma-Bear, haven't you?"

"Quiet, child," Allison said, hiding her grin. "Now, your mom and dad packed all your things and sent them to me, so I took the liberty of unpacking some non-personal stuff, just to make your room feel like home."

Noosh sighed. It had taken her months to find the apartment in Queens, and having to let it go was annoying. *But you're alive, so stop feeling sorry for yourself and buck up.* Noosh smiled her thanks at Allison and changed the subject.

"How are the interviews going?" Noosh had missed the preparation and setting up of the Mobster Heirs series, and was sorry to have been out of action for it. From what Allison told her, it had been an eye-opening experience.

"Good so far, but we have one hold-out...at least, we did.

Christofalo Montecito called the day after our firearms campaign - and your story - got coverage on the national news. Said he wanted to help out with that, and if he could, he would give us the interview we want."

"That's good news. What's his story?"

"Hard to say. We know he's broken away from his family's business, but what he's been doing, what he plans to do, is a mystery. Try researching someone who doesn't want to be found. There are no photos, no gossip about the man at all. Unheard of these days, but the man's a ghost."

Noosh was surprised. "That is unheard of."

Allison grinned at her. "I know what you're thinking – that you can find something on the internet even if an old coot like me can't, but...there's nothing. The man's a private guy. So, him coming in to see us..."

Noosh groaned. "Tell me I can be there! I've missed out on *everything*, Ally."

Allison sighed. "Alright, you can be there, but – and I mean this – you are not to do *anything* but watch and say hello to the man."

Noosh grumbled but agreed. "When is he coming in?"

"Thursday...and as part of the deal, until then, you rest."

"Fine."

"Grumpuss."

"Shut up."

CHRISTO WALKED out of his bathroom to find Bartie waiting in his kitchen, helping himself to Christo's coffee. He smiled at his friend. "How do I look?"

Bertie looked him up and down, snickering. "Ugly as sin, but smart enough."

"Thanks, dude." Christo laughed. He knew he looked good

in the navy sweater and dark jeans, but he was nervous as hell. Bertie studied him.

"Dude, relax. This will be a breeze. All you have to do is talk about your new business."

Christo rolled his eyes. "We both know that's not true."

Bertie grinned, unrepentant. "You got me. Look, just stick to the truth – it's easier to remember. Mr. Montecito, did you ever knowingly participate in illegal activities?"

"No."

"But you knew your father's business was linked to organized crime?"

Christo sighed. "Yes."

"Don't sigh. Just say yes. Look, buddy, of course they're going to ask you the hard questions. You knew this and agreed to the interview anyway."

Christo nodded. "I listened to the other interviews." He began to smile. "Helena really met her match, huh?"

Bertie clutched his heart dramatically. "Do not speak ill of the lovely Helena."

Christo laughed. "Bert, you know what would actually make your fantasy real? Asking Helena out. Come on."

He grabbed his keys and Bertie followed him out of the apartment. "That," Bertie said sniffily, "would involve me speaking to her, which I am not."

"Because she beat you at squash?"

Bertie grumbled under his breath and Christo snickered. "Dude, let it go. Trust me, Helena is a pussy cat."

"God, you've fucked her, haven't you?" As they got into Christo's car, Bertie sounded half-angry, half-admiring. Christo shook his head.

"No, I promise you I haven't. Not Helena, not knowing how you feel about her. I'm glad I didn't sink that low."

Bertie clapped his friend's shoulder. "Good boy." Bertie sat back as Christo pulled the car out into traffic. Christo had always insisted on driving himself, even when he worked for his father, and Bertie watched the streets flow by. After a while, he turned to his friend.

"So..."

"Yeah?"

"You still obsessing over the club girl?"

Christo shot him a look. "I don't want to talk about her."

"But you're still hung up?"

Christo sighed, then nodded. "I can't get her out of my head, Bert. She was so lovely, and I treated her like crap. I would be damn lucky to find a girl like that, and I blew it. All I think about is finding her and apologizing."

"One of your twelve steps?"

Christo grinned despite himself. "You're such a douche bag."

"True dat."

They drove in companionable silence for a while, then Bertie cleared his throat. "How about putting a private detective on the case? See if he can find her?"

Christo rolled his eyes. "Yes, dude, because invading her privacy just so I can feel better *is* the way to go."

"Fair point. Thought about going back to the club?"

Christo shook his head. "No. Look, can we change the subject?"

"Of course, brother."

Ten minutes later they were pulling into the parking lot of the radio station, and Christo hesitated. Bertie waited until Christo nodded. "Let's do this."

They were greeted by a bubbly blonde intern, Liam, who was flirtatious and fun and made them relax a little. "Now, once you have your studio i.d., take the elevator to the third floor and follow the hallway around to Studio C. Noosh will look after you from there. You can't miss her – gorgeous, sexy, and going hell for leather in a wheelchair at the moment."

Christo and Bertie rode the elevator, and Christo blew out his cheeks. Bertie grinned at him. "Not too late to back out."

Christo shook his head. "I'm good."

They followed the hallway as directed and finally came to the door of Studio C. Christo, his mouth dry, stopped at the water cooler outside of the studio as Bertie knocked on the door, opening it to speak to the woman inside.

"Hey, are you Noosh? Hi, I'm Bertie, Mr. Montecito's assistant."

Christo heard a soft voice. "Oh, hey, nice to meet you, I'm Noosh Taylor. Come on in, Ally's just setting up. I'll tell her you're here."

"Oh, hey, do you need a hand?"

"No, it's okay, I'm just getting used to this thing. I don't really need it, but Ally insists. Won't be a moment."

There was something familiar about the voice, and Christo stepped into the room just as the woman turned away from him. *No. No way.* His heart began to beat faster as he recognized the soft wavy hair falling down her back, the caramel skin, the curvy body, now sitting in a wheelchair. *How? Why?*

He made an involuntary noise, and she looked up. Her face paled as she stared back at him with a mixture of horror and shock.

It was her. It was his sweet girl.

CHAPTER SIX

Noosh stared at him, her heart pounding painfully against her ribs. After a moment, she remembered where she was and cleared her throat. Unsmiling, she nodded to him and turned back to Bertie. "Ally will be out in a second. Can I get either of you some coffee?"

"Please, don't trouble yourself," Christo Montecito said in that deep, sensual voice of his, and Noosh felt her belly quiver with desire. *No. Nope, this wasn't happening.* She looked away from that intense green-eyed stare, the curiosity in them. She knew he was wondering about her wheelchair and felt a wash of embarrassment. She leveraged herself out of the chair, wobbling, and both Bertie and Christo stepped forward to help her. She waved them away, her face burning. "I'm fine."

Ally opened the door at that particular moment – *damn it* – and made a frustrated noise. "Again, Noosh? What was our deal?"

Noosh's face flamed even redder. "I was just practicing. Anyway, our guests are here."

Ally immediately switched into her professional mode. "Bertie, how nice to see you again."

Bertie winked at her. "You too, Ally, looking good. Can I introduce my friend, Christofalo Montecito?"

Ally shook Christo's hand and Noosh could see her boss sizing him up. She risked another glance at the man. If it were possible, he was even more beautiful than she remembered, and he looked better, healthier than when she'd met him in the club. His olive skin was smooth, his beard neatly trimmed, his dark curls freshly washed and brushed neatly. Noosh longed to run her fingers through them.

Stop it. You're hardly in any condition to think about sex. She realized Ally was speaking to her and dragged her attention back to her boss. Ally was hiding a smile, obviously having noticed her preoccupation. "Sorry, Ally, I missed that."

"You'll be sitting in on this interview today, Noosh."

Oh, god damn it. She could barely stand the tension between them as it was, and to have to sit by him for the next couple of hours...

Even worse, once they got in the small studio, Ally managed to sit Noosh beside Christo, where she could feel his body heat, breath in his scent of fresh linen and spice. It drove her senses wild and she struggled to maintain her composure. Just before the interview began, Christo looked around at her, and she met his gaze, feeling something shift in the air. She could see he was nervous, and weirdly, she sensed he was looking to her for confidence. She gave him a small smile and a nod, and she saw his shoulders relax. It was such a small moment, but it made her feel... How did she feel? Flattered? Happy? She couldn't tell.

Christo made for an honest, interesting interview. He told Ally about his plans to go into the bespoke furniture business, discussed the stark change of direction, and when Ally questioned him on his father's business, he was honest and forthright.

"I don't pretend that I don't know what my father's business is, and yes, for a long time I took his money and turned a blind eye. From now on…I'm going to try and make up for that. For a lot of things."

Ally nodded. "Do you regret anything?"

Christo was silent for a long time. "Yes, one thing. One thing I regret very much…but it has nothing to do with my father."

Noosh felt a jolt – he was obviously talking about their tryst now…but was he regretting making love to her, or what happened afterward?

WHETHER BY ACCIDENT or by design, Ally bore Bertie off to talk to him after the interview, and Christo was left alone with Noosh. God, he'd forgotten how beautiful she was, how sweet. For a few minutes, they stared at each other then he smiled at her. "Hi."

"Hi." Her voice was wary but soft. He wanted to touch her so badly, stroke her face the way she had his, tell her he was sorry. Instead, he touched the arm of her wheelchair.

"What happened?"

Noosh looked away from his gaze. "An accident."

"I'm sorry."

Noosh gave a strange laugh. "Me too."

Another long silence. "Noosh…that's an unusual name."

"It's short for Anoushka."

"I like it."

She met his gaze, and all he wanted to do was kiss that sweet mouth of hers, hold her in his arms. Christo felt his blood pumping hard through his entire body, his cock twitching, reacting to her. He reached out and stroked her cheek. "Noosh…"

"As I say, Bertie, I'd be most grateful if you would think about it."

Christo dropped his hand as they heard Ally and Bertie return, and Noosh, her face red, looked away from him. Ally and Bertie finished talking about whatever they were talking about, and Christo was saying goodbye.

Noosh shook his hand and he bent down to kiss her cheek. So close to her he could barely stand it, but then goodbyes were said, and he was back in the car with Bertie, feeling bereft now that he was out of her company.

Bertie shot him an amused glance. "I see you were quite taken with the lovely Noosh."

Christo said nothing but gave him a look. After a moment, Bertie's mouth dropped open, having made the connection. "No. *No way. That's* the girl from the club?"

Christo nodded. "She wasn't in a wheelchair then...something happened to her. An accident she said, but...I had the feeling there was more to it."

"But she's the one?"

Christo sighed. "Yes, she's the one."

ALLY DIDN'T MENTION Christo again until they were at home that evening scarfing down pizza. She studied Noosh, who could feel the questions looming. "So, I take it you've met Christofalo Montecito before?"

Noosh sighed. "I have."

"When? Because it seems like, well, the tension between you was pretty smoldering. You sleep with him?"

"Ally."

"Come on, give me details," Ally was grinning. "The man is gorgeous and clearly into you. How come you're not dating him?"

"Because how we met... It wasn't like that – and he wasn't the same man we met today. And besides, I have been occupied with other things. Like almost being murdered, for example."

Ally's smile faded. "Of course, darling, I didn't forget." She put down her slice of pizza. "Listen, Seth and I were talking…I'm sure our listeners would love to hear about how 'Sarah' is doing now."

Noosh chewed her food thoughtfully. "I'm not sure I'm cut out to be on the air," she said slowly. "I've been doing a lot of thinking since the shooting. Maybe my future lies with being your researcher – your best researcher, obviously." She grinned, but Ally didn't smile.

"Anoushka Taylor, you were born for this job. Hell, I've been grooming you for my job since that first day. I've never met anyone with such raw talent, curiosity, and tenaciousness. Cards on the table, Noosh – you're scared."

Noosh swallowed her pizza. "Yes," she said honestly. "I am. I'm scared as soon as I wake up in the morning that whoever tried to kill me will finish the job. I'm scared that everything I've ever worked for is out of reach because of it."

Ally got up and wrapped her arms around her young friend. "Nothing is gone, baby girl. And we'll keep on pushing the police to find out who hurt you. It's okay to be scared, just don't let it rule you."

Noosh wondered if that went for how she felt about Christo Montecito as well. Later, when she was in bed, she couldn't help recalling the way he looked at her, remember his body heat as he sat next to her, maddening her senses with his fresh, clean scent. The way he'd touched her face just before they'd been interrupted. There was an intimacy between them, it seemed, and Noosh wanted to hold on to it, cradle it because it seemed so fragile and yet so right.

Part of her wished she could call him right now and talk, that there was something more between them, that they actually knew each other better so she could reach out. She would give anything to be in his arms right now.

You're being ridiculous, painting him as your knight in shining armor, especially after the way he treated you. But she indulged in the fantasy a little more anyway, thinking back to when his big, thick cock was inside her and his mouth, god, his sexy, soft lips, were on hers.

She groaned and rolled over, pushing away the thoughts. Her back throbbed with pain, and she used that to distract her from Christo, finally falling asleep just before midnight.

WHEN SHE WOKE, all thoughts of Christo vanished when she heard the news that Destry Papps was now his party's official Presidential candidate.

CHAPTER SEVEN

Destry walked off of the stage, the convention crowd still cheering wildly. He grinned to himself and then patted his assistant's arm. "Gerry, they love me."

"They certainly do, Senator." Gervais 'Gerry' Noll grinned at his boss. Ambitious but kind, Gerry had been with the Senator for years, through everything, through the divorce, and Destry's fling with Anoushka Taylor. Gerry and Noosh had become friends, but since the split – or rather, Anoushka's escape – Destry knew Gerry hadn't seen her.

He'd kept the bad stuff from Gerry all this time – he didn't want his closet advisor and probable Chief of Staff, should Destry win the election, to know about his poor treatment of the young girl, or of the attempt on her life.

When Destry discovered Noosh had survived the shooting – barely – he'd panicked. Would she go to the police? There was no way she could prove it was him, after all. Was he stupid to have done the deed himself? No. There was no way anyone could prove it was him, and besides...he wouldn't give up the memory of that night for anything.

. . .

TELLING his staff he was headed for an early night, he'd instead sneaked out of his house and into the rental car his contact had procured for him. He'd driven the near four hours to get to her apartment, then broke in easily and waited. When she'd come home, he'd watched her for a while from inside her closet, then when she had fallen asleep, walked to her couch and gazed down at her.

So beautiful...with her long dark hair clouded around her head, her blankets kicked off in the late fall heat, and her top riding up to show the most delectable expanse of midriff. Destry had felt his cock harden. He couldn't risk fucking her and leaving DNA...he'd said her name, hoping she would wake, hoping she would realize she was being murdered...

When she opened her eyes, he grinned to himself, leveling the gun at her belly and firing point blank at her. Noosh had gasped in shock, in agony as the bullet tore into her soft skin and blood began to gush from the wound. Her breathing quickly became labored, but Destry could not tear himself away just yet. He knew he should put a bullet in her pretty head, but he couldn't bring himself to do it, couldn't ruin all that beauty. Instead, he pressed the muzzle against her navel and shot her twice more, her beautiful body jerking from the impact. So much blood. Noosh lost unconsciousness quickly, and Destry knew she couldn't survive the terrible injuries he had inflicted on her.

As he left her to die, he bent down and kissed her mouth, just once, quickly. "I told you I'd kill you if you ever left me, Anoushka."

But she *had* survived. Some nosy neighbor had seen him leave her apartment – thankfully, he had been masked – and called 911. As he drove back to Washington, he scanned the local news for any mention.

Only a few days later did he catch something on the internet.

A news report buried in the pages of *The New York Times*.

A YOUNG BRITISH-INDIAN woman working in New York was shot by an intruder in her home in Queens Wednesday evening. The young woman, named locally as Sarah Marsh, was asleep at the time – police say there was no robbery involved and the victim remains in critical condition at a city hospital.

SARAH MARSH? *So that's the name you gave yourself to escape me,* Destry thought, but it irked him that she had lived, even if she was in critical condition. This is what comes of not using a professional, of making it personal. He should have had his guy kill her, he knew, but then again…

Since the shooting, he had stayed far away from her. His star was rising in the political world, and any scandal was out of the question if he wanted the big job. That Noosh hadn't told the police about him…well, he could see why she hadn't. Who would believe her? Even her parents, who hated him with a passion and who must have guessed it had been him, had said nothing to the British press either, and Destry knew Noosh must have forbidden it.

Destry was deep in thought. When he was President – and he knew he *would* be, come November – then he could make sure she was silenced forever. But any whiff of controversy now… no. He'd let her think he wouldn't try again. Let her think she was safe. Then he'd take it all away, like she'd done to him.

I'll make you suffer, Anoushka. Make the most of the time you have left, my beautiful girl…

NOOSH SAW the note on her desk as she wheeled herself into the office the next morning. "It came with these," Liam said, following her in. In his hand he held a vast bouquet of dusky pink peonies. Noosh took them from him.

"God, they're beautiful."

"Like yourself," Liam said matter-of-factly. "If I weren't totally gay, I would so turn for you, Nooshy."

Noosh giggled. She and Liam had always flirted with each other, safe in the knowledge that both of them liked men. "You're such a slut," she teased him, and he grinned. He made no move to leave her alone.

"Come on, open the card, I want to know who they are from."

Noosh rolled her eyes and picked up the envelope. It was expensive paper, heavy, the color of thick cream, and the writing was flowing and confident. *Noosh...*

She caught a faint hint of fresh linen coming off the paper, and her heart began to beat faster. She pulled out the letter inside.

Christo had written only a few words, but they made her head spin.

Lovely Noosh,

I cannot begin to tell you my happiness at seeing you again. I have wanted to apologize for my appalling behavior that night for months, and now it doesn't seem enough to say I'm sorry.

My one regret in life is ever letting you go that night. Can you forgive me?

Please, if you would like, please call me.

For my part, I cannot stop thinking about you.

. . .

Yours always,
   Christofalo Montecito

HER KNEES SHOOK, her legs felt weak. He was so formal, almost old-fashioned. *I cannot stop thinking about you. Nor I you,* she thought and grinned to herself.

"Well?"

She had forgotten Liam was in the room. She smiled at him. "From Mr. Montecito, thanking me for looking after him and Mr. Franklin-Hart yesterday. That was sweet of him."

Liam grinned. "I knew it. I knew some rich mukety-muck would take one look at you and want to sweep you off your feet. And he's dreamy, too."

"*Dreamy*?" Noosh hooted as Liam rolled his eyes. "What are you, six-years-old?"

"So cynical. Okay then, he's very fuckable, is that better?"

"Much."

Liam hopped onto her desk and studied her. "You should get on that."

For a second, Noosh wondered how Liam would react if she told him she had already 'gotten on that.' No. That was her secret, hers and Christo's.

"Did he ask you to call him? I bet he did."

"Mind your own beeswax."

"Huh?"

"Never mind."

AFTER THAT, Noosh couldn't concentrate on anything else. She kept re-reading the note, feeling like a lovesick schoolgirl, but still, she couldn't bring herself to pick up the phone. What the hell would she say?

One decision she did make was to get rid of the wheelchair, no matter what Ally said. Noosh had brought her cane in with her today, and although her back was painful, it felt good to work her muscles, which were almost atrophying from lack of use. She made sure she walked everywhere today and told herself it wasn't just because she felt like she needed to get things…going. Working. Just in case she needed to expend some extra energy…maybe…hopefully…

It was five p.m. when Liam called up from reception. "Honey, there's a delivery for you, but the guy says you need to sign for it personally."

"God, does he look like a process server?"

"No, sweets. Can you come down?"

"Be right there."

NOOSH TOOK THE ELEVATOR – she wasn't confident enough with stairs yet – and hobbled out to the reception. Liam was nowhere to be seen. She glanced around then heard a voice behind her.

"I'm sorry, I made him say that."

She turned to see Christo smiling at her. God, that smile – boyish and warm all at once. He stepped towards her. "I knew you wouldn't call, you see, and so I thought I'd give you the option of telling me to leave you alone in person."

He was close now, and Noosh gazed up at him. "Do you want me to leave you alone, Noosh?"

She shook her head, and he smiled. She wobbled, her legs shaking, and he slid his hands onto her waist, steadying her, pulling her into his hard body to balance her. He stroked her face. "I hate that you got hurt."

"No biggie." Her voice was gravelly, but all she could think of was how nice it was to be in his arms. She couldn't stop staring at his handsome face, his eyes, so soft and full of sweetness. He's looking at *me* like that, she marveled, and then a second later, as he bent his head and brushed his lips against hers, she gave an involuntary moan of desire.

"That," he said in a whisper, "that right there is how *you* make *me* feel."

He kissed her again, his lips firmer this time, his tongue sweeping into her mouth to caress hers, his fingers tangling in her long hair. "God, Noosh...*Noosh*..."

She wanted him to touch her everywhere as he whispered her name over and over, but then she remembered they were still in the very public reception of her building. Ruefully, she broke away, smiling up at him. "Maybe we should go somewhere less, um, open."

Christo grinned. "That sounds promising. How about I take you to dinner?"

"I would love that. Let me just get my bag."

"No need." Liam suddenly appeared out of nowhere, clearly having been spying on them. He grinned unashamedly at them and handed Noosh her bag. "Here you go, sweets, I thought you might need this. Ally says have a good night, by the way."

Noosh gave him a mock-scowl. "All of this seems very...planned."

Christo laughed. "Don't blame Liam, blame me. I'm afraid I've had my spies out for a couple of days – and Liam is remarkably easy to bribe."

Noosh gaped at them both for a moment, then laughed. Who the hell cared? "Well, then you'd better buy me a *really* good dinner, Montecito."

"Warning, she can out-eat a water buffalo," Liam ducked away from Noosh's slap. Christo grinned and offered Noosh his hand.

"Shall we?"

CHAPTER EIGHT

Christo led her to his waiting car and helped her in. "Comfortable?"

She beamed at him, not really believing this was real. "Very." The Mercedes had wide, comfortable, supple leather seats, but Noosh barely glanced around. She only had eyes for the man sitting next to her. He held her hand as he drove, probably breaking a myriad of laws, but he didn't seem to care. "Where are you taking me?"

"Well, I thought somewhere quiet, somewhere we could talk."

"Sounds good to me."

Christo, pulling up at a red light, leaned over and kissed her again. "God, Noosh, I've dreamed about kissing you for months now."

"Me too," she whispered then grinned. "Green."

"What?"

"The light is green." She giggled as he shot back into a sitting position, waving an apologetic hand at the cars honking behind them. Noosh grinned at him and he shrugged, smiling back.

"If they could see who I was kissing, they'd understand."

She flushed at the compliment and risked sliding her hand onto his thigh. He smiled at her. "Sweetheart...I was thinking... what if we skip..."

"And go straight to your apartment? I think that's a great idea." Noosh was flushing madly, but she knew he was thinking the same thing.

His eyes seemed to darken with desire, and for a moment, Noosh got a little nervous. "Christo...because of my injury..."

"Baby, we don't have to do anything you're not ready for," he said in an even voice. "I just want to be with you."

Noosh nodded and she felt tears spring into her eyes. *In a minute,* she thought, *I'm going to wake up and find I've dreamed all this. That we didn't find each other, that we didn't get so lucky...*

But it wasn't a dream, and when Christo walked her up to his apartment, she could feel her entire body yearning for his touch. In his spacious open concept apartment, he took her coat and then wrapped his arms around her, gazing down at her. "Hello again," he said softly, "I'm Christo."

"Anoushka...Noosh."

"Noosh..." His lips were firm against hers and his hands stroked down her sides. "Noosh, wanna get naked with me?"

She gave a moan of pure desire, and he swept her up into his arms. Noosh's injured back protested, but she didn't care. She wanted this man as much as he clearly wanted her.

In his bedroom – all muted navy blues and greys, and hand-turned furniture – he laid her on the bed and slowly began to unbutton her dress, pushing the fabric aside and kissing every inch of exposed skin. As he pulled down the lacy cup of her bra and fixed his mouth on her nipple, Noosh closed her eyes, drawing in a long breath. God, the way his tongue flicked around the little nub, making it hard and so sensitive she could have cried. He worked his way down her body, his mouth on each breast, but as he reached her belly he stopped.

"What's this?"

Noosh didn't even need to look. He had seen the scars, and now there was no other way but to tell him the truth. "Those are the scars from my surgery."

Christo looked up at her. "These are *bullet* wounds."

She nodded. "I was shot. Someone broke into my home and shot me as I slept."

Christo made his way up the bed, gazing into her face, the horror in his eyes searing. "What the fuck?"

Noosh didn't know what to say. "Some random...guy... decided he wanted to kill someone that night, and I was unlucky." So, she was lying, she knew who had shot her, but from the anger on Christo's face, she knew she could never tell him. How was it that this man cared so much about her already?

"Jesus..." He traced the scars. "So that was your accident?" She nodded. "How long ago?"

She tried to smile. "About two weeks after we met."

Christo stroked her cheek. "God...Noosh...I'm so sorry."

She moved closer to him, her bare skin pressing against his still clothed body. "It's over now, I'm healed. Healing..." She amended, and he sighed.

"How are you? Really? Because I don't want us to go too far and risk your health."

She sighed and nodded. "I am still getting there, and I do have problems with my back still. The docs have told me it will get better, but yes..."

"I told you we didn't have to do anything, that I'm happy to wait." Christo pressed his mouth to hers, his kiss leaving her breathless.

"Just touch me...please," she murmured against his mouth and felt his lips curve up in a smile.

"It would be my pleasure, ma'am." He rolled her onto her

back, making sure she was comfortable. "You just lay back and let me do all the work..."

He began his journey down her body again, kissing her throat, her breasts, her belly until his fingers snagged in the sides of her panties and drew them gently down her legs.

As soon as his tongue touched her clit, Noosh shivered with pleasure. This man was clearly an expert, his tongue lashing around her clit before dipping into her cunt. Noosh forgot about her back pain, forgot about everything except him, and as she neared a shattering orgasm, she cried out his name over and over.

As she caught her breath, Christo quickly stripped his clothes off and cradled her in his arms, his lips against hers. She could feel his huge cock, hard against her belly. "I want to taste you, baby."

She moved down his body and took his cock into her mouth, sweeping her lips over the wide crest, licking up the salty pre-cum, and trailing her tongue up and down the thick length of it and over the sensitive tip. God, she wanted him inside her, but until her back healed some more, she knew it would hurt like hell – and not in a good way.

She hollowed out her cheeks as she sucked him, then swallowed his seed down as he came, groaning and bucking beneath her. As he caught his breath, he pulled her into his arms. "God, Noosh...thank god we found each other again."

She kissed him. "Thank god, indeed." She snuggled into his arms, again feeling how perfectly their bodies seemed to fit together. She chuckled a little, and he smiled down at her.

"What?"

"Just...we don't know anything about each other, and yet this feels so...natural."

Christo laughed softly. "I know what you mean...and we have all the time in the world. Besides, we do know some things.

I know you like your belly and the nape of your neck kissed. I know you love your job – that was obvious yesterday."

"Did you like Ally?"

"Very much. I knew she would give me a rough ride, and rightly so." His smile faded a little. "There are a lot of things in my past I'm ashamed of, Noosh, but none more than what I did to you that night."

Noosh cupped his face in her palm. "Tell me. Tell me what was going on with you that night."

So, Christo told her, and they talked late into the night, pausing now and again to kiss and caress each other. Noosh felt something shift in her soul, and she didn't want this night to end. Not being able to have sex, full, hardcore penetrative sex at the moment had meant their tryst was more than just a fuck, that they were forging a connection that neither of them could deny. They ordered pizza at 2 a.m., Christo going down on her again as they waited for it to be delivered, then gorging themselves on the pie, joking and laughing around with each other.

THEY FINALLY FELL asleep as dawn began to break. Upon waking, they showered together and, after a breakfast of eggs, Christo drove her back to Allison's apartment. As they rode through the streets of Manhattan, Christo asked her about her home in London, and she told him all she could.

"Why do I get the impression you're leaving something out? Why did you leave? Why did you come to New York?"

Noosh hesitated. "I *had* to leave. Let's just say a relationship went wrong and I had to leave."

Christo stopped and turned to her. "Was it him who shot you?" His face was hard, and Noosh couldn't lie to him. She nodded. *Please don't ask me who he is.*

But she knew he would. "Who?"

For a moment, she was silent. "I can't tell you. If I told you, your life would be in danger too."

Christo studied her, his expression still hard. "You think he'll try again?"

She gave him a sad smile. "I know he will."

"Not going to happen."

Noosh touched his face. "You're sweet to care, but I survived once."

"The police know, right?"

She nodded. "They can't do anything. There's no proof."

Christo gave a frustrated hiss. "Noosh…"

"Christo, please, let's not drag that into whatever this is. Last night was the happiest night I've had for years, but technically we are still strangers to each other. Let's just concentrate on getting to know each other – if that's what you want, I mean." Her voice shook as she suddenly had a dip in her confidence, but Christo smiled around at her.

"There's nothing I want more. Noosh, do you have to work this weekend?"

She shook her head, and he raised her hand to his lips and kissed it. "Would you spend it with me? I'd like to take you out to my place upstate, where my workshop is, so you can see how I really love to live."

Noosh smiled back at him. "I would love that."

At the entrance to her building, he kissed her then leaned his forehead against hers. "I hate to leave you, but I know you have to work. Can I call you later?"

"I can't wait," she whispered, and he smiled.

"Until later then."

They said goodbye and Christo waited until she was safely inside before he drove away. Noosh waved goodbye, then got into the elevator, feeling bereft at the parting. Suddenly she realized something else; she had left her cane at his place. Grinning to herself, she tested her legs again, hopping gently from one to the other. Yes, her back still protested but she felt different, better – maybe it was just the shot of confidence that last night had given her.

In the apartment, Ally had already left for work, leaving Noosh a note not to worry about coming in late. Usually, Noosh was there earlier than anyone, but today she took Ally's note at face value and took a long soak in the tub, hoping to ease some more of her back pain, then called her doctor and asked if there was anything she could do to speed up her recovery.

"Well, this is a good sign," Beth said cheerfully. "You sound more motivated than ever. Well, it's been almost seven months, so you should have started noticing improvements regularly. But, yes, I think you could help yourself along – maybe a yoga class or two a week, and swimming. Don't try running yet, that may be too much."

Noosh laughed, cheered by the thought of improving her situation. "I hated running before I got shot, so that won't be hard. But yoga and swimming, there's no problem there. In fact, my building has a pool, and my boss does yoga so I can piggy-back on her class, hopefully."

"Wow," Beth chuckled, "what happened? Not that I'm not over-the-moon about this change in attitude, but what gives?"

A gorgeous man, whose magnificent cock I'm dying to ride. Noosh thought about saying it aloud, grinning to herself, then merely laughed. "Just want to get my life back."

"Good for you, Spud."

Noosh burst out laughing. *"Spud?"*

"I'm trying out an English nickname on you. *Spud.* Such a satisfying word to say."

"You nutter," Noosh said in her best London accent, laughing. "Listen, when you're not my doctor anymore, let's go out for drinks. I owe you."

Beth laughed. "It's my job, but yeah, I'd like that. You have my cell phone number."

HE WATCHED her get into the cab from the black-out sedan he had rented. It was becoming more and more difficult to go on these excursions without telling anyone. A lot of burner phones and sneaking around, but the Secret Service were antsy now that he was officially the nominee. Destry's hands gripped the steering wheel, his anger a slow-burning thing. He had seen the Mercedes pull up a couple of hours earlier, seen her kiss, of all people, Christofalo Montecito. That bastard had his hands on Destry's property. He and Christo had history – yes, it had been a long time ago, but still. Christo had come out on top then, and now he was fucking Anoushka.

No. This was a good thing, he thought to himself. Let them have their moment, let them fall in love. Because at the end of it all, Destry would have a double victory when Christo mourned the death of his Anoushka. Yes, that was it.

But Destry wasn't satisfied with just that. He wanted Noosh to be scared, to know he was watching. He wanted to test her.

And he knew exactly how to do it.

CHAPTER NINE

Fogliano Montecito listened to the radio interview with his only son with a neutral expression. He had to admit; Christo came across very well. He even managed to answer the difficult questions about Fogliano's business without disrespecting his father, which Fogliano found astonishing.

And *moving*. Ever since that night at the mansion when he'd beaten his son, humiliated him in front of his friends, his family, Fogliano hadn't been able to sleep. What had Christo done to deserve it? *Nothing*. But Fogliano, anticipating the sneers of the other heads of the families, had been thinking only of himself. And what was worse, he had known Christo's defection had been coming.

Defection. Fogliano shook his head, rebuking himself. Going off to make beautiful, bespoke furniture was hardly *defecting*. He also had to admit he admired Christo for wanting to break free – he knew his son had serious moral doubts about some of Fogliano's practices.

Fogliano had himself been born into this life. His father, Fausto, an immigrant from Sicily, had come to New York seventy years ago, already a consigliere to Maximo Gaboni. When Max, childless, had anointed Fausto heir, he had taken over the running of the family.

Fogliano had been his father's trusted advisor, and he had hoped Christo would be his. And for years his son had been there to advise – on legal matters. Christo was very careful never to get involved with the seedier, more violent side of the business, and now that Fogliano looked back, he could see that from a young age his son was determined to tread a different path.

But Fogliano was a proud man, and that night, a drunk one too. He had showboated and lost his son in the process. *God damn it.*

He called in his second, a serious young man called Lucio, and asked him to call Christo. "Tell him I'd like to meet."

Ten minutes later, Lucio got back to him. "He respectfully declines, Don Montecito."

Fogliano sighed, but he wasn't surprised. "Then we'll have to do this from left of field. Have someone watch him – from a distance, don't intrude. I want to know his daily routine, who his friends are, if he's screwing anyone."

"Yes, sir."

Fogliano sat back. If his son wouldn't bend for him, then he would have to be the one to do it. By finding out as much as he could about how his son lived now, he would find a way in, something to bond over. He wasn't yet ready to give up on Christo – his only remaining blood family. Because despite everything, he loved his son.

Noosh made a face when she walked into the meeting room to find them all watching a press conference Destry was holding. She dumped her bag on the table and nodded to Ally, who smiled and turned back to the television.

Even the sound of Destry's voice made Noosh's teeth grind, but she studied his image on the flat screen television. *How could I ever have found you attractive?* she thought, then sighed. She'd *never* found him attractive – she'd just gotten swept along by his love-bombing of her. She'd had no agency whatsoever in that relationship. A flashback of her shooting blasted into her mind, and she winced, her stomach twisting at the memory. She knew it had been him, knew he hadn't sent a hitman, that he had wanted to do it himself. She remembered the pain of that first bullet slamming into her stomach, then the cold muzzle pressed against her belly and the fire that exploded in her as he shot her again so coldly. Noosh felt sick.

"You okay?" Liam nudged her, but she nodded, looking back at the television screen. Destry was playing the role of the benevolent nominee, his face set in a serious but caring expression.

"My hope is this – that this initiative will once and for all open up people's hearts and minds to this spiraling situation."

Vomit. Noosh leaned over to Liam. "What's he talking about?"

"A new campaign to stop violence against women. He's specifically talking about gun crime against women."

Noosh stared at Liam as if he were mad. "Are you kidding me?"

"Shhh."

Noosh gaped back the television screen. Destry had contorted his face into one of sorrow. *Disingenuous bastard.* Noosh's hands, sweating, curled into fists under the table.

"Too often, because of the prevalence of privately-owned firearms, we see domestic situations escalate to murder twice as quickly when a firearm is involved."

"Because it's not so bad when they just beat, stab, strangle, or otherwise abuse their partners, is it, fuckwad?" Noosh said bitterly. Ally shot her a strange look, and Noosh realized she'd said too much. Impartiality. A journalist's mantra.

She wanted to stand up and scream that this man had subjected her to horrific abuse even before he'd broken into her home and tried to kill her. That he was the last person on earth who should be bloviating about violence against women. Her nails dug hard into her palms.

But still, she knew no one would believe her. And if he ever caught wind of her talking about him, Noosh knew Destry would come back to finish her for sure – and make her suffer even more this time.

Noosh dragged her attention back to the screen. Destry paused and looked around at the audience.

"In these cases, there are too many victims, too many people who deserve to hear their names heard, and it seems wrong to highlight any one case, but I was listening to a late-night radio show here in New York a few evenings ago and heard the story of a young woman who was shot and almost killed in her home."

No. No. This couldn't be happening. He wasn't really going to call her out on live television, was he? He wouldn't *dare*... Noosh realized everyone in the room was looking at her.

Destry smiled kindly into the camera. "Sarah Marsh was almost killed by gun-violence six months ago and has been kind enough to share her journey with the listeners of Allison Monroe's *Late Night with Ally* over the past months. I understand that the perpetrator has never been found. What must it be like for Sarah Marsh to know that her would-be killer is still out there? That, whether or not he is known to her, he could... *try again?*"

Noosh felt as if a wrecking ball had been slammed into her chest. So, not only was he calling her out, but he was also threatening to kill her. On live television. The shock was constricting her chest and she couldn't breathe. She stood, staggering as she pushed her chair back, and stumbled from the room. She heard Liam and Ally come after her as she moved towards the restrooms. "Please, let me be..."

Ally, of course, didn't listen, and steered Noosh into the bathroom, ordering a startled woman out. The woman took one look at them both and skittered away in alarm. Ally locked the door behind her and wrapped her arms around a sobbing Noosh.

"It's okay, sweetheart, get it out."

Noosh couldn't stop the tears, but she had enough control to know that she couldn't tell Ally the real reason she was crying. She played it off as being reminded about the shooting and being upset at hearing that her killer hadn't been caught, and Ally seemed convinced.

Ally shook her head. "I was all ready to give the guy a parade until he said that. He'll lose some of the ground he gained by saying it. Insensitive jerk."

It was such an understatement of Destry's evil nature that Noosh couldn't help give a laugh, wiping her tears. "I'm okay. It just sometimes catches up with me."

"I'm not surprised – I'm just shocked it didn't happen sooner. You guys not heard of PTSD over there in Blighty?"

Noosh smiled. "Oh, we have. We just have that stiff upper lip thing going on."

Ally smiled and let her go so she could splash water on her face. "Noosh, we can arrange counseling, it's not a problem."

Noosh hesitated. "I just don't know if I'm ready, Ally. Not yet. I'm trying to get back on an even-keel. So much has changed."

Ally grinned. "Like a certain handsome Italian-American?"

Even the mention of Christo made her whole body relax, and she smiled shyly at Ally. "He is...very sweet."

"The sweet Mafioso's son." They both laughed. "Come on, details…are you seeing him again?"

Noosh nodded. "We're going to his place upstate this weekend."

Ally's eyes widened. "Wow."

Noosh chuckled, some color returning to her face. "I want to say it's not like that…and, for the moment, it isn't. Sort of. Because of my back."

"Plenty of things you can do without, um, straining yourself."

Noosh giggled, her cheeks now burning pink. "Oh, I know."

Ally hugged her. "He's gorgeous, and he clearly likes you a lot. I'm glad, honey. You deserve a good one."

Noosh returned to her desk, ignoring the curious stares of her co-workers, knowing that only Ally and Liam would be brave enough to question her. She checked the time. It would be about four p.m. in London, and seeing as Destry obviously knew where she was, she risked a call to her parents.

"Hello, love, how are you?" Hearing her mom's soft voice made her want to cry again, but a half hour later, she hung up with a smile on her face.

There was no way she was letting Destry ruin her life. He could go fuck himself. If he messed with her, she would go to the press, and whether people believed her or not – she would bring him down.

With new resolve, she got back to work.

Destry Papps walked away from the podium and greeted some of his well-wishers, all the while thinking about Noosh and whether she had seen the conference. Yes, he was playing with fire by goading her, but he wanted her cowed and terrified before he inevitably killed her, to know that she was his, that he controlled every aspect of her life…

. . .

...WHAT REMAINED OF IT.

CHAPTER TEN

"So," Christo said, steering the car out of the city, "why on earth was a girl like you at that club that night? I mean, not that there's anything wrong with that club."

Noosh grinned at him. "Well, *you* were there, so there really *was* nothing wrong with it. But I was doing a story on BDSM culture in New York, and that was a research trip." She reached over to touch his face. "And no matter how it ended, I'm glad I did go there."

Christo kissed her hand. "Me too, sweetheart. So, what happened to the story?"

"I canned it," she said, uncomfortable, and smiled wryly as he turned to frown at her. "I didn't feel I was qualified to write it. Amazing sex doesn't count as BDSM. But I'm more interested in why *you* were there."

Christo hesitated. "I admit...I behaved appallingly that night. I was drunk and sad, and you were too good for that place. But I have been a...client of that type of club in the past. Does that shock you?"

Noosh shook her head. "No, actually...it's kind of hot. So, are you into being dominant, or submissive?"

Christo grinned. "Look at you with the terminology. Well, have you heard of a switch?"

"Like a whip?"

"Ha, no, I mean someone who can either be a sub or Dom depending on their mood, or the person they are with." He wiggled his eyebrows at her suggestively, and she chuckled, feeling her face redden.

"Either, huh?"

He grinned at her. "Curious?"

"Yes, actually...if I was with someone I trusted."

He squeezed her hand. "I'll strive to be that person."

Feeling brave, she took his hand and slid it under her skirt. Christo grinned and caressed her through her panties.

"God, Noosh, I want you so much."

Noosh put her hand on his crotch, feeling his cock harden beneath her fingers. "That night in the club...I've never, I mean, that was the most exciting night of my life – up until now. I wish so much that I was well enough to say to hell with it. Believe me, I would fuck you right here, right now, if I could."

"Baby, there's plenty we *can* do...and think of the anticipation. I'd never risk your health, even if you are the sexiest woman on this planet."

It seemed strange that *he*, he who could have *any* woman in the world, would say that about *her*. Her old insecurities bubbled just beneath the surface and she was quiet for a time. Christo held her hand the whole way into the countryside, and when he turned down a long track, Noosh was surprised to see a relatively modest farmhouse in front of them. It was such a stark contrast to his polished Upper East Side apartment that she gave a little laugh and Christo grinned at her reaction. "You like?"

"It's beautiful." She beamed at him. "More how I imagine you living."

They got out of the car and Christo offered her his hand. "I bought it because it reminded me of where I spent summers in Italy with my Mom. Despite Dad's fortune, she insisted that she wanted a smaller place, no staff, no hangers-on. Something that was a family home."

"Is she still with you?"

"No, she died when I was seven."

"I'm sorry."

Christo nodded tightly and Noosh could see he was upset. She stopped him and stood on her toes to press her mouth to his. "I'm sorry, baby, you must miss her."

He leaned his forehead against hers. "Thank you. I wish she could have met you, she would have loved you."

"Me too." God, this man was driving her crazy, and yet he was still so sweet, so sensitive she could hardly believe he was the same man who'd roared at her in anger the night they met.

It wasn't him then, she told herself, *he was in pain.* She remembered, in the first days after she had been shot, angry, scared, frustrated in the hospital, she had taken it out on her parents, Beth, the nurses, even Ally. She had, of course, apologized for her angry behavior, but she could understand how he felt, and she was way past forgiveness with him.

Being with Christo as he showed her around the small farmhouse, she felt closer to him every moment. He made her laugh one moment, and then the next he would look at her with such skin-scorching desire that she felt weak. Right here, right now, if the rest of the world faded away, she wouldn't be sorry.

"Are you hungry? We might have to go to the local farmer's market to stock up. Like Mom, I don't have staff here, so it'll be just us for the weekend."

Noosh smiled. "Good, and yes, I could eat a walrus."

Christo laughed. "That's...random. Let's go see if the market has walrus."

. . .

It was weirdly domesticated, but a lot of fun, pushing a cart around the market, choosing fresh produce. *This man comes from a mafia family, and here he is discussing the merits of pomegranates over grapes,* she laughed to herself.

She let Christo take the lead in buying ingredients; he clearly knew what he was doing, and when they were packing their paper sacks into his car, she asked him about it.

"Mom, again," he said, shrugging good-naturedly. "While Dad taught me the harsh truths of the world, she taught me the finer things. Cooking, painting, even carpentry."

"And now you're a full-time carpenter?"

Christo nodded, pride in his eyes. "After lunch, I'll show you the workshop. Get you all sawdusty."

Noosh giggled at the playfulness in his eyes. "Nutter."

"Excuse me?"

But she just laughed and he leaned over to kiss her. "I'll take it."

"Drive faster, man, I'm starving."

For lunch, they sat outdoors at a picnic table he had set up, enjoying freshly baked bread, soft oozy Brie and sweet peaches, and cold white wine. Christo had arranged their chairs so that she could lean back against him afterward. The view looked out over rolling fields and she gave a laugh. "Only an hour or two outside the city and we could be anywhere else but New York."

He pressed his lips to her temple. "You like?"

"I like very much."

"I'm glad."

She turned to face him then. The desire was back in his eyes, and Noosh gazed back at him, then began slowly unbuttoning her dress. Christo put down his wine glass and watched her, a lazy, sexy grin on his face. Noosh pulled the top of her dress aside, revealing her lacy pink bra. Christo bent his head, and pulling the lace of the cup down, he took her nipple into his mouth, flicking his tongue around the nub, sending shivers of pleasure through her body.

She reached down to unzip his jeans, taking his cock in her hands and stroking along the length of it. She heard Christo moan. "God, I want to fuck you so badly, Noosh."

She gave a little chuckle. "Anticipation, baby."

Christo gave a growl and in one swift movement, swept her into his arms and to his bedroom. "We may not be able to fuck yet, baby, but I'm going to kiss every inch of your heavenly body, and then suck your clit until you weep."

Noosh felt her sex flood with arousal as he dropped to his knees between her legs. Always checking to make sure she wasn't in pain, he buried his face between her legs and began to lick and gently bite at her clit until it was rock hard and she was moaning his name over and over.

Christo gently slid two fingers into her cunt as he pleasured her, moving them in and out until Noosh was screaming and crying out as a shattering orgasm hit her. Christo kept his promise and tears of joy, of ecstasy, flooded down her face.

"I want your cock inside me so badly," she said breathlessly, kissing him. She hooked a leg over his body to test if she could do it, and then winced. "But my bloody back..."

"Don't stress out, baby, we have all the time in the world."

"There is something I *can* do for you." She clambered down his body and took his diamond-hard cock into her warm mouth. She loved the silky feel of the skin over the hardness of him. He was so huge she couldn't take all of him into her mouth. She kissed, licked, and teased the tip, her hands stroking down the length of him. She massaged his balls gently, then milked him dry as he shuddered and came, swallowing every salty drop of his cum.

Noosh crawled back to his side as he caught his breath and grinned at her. God, she *adored* this man, his boyish grin, his devastatingly handsome face, his playful nature that was so at odds with her first memory of him. *You would be so easy to fall in love with,* she thought with a shock.

Christo opened his arms and she went into them, pressing her skin against his. It was still only mid-afternoon, but they fell asleep together, waking only when Christo kissed her mouth so tenderly that she had to wake up to gaze at him.

IT WAS early evening when they dressed, and Christo showed her around his workshop. Noosh marveled at his, running her hand over the hand-turned pieces of wood that would eventually fit into a beautiful love seat, or a table or chair. She laughed a little. "From organized crime to this...not that *you* were a criminal," she added hastily, but Christo just smiled and shrugged good-naturedly.

"However innocent I want to think I am, yes, my family business is crime. Corruption."

"Not anymore."

"I hope not. Although if I ever find out who hurt you, my darling..."

Feeling uncomfortable, Noosh looked away, admiring a small side table he had almost finished. "This is gorgeous."

"Not compared to what I'm looking at."

Noosh flushed as he came to her, tilting her chin up so he could kiss her. "You're completely intoxicating, Anoushka Taylor."

"Right back at you, dude." They both laughed then Christo turned to retrieve something from a cupboard.

"This is something else I've been working on...not furniture, but a little project I began when I was in rehab. Don't freak out, but..."

He handed her a small wooden bust, only a few inches high. Noosh studied it then gasped a little. The female figure, her head and shoulders only, had long wavy hair that fell over one eye and fell in a cloud down past her shoulders. Her lips were full and her one visible eye was large and soulful. It was Noosh.

"I did it from memory, but I think I caught your likeness." He sounded a little nervous, and Noosh turned tear-filled eyes to him.

"It's incredible. God, Christo, I'm so moved."

He stroked her face. "You've been haunting my dreams, Noosh Taylor, for months now. Is it too much?"

"It should be, but it isn't. Not from you." Her voice was a whisper and he kissed her gently.

"You know, I was strangely superstitious about this little woman. I thought if I kept her in the house, you would never actually come here. So that's why she's out here."

Noosh grinned and he chuckled. "I know, dumb, huh?"

She shook her head. "Not at all. But...I *am* here."

"So, we should bring her in."

They walked back to the house. "Hungry?"

"Always." She grinned. Together they prepared roast chicken with rosemary and lemon, and roasted vegetables.

"Almost a traditional roast dinner," Noosh nodded approvingly and Christo grinned.

"The last time I was in London, I was unfortunate to try something called Marmite." He grimaced at the memory of the savory salty spread and Noosh looked outraged.

"Marmite? On a piece of buttery toast, with a cup of tea? You haven't lived, Montecito."

"It was beyond gross."

Noosh giggled. "You want to talk about gross? What about that sorry excuse you call chocolate over here? Waxy vomit bars."

"Have you never heard of s'mores?"

"I hate marshmallow."

She laughed as Christo threw his hands up in the air. "It's over between us."

She slid onto his lap. "I'm sad."

Christo's eyes lit up. "I'll make you happy."

You already have... She kissed him, the intensity growing between them until he laid her gently on the floor. He slid his hand under her t-shirt and stroked her belly, making it quiver with desire. Noosh traced the line of his full lips, and then brushed her fingertips through his thick, dark, eyelashes. "You are so beautiful," she whispered, almost incredulously, and he chuckled.

"You stole my line."

Noosh smiled at him, but her eyes were serious. "I keep waiting for something to ruin this perfect day, but it hasn't. How cynical is that?"

"After what you've been through in your young life, it doesn't surprise me."

"Not that young."

"How old are you?"

Noosh grinned. "I'll be twenty-five in a month."

"Old woman."

"Hey!" She mock-punched his jaw and he laughed. "Then how old are you, crumbly?"

"Thirty-nine." His smile faded. "Does the age difference bother you?"

She shook her head. "My mum always told me I was an old

soul, and I am. The guys my age? Good god." She shuddered and he laughed.

"I'm serious. When you're forty, I'll be nearly sixty."

"And still the most devastating man on the planet," she countered, a thrill running through her when he talked about the future as if they would be together. *If Destry doesn't kill you first.*

The thought came out of nowhere and she faltered. She tried to hide it but Christo, watching her closely, noticed. "What is it, sugar?"

"Honestly, nothing." She wriggled closer to him. "Everything's perfect."

Christo looked unconvinced but she was relieved when he seemed to let it go. "Wanna watch a movie together?"

"Love to."

LATER, after they'd gone to bed and Noosh was asleep, Christo slid from the bed. For a long moment, he stood at the end of the bed, watching her sleep. God, she was lovely. Christo knew he was falling for her – *scratch that,* he thought, *I'm in this deep. I'm crazy about this little girl.*

He crept downstairs and snagged his phone. He'd had the idea after Noosh's little hesitation earlier, but he didn't want to scare her, nor did he want to make her uncomfortable.

It was just...he didn't want her to live in fear for the rest of her life. If whoever shot her – Christo couldn't think of that without cringing – came after her again... If they actually finished the job and killed his beloved Noosh...*no. No fucking way.*

He called Bertie, who he knew would still be awake at this late hour. "Hey, buddy."

"Hey, Bert. Listen, I need to ask you a favor."

"Go for it."

"That guy you used when Dimitri Engles was trying to blackmail you?"

"The private dick?"

"Yeah," Christo said, his voice grim. "Can you give me his number? There's something I want him to find out."

CHAPTER ELEVEN

"Anoushka Taylor, have you been taking some wonder pill I don't know about? Because the progress you've made since we last met is incredible." Beth shook her head in disbelief as she watched Noosh move around the physio room three weeks later.

Noosh grinned at her. Her back still ached a little but the swimming she had been doing had been paying off – it helped that she had the prospect of finally being able to be with Christo to motivate her. Tonight he was flying them to Europe, to a small island off the Italian coast, and Noosh was determined that they would finally make love, if not for the first time, then for the first time since their reunion.

And god, she couldn't wait. Every waking moment, she thought about him, a permanent smile etched on her face of late. She had spent every weekend at his farmhouse, and every weekday he picked her up from work and took her back to his apartment. Ally complained that she never saw her roommate, but Noosh could tell that her boss and friend was delighted for her.

Now Beth, laughing, signed off her charts. "Well, kiddo, you did it – I'm so proud of you."

"I couldn't have done it – couldn't have survived – without you, Beth. I'm serious. You made this so much easier than I thought it would be."

"Aww shucks," Beth grinned and Noosh laughed.

"And I meant it about keeping in touch. You've become a real friend to me."

"And you to me, honey. Let's get together soon."

IN THE CAB back to work, Noosh called Christo. "It's on, baby."

Thrills ran through her body when she heard his low, throaty laugh. "I can't wait, baby. And those toys we talked about? I've ordered a bunch."

Her sex quivered and she lowered her voice. "I'll be thinking about you inside me all day."

"The same, my darling. Later."

"Later."

It was on the tip of her tongue to tell him she loved him, but she held back. She wanted to be one hundred percent sure of her own feelings and of his as much as she could. The last thing she wanted to be seen as was a silly little girl with a crush. Christo had a gravitas about him, even with his fun-loving side, that made her feel as if this were a real, adult relationship that she needed to be wholly mature about.

Still, the thought of his cock, huge and thick, gliding inside of her made her quiver with anticipation. At work she was distracted and Ally nudged her during a staff meeting to attract her attention.

"This is us, space cakes, you might want to get your mind out of Montecito's pants for this bit." Noosh colored as Ally chuckled softly.

Seth was talking. "We've been granted full access to Destry Papps's campaign team, and the candidate himself. He has asked that 'Sarah Marsh' be his liaison – that's a coup for you, Noosh, so congrats."

Noosh felt her heart sink as the others gave her a little round of applause, and waited for them to stop. "With respect, Seth, being shot doesn't make me qualified for this. I feel that the candidate would be taking advantage of my situation to further his own cause rather than to help women. I'd rather not have anything to do with it."

The room was silent, her work colleagues looking at her in astonishment. Seth was the first to recover, clearing his throat, his shock and a little annoyance clear in his eyes. Noosh's heart thudded uncomfortably. She could feel the tension rolling off her boss.

"Well, that's something you need to work out with Ally, but it would be a big get for the station. But if you're uncomfortable..." He trailed off, but his meaning was clear. She was letting the team down. Noosh felt like crying.

Ally asked her to come into her office as soon as the meeting was finished, and Noosh knew it wouldn't be an easy conversation. She sat opposite Ally, wishing it was six o'clock and that she was on the plane to Europe with Christo's arms around her.

Ally didn't mince her words. "What's your problem with Destry Papps?"

Noosh clenched her fists in her lap. "I find him fake, disingenuous, and a creep." That was the strongest way she could find to express how she felt without giving anything away, but she could see Ally wasn't convinced.

"Noosh, you're not a child and I'm not an idiot. There's something more."

"No. He just gives me the impression that he wants to use my story for his own personal gain." *And besides that, he was the one who shot me.* If only she could say that aloud and have Ally believe her. God.

Ally sighed. "Well, as Seth said, it would be a coup. We'll tell Senator Papps that we'll deal directly with him through me, but Noosh, do you realize the opportunity you're turning down?"

"I do." God, she hated Destry and his manipulative behavior. He knew exactly what he was doing, invading her work life. For once, she was glad Christo was from a mob family – Destry wouldn't dare interfere with that...would he?

No. It was one thing to mess with her, another thing entirely to get tangled with the mob. At least that's what she would tell herself – it was the only thing giving her any sense of protection from him at the moment.

She sighed and rubbed her eyes. "I'm sorry, Ally."

"It's just with this, and the story you abandoned... Seth will begin to wonder if you're really cut out for this job."

Noosh knew it was coming but it was still a shock to hear. "I know. I just need to get my head together...and maybe I'll take another look at the club story. I might have an...in...there now." She colored, but couldn't help smiling a little. The thought of going to Christo's club with him had been growing in the back of her mind, but she'd dismissed it as just her raging lust for him. Now though...maybe she could salvage her story too.

Ally looked mollified and studied her. "Take this week with your man, and come back to me refreshed. We will be working on the Senator's story, Noosh, but maybe we can work around your objections. And," finally she smiled, "if the BDSM club is something you want to revisit, then go for it. That story had wheels."

. . .

When Christo picked her up, Noosh pressed her lips to his for a long time and he laughed when they finally broke away for air. "Well, hello to you too, baby." He cupped her face in his palms. "Did you get even more beautiful?"

Noosh grinned, her whole body relaxing. "Nope, but you did." She loved the way his thick, dark lashes brought out the startling green of his eyes. His skin, olive, was speckled with freckles, his beard as black as his hair. Noosh couldn't imagine a more beautiful man.

He drove them straight to the airport, and she admired the deft, friendly way he dealt with passport control as he and Noosh arrived on the runway. The private plane, borrowed, he told her, from Bertie, was an Embraer Lineage with five cabin areas with every luxury, and a master-suite with a king-size bed and a walk-in shower. Noosh's eyes were huge and she didn't know whether to approve or disapprove of the opulence.

Christo was watching her, his eyes amused. "For your information, this thing cost fifty-three million and yes, it's completely over-the-top and ridiculous. Usually, it's not my thing – I'm a little more environmentally conscious, but just this time... For this occasion, I thought it was fitting." He bent his head to kiss her then nuzzled her neck, finally whispering in her ear. "I don't know about you, Noosh, but I'm not going to be able to wait until we get to Italy...and I owe you the very best for how I treated you the last time we were together. I want this to be perfect."

Noosh leaned into his body, into his body heat, and gazed up at him. "It will be perfect."

He stroked her face as the pilot came over the P.A. and asked them to strap in for the flight. Christo slid his hands around her waist and fixed her seat belt in place, even making that simple move so erotic that Noosh thought she might explode. Christo never took his eyes from her as he belted himself in next to her, and as they took off, he leaned over and they kissed. The kiss was soft at first, but as their desire grew, their tongues caressing the other's, it became an urgent thing, their need for each other almost desperate.

Noosh strained against her seatbelt in her need to be next to him, but when the seatbelt warning light clicked off, Christo put his hand over the belt fastener, stopping her from opening it, grinning as he released himself.

He sank to his knees between her legs and smiled up at her. "I'm in charge now, beautiful."

Noosh shivered with desire as he slid his hands under her dress and gently drew her panties down her legs before beginning to unbutton her dress. She had deliberately not worn a bra, wanting him to see that her nipples were hard and ready for his touch, wanting him to see her arousal. The sigh of happiness he gave when he pushed the fabric of her dress aside was heady. Christo leaned forward and kissed her mouth, her throat, down to her breasts. He sucked each nipple until Noosh was gasping for air, then trailed his lips down her stomach before burying his face in her belly. He kissed each scar before rimming her navel with his tongue, dipping it into the deep, round indentation, tongue fucking it until Noosh was squirming with pleasure.

Christo smiled his devastating smile at her. "Spread your legs wider for me, beautiful."

Noosh did as he asked and Christo took her clit into his mouth, his tongue lashing around the tiny bud. Noosh's body reacted, writhing, bucking against his face until she came, her cunt flooding with arousal as Christo delved his tongue deep inside her, tasting her with obvious pleasure.

When he raised his head to kiss her again, she could taste herself on him. His fingers trailed down her belly, gently stroking her. She gazed at him, her hands cradling his face. "I want you inside me," she whispered, and he nodded, smiling.

He released her seat belt and swept her into his arms, carrying her back to the bedroom. He laid her gently on the bed and stepped back to strip. Noosh watched him, her eyes sweeping over his magnificent body, the broad shoulders, slim hips, and his thick, long cock, which curved upwards proudly against his belly. He rolled a condom down over it, grinning at her obvious lust, then covered her body with his. He stroked her face. "Now?"

"Now...please..."

Noosh wrapped her legs around him as, tantalizingly, he notched his cock into the entrance of her cunt, then waited. She groaned at him, and he laughed. "More?"

"More..."

He pushed in a couple of inches. "More?"

"Christo!" Noosh groaned in frustration.

He laughed out loud then launched himself deep inside her with one firm thrust. Noosh gasped at the feeling of him filling her so completely, his cock plowing her mercilessly as they fucked. Noosh tilted her hips up so he could go deeper, her back only protesting a little, but she couldn't care less. She was lost in this man, his hands pinning hers to the bed, his mouth seeking hers hungrily. The sensation of him driving himself so relentlessly into her, seeing how much he wanted her...god, it was intoxicating.

Noosh was almost delirious with pleasure as Christo dominated her body, his eyes never leaving her face, and when she came, a towering, shattering explosion of pure ecstasy, he was triumphant, victorious as he too climaxed.

Panting for air, they kissed as they recovered. Christo gathered her to him, holding her tenderly. "Are you mine?"

Noosh smiled, her eyes full of tears. "I'm yours, forever." And they began again where they left off.

. . .

BERTIE SAT IN THE BAR, considering ordering another shot of bourbon, when his associate, a private detective called Alan, clapped him on the back. Bertie greeted him, shaking his hand warmly. Alan had been a business connection his family had held for many years – Alan's tenacious work ethic and utter professionalism were second to none in the business.

Bertie ordered them both a drink then raised his eyebrows at his friend. "So, Noosh Taylor. Anything?"

Alan picked a folder out of his case. "Anoushka Eleanor Taylor, twenty-five next week. A graduate of a high-end college in London – left with top honors. Masters in Communications and Media. Came to New York just under two years ago after she was offered a trainee position with Ally Monroe. Been at the same place ever since, but you knew that. A few boyfriends, nothing long-term, until three years ago when some friends of hers told me she was practically stalked by someone until she gave in and had a tentative relationship with him. That lasted for about a month before she was hospitalized after trying to kill herself. Seems the 'boyfriend' – and I use the term loosely – was a psycho who beat her. When she tried to leave him, he threatened to kill her."

"Son-of-a-bitch," Bertie spat. He had grown very fond of Noosh since she had started seeing Christo; both of them had the same silly sense of humor, and they both adored Christo. That was enough for Bertie. "Who was he? I assume we think he's the man who shot her."

"That's just it." Alan took a sip of bourbon. "When I tried to find out, I was shut down. Completely, Bertie. Police, lawyers, friends. All of them shut up. That's unheard of. There's always a leak, *always.*"

Bertie took this in. "So, whoever it was has money, power, influence...enough to show his teeth if anyone spilled. Someone who would kill."

"Yup. One thing confuses me. I don't think this guy – if he is the one who shot your friend – has ever killed before, or at least gotten his own hands dirty."

"Why?"

"Because he left her alive. A professional would have put a bullet in her head or her heart, would have made sure. This was a thrill kill. Shooting a woman in the belly means you want her to know she's being murdered. She has time to bleed out, maybe even identify her killer before she dies – or survives, thankfully, in this case. Which means Noosh Taylor probably knows who shot her and is scared enough to keep it to herself. I saw the records of her police interviews in the hospital. She swore up and down she didn't see who it was."

Bertie winced. "Poor kid. Imagine living with that fear."

Alan nodded sympathetically. "And she *is* a kid, too. Twenty-five, Bertie, and she'd already seen so much horror."

"At least she's with Christo now. He'll keep her safe, and he won't be scared off by anyone. I know Christo – if he finds out who this is…" Bertie's voice tailed off, his face grim, and Alan nodded.

"I would give him some advice. Don't get Fogliano involved."

Bertie gave a humorless laugh. "I don't think that's going to be a problem. Why do you say that?"

"Because Fogliano has spies out on Taylor too."

Bertie was astonished. "What the hell? How do you know?"

"Because us private investigators sometimes cross paths when we're following the same subject."

Bertie considered for a moment. "Any chance you can find out why?"

"I'll try, but I won't ask another detective to break his confidentiality code."

"That's fair enough." Bertie signaled for the check. "Thanks,

Alan...god, why on earth is Fog looking into Noosh? I thought he'd washed his hands of Christo. Christo certainly thinks so."

"Mr. Montecito Senior isn't one to let things go, am I right?"

Bertie hissed in frustration. "Alan, scratch my request. I'm going to the source. I'll ask Fogliano myself. I want to know why he's snooping on my best friend's girl."

CHAPTER TWELVE

Christo walked through the quiet villa, feeling the warm breeze blow through the stone hallways. This place was a find, and he wondered idly how much the owner would sell it to him for. It was perfect, quiet, secluded, and nestled on the side of a cliff over-looking the Mediterranean ocean.

The last few days had been perfect too. Here, with Noosh, making love or joking around, cooking simple meals together, walking along the beaches down below – it was heaven as far as Christo was concerned. No staff, no one else to interfere with their little haven. Here they loved and laughed, and Noosh was safe.

Christo had no doubt that this was what he had been looking for all his life. He had never been so happy. He went to look for Noosh now, and found her in the living room, looking out of one of the windows. All she wore was one of his shirts, which fell to her mid-calf, her long dark hair tumbling in waves down her back. Christo stopped at the doorway and watched her.

"Hey."

She turned and gave him the most devastatingly beautiful smile when she saw him. The white shirt was open, revealing her spectacular body, full breasts, flat belly, long legs. Utterly bewitching. Christo went to her and took her in his arms.

"God, you're beautiful," he murmured, his lips against hers, then he kissed her, feeling her soft lips respond.

He lifted her up and sat her on the stone window ledge. Noosh wrapped her legs around his hips as he freed his cock from his pants and entered her. Noosh shivered with pleasure as they fucked there, trying to keep their balance but inevitably tumbling to the floor, laughing. Noosh straddled him and guided him back inside her.

"Come inside me, I want to feel you come," she whispered with a thrust of her hips, squeezing her vaginal muscles so hard around his cock that Christo groaned. "Fuck me, Christo."

They fucked hard, Noosh wanting to feel his cum fill her. When he came, he pumped his thick creamy seed deep into her and she cried out with delight. Christo flipped her onto her back and fucked her again and again until they were exhausted, laughing, laying side by side on the floor. Christo, panting, kissed her. "It's a little late to ask now, but are you on birth control?"

Noosh laughed, nodding. "Oh yes. It was a little reckless of us, but I just needed to feel you come inside me."

Christo propped himself up on his shoulder and gazed down at her. "Noosh...if this is too soon, then please say no...but when we get back to New York, would you consider moving in with me?"

Noosh grinned at him. "I'm practically living with you anyway, so yes, Christo, I would love to."

Elated, Christo kissed her until she laughingly protested that she couldn't breathe. Noosh stroked her hand down his chest and then smoothed his cheeks with her thumbs. "I wish we could stay here forever. Just you and me."

"Say the word and it's done, but you have your career to think of." He smiled then frowned when he saw her expression cloud over. "What is it, baby?"

Noosh hesitated for a long moment. "I'm a bit persona non grata at work at the moment."

Christo was surprised. "They adore you."

"Not at the moment. I turned down an opportunity, and it could affect the whole station."

Christo sat up, and Noosh followed suit. Christo pulled his shirt around her. "Why would you turn it down?"

"Because it would involve working closely with someone I dislike. Intensely."

Christo's eyebrows shot up. "Who?"

He noticed the tiny hesitation before she answered. "A politician. Destry Papps."

Christo felt like he'd been slapped, and his anger roiled inside him. "That bastard."

It was Noosh's turn to look surprised. "You know him?" She checked herself. "Of course you know him, he's a presidential candidate."

"No, I've known him for years. Or rather, I knew him years ago, but I don't expect he's improved in the inte –"

He was cut off as Noosh pressed her lips to his, fiercely, and he tightened his arms around her, laughing softly when she broke away. "What was that for?"

Noosh grinned. "Because everyone else seems to think the sun shines out of his arse. I can't stand the bloke."

Christo smiled, but he had the feeling she wasn't telling him everything. "So, why don't *you* like him? Apart from his obvious douchbagginess – what? That's a *word.*"

Noosh laughed, and to him, she seemed lighter than she had

been indays – as if a weight had been lifted by him disliking the politician as much as she did. "I'll let you have it, until our dotage and we're playing Scrabble, then no way."

"I like the sound of 'our dotage.'" He pressed his lips to her throat and she tangled her fingers in his dark curls.

"Of course," she deadpanned, "you'll get there *way* before me."

Christo wrestled her back to the floor as she shrieked with laughter. "Just for that, you ain't getting the D tonight," he drawled in a dreadful New Jersey accent, and she grinned, reaching down to cup his already stiffening cock.

"Oh yeah?" She was already wrapping her legs around his waist and guiding him inside her.

"Yeah, this is you not getting the D," he said, laughing as he thrust deep into her velvety cunt, watching her cheeks flush with pleasure, her big brown eyes, so chocolatey and warm, and full of adoration for him. God, he loved this woman, but he was terrified of scaring her off. Which was why instead of telling her he would die for her, he kissed her until neither of them could breathe and made love to her long into the night.

It was only later that he realized she hadn't answered his question about Destry Papps, and he wondered again why his love would hate a man she'd never met so much.

CHAPTER THIRTEEN

"Simple," she told him the next morning at breakfast. She waved a piece of melon around as she spoke. "He wants to use my shooting to shill for his half-arsed campaign for stopping gun violence against women, and I don't believe for a *second* he's genuine. Arrogant wanker. So, he isn't going to get to use me to help him. *Arse. Hole.*"

Christo grinned at her cursing but seemed satisfied with her answer. Noosh felt a wash of relief – he believed her. She'd known he hadn't been satisfied with her answer yesterday, and mind-blowing sex could only distract him for so long. She loved that he cared enough to be angry for her, and the gratitude and relief she'd felt when he sided with her about Destry had been overwhelming. She wondered about Christo's past history with Destry but didn't worry about it. She just enjoyed the fact that Christo felt the same way she did.

She smiled at Christo now. He was wearing a simple cheesecloth top, which highlighted his golden olive skin and green eyes. His dark curls were wild about his head, his beard growing wild too. She leaned over and rubbed her chin against it. "Sexy."

Christo laughed. "I know you are."

"Ha ha. How the hell were you single when I met you? You? Have you seen yourself?"

Christo rolled his eyes. "Because I hadn't met you yet."

"Good answer." She cupped his cheek in her hand. "I'm doggone crazy 'bout cha."

Christo burst out laughing. "Was that your attempt at an American accent?"

Noosh pretended to sulk. "*Noooo...*"

"It was. It totally was."

Noosh started to laugh with him. "Well, let's hear your British accent then, smart arse."

Christo grinned widely. "Pleasure to meet you, Miss Taylor. I'm Christofalo, and I, too, am crazy about you." His accent was flawless, and Noosh gaped at him. Christo smirked.

"Chip, chip, chipper."

Noosh made a mock-disappointed face. "You ruined it."

"I took it too far?"

"You did."

Christo sighed. "Perhaps, then, some sort of punishment is probably in order."

Noosh squirmed in excitement. "For me or you?"

Although they had talked about experimenting with BDSM, they had yet to try it, reveling instead in making love as often as they could between talking and getting to know each other. Now, though, Noosh was excited about the thought of being bound by him, whipped or paddled, or doing the same to him. She wanted to explore everything that made him happy.

Christo's smile widened. "Well, I'll flip you for it, but the beauty of being a switch is that you can change your mind like that." He clicked his fingers, but then his smile faded. He leaned forward and took her hands. "But if you say stop, we stop. That's what a safe word is for, baby. I hope you trust me to stop if you ask, but I will always insist on the safe word. It removes any doubt."

"I have no doubts about you, Christo. Not one." Her voice, already a whisper, shook a little, and she was afraid he'd think she was scared, but instead he pressed his lips to hers.

"We take this slow, baby, so you can get a feel for what you like, or what you don't."

She swept a hand through his curls. "What do we start with?"

"Some light bondage? I could simply tie your hands behind you to start, bend you over the window ledge of our bedroom, fuck you from behind."

Noosh felt her sex tighten with excitement. "Maybe you could use a crop on me? On my bum?"

"You are adorable. Yes, I will use a crop on your...bum...if you like."

Noosh looked sheepish. "Bum isn't a sexy word, is it? How about if I tell you to ream my cunt so hard that I scream your name so loud the people of Greece will hear it."

Christo looked impressed. "Wow, you really changed it up there."

"Does it work for you?"

He grabbed her hand and pressed it against his rock-hard cock. "What do you think?"

Noosh squeezed his cock through his pants. "I think we should stop talking about it and get busy."

Christo offered her his hand. "One last thing – the safe word."

Noosh thought for a second. "Dragonfly."

Christo nodded approvingly. "Nice. Remember, if you're ever scared and you need me to stop, or need my help, just say it. I want you to enjoy what we're going to do."

Noosh pressed her lips to his. "Yes...sir."

Christo grinned and began to unbutton her dress. Exposing her breast, he dipped his head and began to suck on her nipple, flicking his tongue around the nub. His hands slid up her thighs, encountering bare skin. He looked up and his mouth curved up into a smile. Noosh grinned.

"I thought, why bother with panties?"

"Why indeed. Straddle me, gorgeous."

She did ask he asked and he supported her as he pushed her dress up. "Your cunt is the most beautiful thing," he said, "so pink and lush." His voice was gravelly with desire, and he slipped two fingers inside her and began to rub, searching for her g-spot. She cupped his face, but he shook his head, smiling. "I'm doing all the touching, baby girl."

Noosh made a face, but the laughed softly. Christo's thumb was stroking a rhythm over her clit, and his eyes were fixed on hers. Noosh felt the power of his machismo, of his control over her, and when he suddenly pinched her clit hard, she gasped and came, giggling at the surprise of it. Her cunt flooded with arousal and Christo pressed hard on her g-spot, making her orgasm again in quick succession.

She recovered, panting. "God, you're incredible."

Christo fisted her long hair in his hand and tugged her head back to kiss her throat. The pain of her hair pulling was brief, but it sent thrills through her body. "I'm yours..."

"You better believe you are." He bit down on her shoulder, hard, not hard enough to break the skin, but Noosh saw he left a mark.

"Please...fuck me. Fuck me hard...*hurt* me..."

Christo gave a growl, and in a flash he had thrown her over his shoulder and was marching towards their bedroom.

He threw her face down on the bed and Noosh wriggled as he pulled her wrists behind her back. She felt him wind something around them.

"Do you want it harder, pretty girl?"

She nodded, and he tightened the knot, making her shoulders burn. The thrill of being totally under his control was heightened as he slipped her onto her back and stood over her, his cock so hard she could see it bobbing under its own weight. "I want to taste you. May I suck you, sir?"

Christo nodded, and she took him into her mouth, curving up her body to meet him. He placed his hands on her shoulders, supporting her as she pleasured him and when he was close, he pulled out and came on her belly. Excitement zipped through Noosh's body as he pushed her back and massaged his seed into her skin. He covered her body with his, using his weight to push down, making her shoulders ache, but Noosh didn't care. The way he was looking at her took away any sting from the pain, turning it into the sweetest pleasure.

"Open your legs, pretty baby."

She did, wrapping them around his waist, and he thrust his cock deep inside her, kissing her so passionately she tasted blood as her teeth cut her skin. It added to the danger of it all, and yet she had never felt more loved.

Christo fucked her hard and fast, coming inside her and withdrawing so she felt his seed spilling down her thighs. He disappeared for a moment, coming back with a crop. He gently stroked the end along her skin. "Where do you want this, baby? Thighs?"

She nodded, and he swatted at her, testing her tolerance. "Harder?"

"Yes, yes..."

He brought the crop down on the soft flesh of her inner thigh, and she gasped at the sting but smiled at him. "Would you strike my belly, sir?"

Christo grinned and swept the crop across her belly, leaving a pink stripe. Noosh groaned, the pain so sweet as he struck her again, leaving a crisscross pattern on her skin. "Yes, yes..." she moaned, and he brought the crop down hard on her breasts, making her nipples sing out with exquisite agony. Christo flipped her onto her stomach and whipped her buttocks, responding to Noosh's urging to hit her harder.

Finally, as Noosh gasped, he dropped the crop and covered her body with his. "I'm going to fuck you from behind now, beautiful."

Her cunt was dripping wet as he pushed into her, his cock swollen so hard it was almost painful. He bit down on her shoulder as he fucked her, murmuring all the while. Telling her what he'd like to do to her, making her moan with desire. When she came, it was an explosion of ecstasy that made her head whirl.

She felt Christo release her hands and, turning her, he gathered her in his arms. His eyes were concerned. "Are you okay?"

Noosh gave a little laugh. "More than okay, baby. God, that was intense."

His furrowed brow eased. "I'm glad, really glad. Thank you for being my partner in this."

Noosh brushed her lips against his. "I'm a more than willing partner. The dominance you had over my body...incredible."

"Are you sore?"

Noosh debated. "A little, but it's a good ache. You were holding back, though, weren't you?"

Christo nodded. "For your first time. It can get quite dark, quite intense, and I never want to put you in a position where you're frightened." He traced her scars with his finger. "I never want you to be scared again."

Noosh gazed up at him, knowing she could never be scared of this man. She brushed her finger tips along his dark lashes. "I would try anything with you...except for maybe anything where I can't breathe, or knife play. Nothing with blood."

Christo frowned. "That's not something I'm into, Noosh. I'm not going to put you at any risk, I swear to God. I couldn't live with myself if I hurt you. I couldn't live without you now."

His tender words made tears swell in her eyes, and she began to cry, waving away his concern, smiling through her tears. "Happy tears, I promise."

He crushed his lips against hers. "I'm in too deep, Noosh. Too deep."

"Me too, baby. Me too."

Okay, so it wasn't 'I love you,' but it felt right to say now, even this early in their relationship. But Noosh knew, without a single doubt, that this man was her future. She wanted to spend every minute with him, travel the world, discover new things. He gave her so much confidence that Noosh felt she couldn't hope to reciprocate enough, but Christo seemed to delight in being with her, and that was enough for her.

They made love again, slowly this time, gazes locked, hands caressing each other, until they were exhausted. They fell asleep wrapped around each other as the late morning breeze drifted gently over their hot bodies.

THIS WAS different from the nightmares she had been having since the shooting. In those ones, her shooter was a faceless figure, his gun oversized, and she always woke before he pulled the trigger.

In this dream, there was no doubt who was coming for her. Destry. And he was chasing her through the cold, barren halls of a great house. No matter how fast she ran, he was always one step behind her. She was screaming for Christo, but he was nowhere to be found at first, then just as Destry grabbed her, she saw him.

Tied to a chair, beaten, bloody. Destry pulled her back from him as she lunged for her stricken lover. Christo looked up, and she saw tears falling down his cheeks.

"I always knew," he whispered, "I always knew he'd take you away from me."

She reached for Christo as Destry plunged a knife into her belly again and again...

NOOSH SAT UP, breathing hard. God, what a dream to have *now*. Christo woke and was immediately by her side. "Are you alright?"

"Bad dream, is all," she said, trying to smile. Her back ached, and her skin felt like it was on fire. She dragged a couple of deep breaths into her lungs, trying to stop her heart from beating so hard. Christo stroked her face, his gaze intense.

"Is it him? The man who shot you?"

She nodded; there was no reason to lie. "I've been having these nightmares ever since. Usually, it's just a replay of that night, but this one...you were there, and you told me you always knew he would take me away from you. Then he stabbed me to death in front of you."

"*Jesus.*" Christo ran his hand through his curls, looking distressed. He pulled her into his arms. "No one will ever take you away from me. The only way I'll let you go is if you, and only *you*, ask me to let you go."

She rested her head against his shoulder, kissed his jaw. "I'll never say those words to you. Never."

His tension eased a little, and he smiled down at her. "You and me from now on."

"You and me," Noosh agreed, "always. *Always.*"

CHAPTER FOURTEEN

Christo smiled over at her in the car as they drove back into Manhattan. "You have a sulky face."

Noosh grinned. "Just thinking about our little piece of heaven. That week went too quickly."

He touched her cheek. "Say the word and we'll go there forever. Italy has radio stations too."

"So tempting." She sighed. "But I still owe Ally so much, and I need to fulfill my obligation to her. She's really helped me so much, and she's become like a big sister to me. I can't just up and leave." She leaned over and kissed his cheek. "Ask me again in a year."

Christo grinned. "Don't think I won't."

She chuckled as he pulled the car into the parking garage of his building. "I'm getting way too used to living in luxury."

"No more than you deserve."

"Well, you see? I need to make my own money so we can have some kind of parity. *Some* kind," she added when he rolled his eyes. "I know I can't compete with Mr. Moneybags, but I need to contribute. I'm no gold-digger."

"I know that," Christo said as they got out of the car and

walked to the elevator. They kissed on the way up to his penthouse apartment and were fooling around, teasing each other, as the elevator doors opened.

Christo stepped out and stopped. Noosh moved around to his side, confused, and then she saw him. The older man who looked so much like Christo he could only be his father. Fogliano Montecito nodded politely to her and then turned his attention to his stony-faced son.

"Christofalo. I've come to talk to you."

"Then you wasted a journey," Christo said coldly. He squeezed Noosh's hand. "As you can see, I'm with my partner, and I have no wish to hear anything you say. Goodnight."

"Please, son." His father's voice quivered with real emotion, and Noosh was taken aback to see tears in the older man's eyes. "I have come to make peace with you – and your lovely companion. Hello, Miss Taylor. Your beauty has not been exaggerated."

Noosh looked with uncertainty at Christo, then spoke. "Hello, Mr. Montecito."

"No, no, Noosh, it's *Don* Montecito, don't forget. Sweetheart, will you go inside while I deal with Don Montecito?"

She nodded, but before going into the apartment, she looked back at him. "If you need me, I'm right here."

She heard Fogliano speak before she closed the door. "Your lady is lovely, son."

She closed the door and moved away, wanting to give them privacy. Their idyllic vacation seemed a million miles away now. *Reality crashes in*, she thought, and went to shower.

CHRISTO WAITED for his father to speak. Fogliano studied his son. "You look well."

"I am."

Fogliano sighed. "Look, Christofalo, there is no way other

than this, to say I'm sorry. I'm sorry for my behavior, for striking you."

"For humiliating me?"

"Of course. Son… I reacted badly to something that was out of my control – it is a failing, I know, and I have no explanation."

"Your anger issues are longstanding, Dad. Mom knew that."

Fogliano's face shut down. "Let's not bring your mother into this."

"Why not? You beat her too."

Christo could see his father's anger roiling beneath the surface, and he was glad. He was deliberately goading Fogliano now, wanting to prove his father hadn't changed one little bit.

To his credit, Fogliano kept his cool. "Christo, whatever my past mistakes, I am trying to settle things between us."

"You've apologized. Things are settled. Now we need never see each other again."

"That's not what I want." Fogliano looked towards Christo's apartment. "From what I have seen, what I have heard…I might soon have a daughter-in-law whom I would like to know."

"From what you've 'seen and heard?' So you're spying on us, on Noosh? Great way to build fences, Dad." Christo's laugh was humorless, and he turned away from his father.

Fogliano stopped him, a hand on his arm. "I will go now, but remember…if you need me…"

Christo shook his father's hand off. "We won't. Goodbye, Dad."

Christo went inside the apartment and closed the door in his father's face. For a long moment, he stood in the dark hallway, breathing deeply, letting his temper calm. He closed his eyes and wondered why his father still had this power over him, to make him feel like a kid, a naughty child, instead of a man. He knew his father of old; there was no way he was making these overtures without a motive. And the fact that Noosh was now on his radar made Christo feel sick. His father would have no qualms about using Noosh to get to Christo, and with Noosh's sweet nature...

"Baby?"

At the sound of her voice, he opened her eyes. She looked at him uncertainly. "Are you okay?"

He opened his mouth to say yes, but he couldn't lie to her, and just shook his head. Noosh came to him and pulled his head onto her shoulder, cradling it, pressing her lips against his forehead. "It's okay," she whispered, "it's okay, baby. I'm here."

Christo knew at that moment that he was deeply in love with her, and that nothing, *nothing,* would ever come between them.

But, of course, he was wrong.

CHAPTER FIFTEEN

It began the morning Noosh returned to work after her vacation. Held up by Liam at reception, who wanted to know every detail of her 'sex-a-thon' (Liam's description, but she couldn't disagree), she finally managed to make it upstairs to her office. In the elevator up, she closed her eyes, remembering making love with Christo that morning, waking up next to him. His mouth on her lips, then on her breasts, her belly, and finally closing over her clit. He'd brought her to the point of orgasm before slamming his huge cock deep into her. Her cunt, her thighs still ached from the pounding of his lovemaking. Noosh bit her lip, trying not to moan aloud at the memory.

She was still smiling when she pushed her way into her office and dumped her bag on her desk. Allison poked her head out of her own office, smiling at her. "Hey, good morning. Great to see you. Have you got a moment for me?"

Noosh grinned at her. "Sure thing, boss, I've missed you."

She walked into Ally's office...and her smile disappeared. Her body went cold, and every instinct told her to run.

Destry Papps stood in Allison's office. "Miss Marsh, how

good to meet you. Allison has been singing your praises." And he leaned forward to shake her hand, this man, this man who had stalked, raped, beaten, and shot her – he smiled at her as if he was, for all the world, a stranger to her, and not her worst nightmare come true.

Noosh felt numb as the three of them sat in the office, discussing the upcoming interview.

Noosh realized she'd been kidding herself, thinking that anything could have kept her safe from Destry. Lying low, trying to act non-threatening – not even the notoriety associated with Christo's last name would keep Destry from her. But still, what could she have done differently these last few months?

She still didn't think the police would help her. Hell, they'd been investigating the shooting and hadn't gotten any answers – for all she knew they had already figure out it was Destry and weren't going to do a damn thing about it.

She should have run away again? No. Even if she ended up dead at the end of this, at least she had gotten the opportunity to spend this time with Christo – she couldn't regret that.

Allison didn't notice the tension between Noosh and Destry, or if she did, she was obviously putting it down to Noosh's apprehension about working with the politician.

So Noosh went along with discussing the interview. She could feel Destry's eyes on her, but she barely glanced in his direction, letting Ally take the lead.

"I think this will be great for your campaign, great for the station. Look, why don't I run and get Seth? He'll want to see you, Senator. Noosh, why don't you run through dates with the Senator and narrow down some windows where we can record the interview?"

No, don't leave me alone with him... But Allison was already out of the door, closing it behind her. Noosh didn't look at Destry.

"You're even more beautiful than I remember."

"Go fuck yourself," Noosh shot back, and Destry laughed.

"I'd much rather fuck *you*, Anoushka, and in fact, before long, I'll get to do just that."

Noosh gritted her teeth and looked at him. Destry wore a supercilious smile, arrogant, utterly certain. "You'll never touch me again, Papps. *Ever.*"

"Oh, I don't think that's true. Before long, my cock will be inside your heavenly cunt again, Anoushka, and I will fuck every memory of that criminal you're screwing out of your pretty head."

"Christo isn't a criminal, and I'd rather be dead. But of course, you've already tried that, haven't you?"

Destry laughed. "I have to admit, putting that lead in your belly was almost as much of a turn on as fucking you. But you lived." His smile disappeared. "Or should I say, you'll get to live as long as *I* decide to bestow life on you, Anoushka. You belong to me, and you need reminding of that fact."

Noosh's eye narrowed, his threats merely making her angry. "What's to stop me from going to the press about you? From telling everyone that you shot me – after you had raped me on multiple occasions? Where would your campaign be then, Senator?"

He moved so quickly that she had no time to react. He trapped her in the cage of his arms, and she struggled to get away from him. Destry kissed her neck, her cheek before his lips went to her ear. "My campaign would be over. But remember this, Anoushka, you'd be dead."

Noosh felt something cold and hard press into her belly. Something sharp. A knife. *God.*

Destry laughed. "That's right, my darling, I'll gut you

without even thinking about it. When you're living with me permanently, by my side, I want you to know that this knife will always be at hand, that I'll kill you whenever it takes my fancy. I'd rather go to prison for life than let you live without me."

He released her, and she skittered away from him, her eyes wide with horror, anger, and terror. Destry smiled his too-white smile at her. "I'll leave you alone for now, Anoushka, but I'll be in touch with instructions soon. Believe me, my darling, you'll follow them."

Noosh couldn't speak. Was this really happening?

Allison returned then, with Seth at her side, and they and Destry began to talk schedules. Noosh stayed silent. What the fuck was she going to do?

Tell Christo.

She closed her eyes. *No.* She couldn't, she didn't want to drag him into this, drag him into something where he could get hurt. But she didn't know who else to turn to. But given his history with Destry…what *was* his history? She needed to know before she asked him for help.

LATER, at dinner, she asked him. Christo looked surprised. "Why do you ask?"

"The dirt bag was at the office today, sucking up to Ally and Seth. He's obsequious and I realized I never asked you what your actual history with him was."

Christo nodded. "Before I tell you, he didn't upset you, did he? Because if he did, I'll fucking kill him."

No, he just threatened my life…again. "No, I just think he's a sleaze." These lies were coming too easily. "Tell me."

Christo sighed, putting down his fork. "He came to my college as an associate professor in my last year."

Noosh blinked. "Papps? *A professor?* Of what, cuntiness?"

Christo snorted with laughter. "That wasn't his official title, but yes. Anyway, he and I didn't see eye-to-eye from the start. He was sexist, misogynistic, and unprofessional. He targeted the women in our class and spent his time belittling them. I took him to task, and he failed me. Luckily for him, the faculty reversed the decision. I was, after all, a Fulbright scholar, and my grade point average was 4.0 from the start."

"Nerd."

Christo grinned. "You know it. Anyway, if it had just been that, then maybe I could just put it down to egos clashing. I was somewhat of a player back then. Anyway, there were rumors, *many* rumors, about him working his way through the female students. And then there were the rumors that he got violent with some."

Noosh's heart felt frozen. *Oh, I believe it.* She waited for Christo to continue.

Christo sighed. "And then there was a friend of mine, Jasmine. She was amazing, Noosh, you would have loved her."

"Did you and she...?"

"Oh, no, I wasn't Jas's type. *You* might have been."

"Ah, okay."

"Come to think of it..." Christo broke off, staring at her, and Noosh frowned.

"What?"

Christo was silent for a moment. "You look like her. It's never occurred to me before, but you do. You look like Jas. Both biracial, with part-Indian heritage. Both beautiful, long dark hair, big brown eyes...*God.*"

"Focus." She gave him a small smile, rubbed his arm. Christo gathered himself.

"He pursued her, quite blatantly, after graduation. She complained to the authorities, but he already had so much influence that they did nothing." Christo's voice broke. "She disappeared, Noosh. I'll never know whether she went into hiding, or if he had something to do with it. I know what I think, but I can't prove it."

Noosh closed her eyes. She would bet her life Jasmine was dead, killed by the monster that was Destry Papps – and he was going to kill *her* too.

Well, Destry, even if you manage to kill me, I'm going to go out fighting. Fighting to live, fighting for a future with this incredible man...

"Christo?"

Christo, lost in his own memories, blinked and smiled at her, touching her face. "Yes, darling?"

"I love you. I'm in love with you." Her voice was strong, not wavering in the least, her gaze steady on his. His answering smile was all the proof she needed, even before he spoke.

"I am so in love with you, Noosh Taylor. I have been, I think, since the start. I think about you every moment. When we're apart, my whole body aches for you. When we're together, I just want to hold you, kiss you, make love to you. You are my world."

She couldn't stop the tears then, and he pulled her into his arms. "This is endgame, right? You and me? We can get through anything as long as we're together."

Noosh nodded, pressing her lips to his. "I just love you so much," she whispered, leaning her forehead against his, drinking him in. "I've wanted to tell you for such a long time, but I didn't want you to think I was just some silly schoolgirl with a crush. With you, I've never felt more like a woman, like an adult, with my own agency. You've given me that."

"I promise to make you the happiest woman in the world."

"No," she said suddenly. "No promises. Let's not make promises to each other. Not while..." She couldn't finish the sentence. *Not while my life is in danger, not while I could be killed at any moment.* "No promises. Deal?"

He didn't look convinced, but he nodded. "Deal. No promises...for now."

"For now. It doesn't change how I feel about you." She looked at him, her warm brown eyes wide and serious.

"God, Noosh..." He swept her up into his arms and to their bedroom – and it was *their* bedroom now, Noosh knew – and onto their bed. He lay on top of her, stroking her face, his eyes full of love and incredulity that she was his, and Noosh knew it was a reflection of her own eyes. *Screw the rest of the world.* This was real, was the happily ever after she was owed. Here, with this beautiful man.

They made slowly, forging a deeper connection than ever before, knowing that the rest of the world would soon interfere again and that stress and worry would invade.

But not this night. This night was about the two of them, and love and being together. As dawn broke over Manhattan, they finally broke apart, gasping for air, laughing, and knowing that just for this night, no one could touch them.

16
CHAPTER SIXTEEN

Allison sighed but nodded. "If that's how you feel, Noosh, then so be it."

"I'm sorry, Ally. I just can't be impartial towards the Senator. I find him...objectionable. If you want to fire me, then it's your right. I just don't feel comfortable working so closely with him."

"I'm not going to fire you, Noosh, don't be silly. I would never make you work with someone you're obviously uneasy with. To be honest, and don't tell anyone I said this, I'm not wild about the man."

Noosh's eyebrows shot up. "Then why...?"

"Because that's journalism, Noosh. More often than not, we have to deal with subjects and people we're not comfortable with. And getting a presidential candidate, especially a popular one, is a huge coup for the station."

Noosh felt a little ashamed. "I guess I'm showing I'm not cut out for this job. The story I canned, the BDSM one...what if I told you I was thinking about finishing it?"

Allison perked up. "Really?" She grinned. "And it has nothing to do with that gorgeous man of yours?"

Noosh laughed, her chest lightening. "Actually, it has *everything* to do with him. You asked me how we knew each other... remember when I went to that club back then? Before the shooting?"

"Of course." Realization dawned. "Oh! He was the guy?"

Noosh nodded. "Cards on the table. He was there and I wanted him. So, I slept with him, but then...he was in a bad place. He wasn't ready for me. I could see it in his eyes, Ally, he was in so much pain. But he never forgot me." Her voice was soft and Ally smiled gently at her.

"You love him."

"I do. So much, Ally. He really is the best man I've ever known."

Ally got up and hugged her friend. "I'm very happy for you, sweetheart. Christo is the polar opposite of his father – and of someone like Papps. Don't worry, when the Senator comes to the station, I'll make sure you're out on assignment or something."

"You're the best."

Ally grinned. "I really am. Now, let's get to work."

IN THEIR FAVORITE BAR DOWNTOWN, Christo greeted Bertie with a hug. "Been a while."

Bertie gave a filthy laugh. "And how is the delectable Noosh?"

"Gorgeous, beautiful, sexy, wonderful. All the adjectives." Christo laughed. "She sends her love, tells you she owes you an 'ass-whooping' at poker the next time you're free."

"She actually said 'ass-whopping?'"

"Okay then, 'arse-whooping.' How are things with you? Any progress with Helena?"

Bertie made a face as the bartender brought their drinks

over. "Helena is seeing a hedge fund director from Paris," he said with undisguised disgust. "*Bertie, darling, you simply must come and meet Holland. He's ex-twor-dinawy.*"

"Oh dear," Christo said with a grin, "someone's jealous. You don't break out the speech impediment unless you're really pissed off."

Bertie shrugged grumpily. At almost forty, with short mid-brown hair and a neatly shaped beard, Bertie was handsome and attractive, but had the unfortunate luck to be friends with Christo. Christo's overwhelming physical beauty put everyone else in the shade, but Bertie never held that against his friend – Christo didn't give two craps about his appearance.

"Anyway, I'm beginning to think there are other fish in the sea."

"There are, and plenty who deserve you more than Helena."

"Let's change the subject, bro."

Christo's smile faded. "What did your guy find out?"

Bertie filled him in on what Alan had told him. "So, there's this big gap where no one knows – or is telling. Noosh was in a relationship with this man, but whether or not she wanted to be…we just don't know."

"No one is spilling the tea?"

"No one. And Alan would have found out if they were. Shifty."

"I'll say." Christo was lost in thought, a horrific idea floating around the back of his head. "Okay, if you don't mind, ask Alan to keep digging. I want to know for certain who this guy is."

Bertie frowned. "For certain? You mean you have an idea?"

"I do, but I'm not comfortable sharing it just yet. If I'm wrong, it could have serious consequences. If I'm right…god help us."

Bertie looked alarmed. "Christo…are you telling me Noosh could be in danger?"

Christo nodded grimly. "Very much so. But Bertie...I'll do anything to keep her safe. *Anything.*"

And for the first time, Bertie saw a bit of Fogliano in his friend's expression, and he shivered.

WHEN CHRISTO SAID goodbye to his friend an hour later, he stepped out onto the street and pulled out his cellphone. He called a number he knew by heart, that he would never forget as long as he lived, and when a woman's voice answered, he identified himself merely by saying, "It's me. Can we meet? I need to ask you something."

He listened to her answer then nodded to himself and told her, "Okay, an hour. Bethesda Terrace. See you there. Thanks."

He had an hour to kill, but he knew exactly where to go. He'd placed an order for something at a high-end store in the city a couple of weeks ago for Noosh, and now he was going to pick it up. It helped clear his palette for the conversation he was soon to have.

THE FLOWERS CAME as Noosh was helping Ally polish up a segment for the night's show. Liam brought, and she could see by his face that he was disturbed by something. "What is it?"

"Someone sent flowers to you, Ally, and forgive me, you know I can't resist a peak at the card. Only...it's not a card. It's a photograph."

Ally picked up on Liam's distress and stood, taking the flowers from him and holding onto the photograph. Her face paled, and Noosh stood. "What is it?"

Ally hesitated, then handed her the photo. For a second, she didn't understand. Two blood patches on... *Oh god.* She thought she might throw up. It was *her*, it was her belly, shot – newly shot

– blood pouring from the first shot an inch above her navel, which was ringed with soot, and the impression of a muzzle, the deep indentation filled with her blood. The bullet wounds were framed carefully. Underneath, the caption read, "*It could happen to anyone.*"

Destry was threatening Ally. *Bastard.*

"*Sick fuck!*" Noosh was apoplectic with anger. Ally put a hand on her shoulder.

"I'm so sorry, Noosh."

"Why are *you* apologizing to *me*?" Noosh said incredulously.

"Because he's taunting you through me. We need to call the police."

Noosh shook her head, dropping the flowers in the trash. "No. Don't give him the satisfaction."

"But..."

"No, don't engage."

Ally disappeared back into her office, and then Liam and Noosh could hear her crying softly.

Noosh looked helplessly at Liam, who shook his head, answering her unspoken question.

"Well, I'm hanging on to this." She waved the photo. "Whoever took it has made his first mistake."

"How so?"

She smiled. "He's admitting guilt. Who else could have taken this picture?"

Liam, after giving her a hug, disappeared back down to reception and Noosh studied the photograph. Destry was tormenting her through Ally – his determination to invade every part of her life in full swing.

"Well, you won't win, jackass." She wouldn't react to Destry's latest tricks – instead she would quietly gather her evidence and drop it on him at the worst moment of his campaign. She'd had enough....and she knew just who to contact to help her protect Christo in all of this.

His father.

CHRISTO SAW her approach and stepped out of the shadows to greet her. The woman, her red hair cut in a bob, her clothes expensive and efficient, nodded at him, unsmiling. "Christo."

"Telly." He kissed her cheek, and she offered a small smile.

"Still handsome as fuck."

"Still beautiful as fuck. Shall we sit?" He grinned at her, and she gave him a genuine smile and nodded.

They found two free seats on a bench outside the Terrace. "So, why the call? I'm surprised – we haven't talked in years. I heard you had a nutty and went to rehab and now you're in love with some British girl."

"All true." Christo studied her. "Telly, I have to ask you about something. When we...were together...you said your husband was screwing around with someone."

Telly nodded. "Some*ones*. I heard he had a girl in every major city. I had stopped caring by then. I was happy enough to screw you, even though I knew you were just fucking me to get revenge on him."

Christo had the grace to look ashamed. "I'm sorry, Telly."

She touched his cheek. "Don't be. I got to fuck *you*, that was enough for me. I didn't need the feelings that went along with it. But you...that isn't you. It wasn't you then or now. Look at you... you're in love. I can see it."

"I am. Very much so. But I need to know something about her past – something I think you can tell me."

Telly looked surprised. "Why? Who is she?"

Christo watched her expression carefully. "Anoushka Taylor."

Telly paled and stood. "And that's where this conversation ends." She began to walk away, but Christo caught up with her, taking her arm.

"Telly, this is important, please."

She rounded on him, her face full of fear. "You don't understand. My alimony, my very large alimony, is only mine on the condition that I never ever talk about that period of Destry's life. And believe me, it's not just the money."

Christo's heart sank. So his guess was right. "So, he did know her. Telly, please. I understand, but this is my love we're talking about. What was she to him?"

Telly looked around the crowded park. "Not here." She said it in a low voice. "Not in public."

Christo nodded. In twenty minutes they were in the darkest corner of a random bar. Telly was trembling, and it distressed Christo to see her so scared. God, what kind of monster was Papps? He and Telly had been divorced for nearly two years. "Telly, tell me."

She hesitated, and when she spoke, her voice was low, terrified. "She was different than the others. The others were just easy fucks. The Taylor girl...she didn't want anything to do with him at first. He stalked her, bombarded her with affection, and, I believe, eventually wore her down, so she agreed to go on a date with him. Her first mistake. He controlled everything, and she tried to leave. So he beat her, threatened to kill her if she ever left."

Christo felt as if a wrecking ball had hit him in the chest, not only fear for his love, but a twisted kind of jealousy that Noosh had ever slept with Destry Papps. "How do you know all of this?"

"I was having him followed," Telly smiled without humor. "I had his place wired. I saw the photos, heard the arguments, the beatings. The things he threatened to do to her."

"He shot her." Christo blurted out. "About a year ago. He shot her, or had her shot."

Telly shook her head. "Oh, no, if your girl was shot, believe me, Destry did it himself. Can she prove it?"

Christo shook his head. "Or won't. She's terrified, I think."

"With good reason. Christo, believe me, I don't bear any resentment towards the girl, in fact, I felt sorry for her even then. He is obsessed with her. I have no doubt he will try again if she doesn't go back to him – and even if she does, he'll eventually kill her. The best thing you can do is get her far away from him."

Christo felt wrecked. "She tried running away before, I think."

"Not far enough."

"God."

Telly studied him. "If he finds out I talked to you, I'm a dead woman."

"I'll hire you protection, around the clock. Or set you up somewhere else. I can't thank you enough for this, Telly."

She touched his cheek. "Beautiful boy. You gave me something Destry could never have given me in a million years."

"What was that?"

"Myself." She hugged him. "Darling, I'd help you bring him down if I could, but we need to be realistic. You, me, your girl... all our lives are forfeit if it means we're a risk to Destry's campaign – and god help us all if he gets in."

"I mean it, Tels. I will protect you. However much it costs, wherever you want to go."

She smiled at him and kissed him full on the mouth quickly. "You would have been easy to fall in love with, kid. Look after your girl. Look after yourself."

And she got up and walked away, with Christo staring unhappily after her.

17

CHAPTER SEVENTEEN

They were both putting on a performance, Noosh could tell. Something was bothering Christo, but she couldn't reasonably ask him to dish when she had secrets of her own. Instead, they both pretended nothing was wrong, and for now, she'd take it. They shared a meal they'd cooked together, and then Christo asked her to sit with him on the couch in his living room.

"I have something for you."

He brought out a Tiffany bag, and Noosh looked vaguely alarmed. He saw her expression and chuckled. "Don't worry, I'm not proposing...*yet*." Noosh looked relieved. "But," he added with a grin, "it's gonna happen sometime in the *near* future, so suck it up."

She giggled.

"Close your eyes, beautiful."

She felt him fasten something around her neck. "Okay, you can look."

Noosh opened her eyes. A delicate white gold chain hung around her neck, a charm nestled between her breasts. She picked it up. A tiny dragonfly picked out in diamonds. She felt tears in her eyes. "Oh, Christo, it's perfect."

He swept her hair back behind her ear. "I wanted to get you something, but I know you're not into big, flashy jewelry. I love you, little one."

Noosh pressed her lips against his, and they kissed for a long moment. "I love you too, big guy. Thank you for my present."

She stroked his face, gazing into his eyes for a long moment, then grinned. She got up. "Come on, I have an idea. We're going out."

"Where are we going?"

Noosh kissed him again as she pulled him into their bedroom to change. "You'll see."

DESTRY CALLED his detective from the burner phone. "You're following her?"

"Yup. She and the Don's son just got in a cab. We're heading in the direction of the city. What do you want me to do?"

"Just follow them, get photos if you can." Destry's gut roiled with jealousy. "What's she wearing?"

"Red dress, one of the wraparound things. I gotta give it to you, she's stunning."

"Mind on the job, please."

His detective gave a dark chuckle. "Just saying, man. Hang on, the cab's pulling up." He started to laugh. "Oh, my my."

"What?" Destry was getting irritated by the man now. "What is it?"

The detective laughed. "Boss...you're never going to *believe* where they are."

CHRISTO'S EYES widened when he saw they were back at the club where they met. He looked at Noosh, who was blushing but smiling at him. "Are you sure, baby?"

She nodded. "I keep thinking about what we could do here, and I want to try it all with you. Properly, this time. What do you say?"

Christo crushed his lips against hers. "I say," he said when they came up for air, "let's go for it."

He took her hand and they walked into the club together. The doorman, who had been so polite to Noosh the first time around, nodded again and smiled. "Welcome back."

She grinned shyly. "You remember me?"

"Of course, ma'am. I think it would be hard to find a man who wouldn't remember you. No disrespect, sir."

Christo grinned at him. "None taken, you're absolutely right."

As they walked into the club, Christo nodded at the people who knew him well and felt a surge of pride when they looked at Noosh with admiration and unconcealed desire. *And she's with me*, he thought, feeling wiped out by love for this woman, this brave, generous woman.

"I love you," he murmured into her ear, and she pressed her body against his, swaying to the slow beat of the sensual music playing in the club.

Noosh looked up at him from underneath her lashes, and he felt his body react to her, her beauty, the desire in her eyes. "I love you," she whispered and pressed her lips to his. God, she drove him crazy; he could feel his cock harden, pressing against her belly.

"Come with me." He led her to a small room, and for a moment she looked confused. In it, there was no bed, no equipment, and it was barely large enough to fit more than two people. One wall was glass and, grinning, Christo flicked a switch. Suddenly, the rest of the club was visible through the window.

"They call this The Box. It's so people can watch us fucking – if that's what you want. I'd like to fuck you against that window, let everyone see your spectacular body, your tits, your belly, your cunt as I take you from behind."

Noosh gave a soft moan of desire, and he pulled her into his arms, grinding his mouth down on hers. "Fuck me, Christo," she gasped. "Fuck me hard. Make everyone in that room jealous, every woman desperate for your glorious cock as you ream me into submission..."

She didn't finish, as with a feral growl, Christo tore her dress open, dropping to his knees and burying his face in her belly, his fingers tugging at her panties. He drew them down her legs and his tongue found her sex, lashing around her clit, his fingers biting into the soft flesh of her thighs. He ate her hungrily, Noosh quivering and gasping.

She wanted to return his generosity. "I want to taste your cock," she said, and Christo swept her to the floor and turned around so that she could take him into her mouth as he licked and dipped his tongue into her convulsing cunt.

They came quickly, and then Christo was stripping the rest of her clothes off and pressing her against the window. Her breasts, her belly against the cold glass, Noosh had never felt more beautiful than when Christo flicked the switch on the window and the whole club could see her. Before she closed her eyes, she saw the lascivious looks of the men – and some of the women – as they gazed at her. Then Christo's cock was thrusting into her cunt, his hands spreading her legs wide. She leaned her head back on his shoulder as he fucked her, and Christo kept up a stream of filthy talk that made her wetter and wetter.

"I'm going to fuck your perfect cunt until you beg me to stop, beautiful, and then I'm going to take you in the ass. Let the people see you come for me, see that beautiful color in your cheeks as you scream my name over and over."

He pressed her hands above her head, flat against the glass, his lips on her neck as he slammed his hips against hers. "Look at all those men who want you, Noosh, all of them. They all want to kill me because I'm the one fucking you...imagine if they each had the chance to fuck you...does that turn you? Being fucked by two men at the same time?"

Noosh groaned, delirious with pleasure, and Christo laughed. "If you wanted to try it...I'd be okay with it. There are professionals here. I'd make sure it was safe."

Noosh wanted to deny that she found the thought erotic and exciting, but she couldn't. "I love you," she said, searching his eyes for any sign of unhappiness. Instead, she found nothing but lust and excitement. She gave a little nod, and he grinned.

He nodded out at the crowd. "Pick someone."

She picked out a young man who had been staring at them the whole time. "Him."

Christo nodded and pointed at the man, beckoning at him to come inside. The man grinned. "He's a pro," Christo said, "one of the club's best. But remember, darling, the safe word. If you change your mind at any time, just say it. I'll tell Reece the safe word too, and believe me, he'll stop immediately if you use it."

Reece knocked at the door and Christo let him in, shaking his hand. It seemed an oddly formal thing to do – especially seeing as both men were naked. Recce was younger than Christo, but his body was softer, not as well honed. He had a sweet face, friendly smile, and a large cock. Noosh felt a wave of apprehension, which Christo saw. "Safe word is dragonfly, Reece." The young man nodded.

"Understood. Hello." He kissed Noosh's hand. "I'm Reece. You're exquisite."

Noosh grinned. "Noosh, and thank you."

"First time doing this?"

She nodded and felt Christo slide his arms around her. "Baby, relax. Do you want Reece to fuck your cunt while I take you from behind?"

She let out a shaky breath but nodded. She was almost unbearably excited about the thought of doing this. For her, as nice as Reece was, she could only imagine that it was Christo's cock inside her cunt *and* her ass. As Christo eased into her ass, and then Reece thrust into her cunt, she closed her eyes and let the sheer pleasure of it all take over.

Both men began thrusting gently, but soon she was screaming at them to go harder, faster, deeper, until she came explosively and with a scream of pleasure. She heard Christo's deep, low chuckle. "Good, baby?"

"So good....so good..." She panted for air as Reece withdrew, smiling.

"You are beautiful," he said, then nodded to Christo. "You are a lucky man."

Christo nodded at him. "Thank you, Reece. There will be an extra something for you at the reception."

"Thanks, man." Reece gave them both a smile before disappearing.

Noosh was still coming down from her high, but she turned and kissed Christo. "You are the most generous, most loving man. Now...I want to do something. Let's go to one of the other rooms...and we can play master and servant...or mistress and servant, whichever you're into tonight."

"Hmm." Christo grinned as he picked up their clothes, but didn't attempt to dress – why bother? Everyone had already seen all of both of them. They walked hand-in-hand to one of the pleasure and pain rooms.

Inside, Noosh raised an eyebrow at him. "Well?"

Christo chuckled. "I think I know who's in charge tonight... Ma'am."

Noosh grinned widely. "Damn right. Now..." She looked around the room. "So many toys to play with." She plucked out a long strip of leather and nodded at a chair. "Sit down, Serf."

Christo obeyed, and she wound the leather strip around his body and bound his hands behind him. She straddled him, taking his cock in her hands and rubbing the tip up and down her damp sex. "You like this?"

"Hell, yes."

She narrowed her eyes at him. "Did I say you could enjoy this?"

Christo hid a grin. "No, Ma'am."

"Hmm." She got up and went to the cabinet again, choosing a riding crop. She flicked it lightly against his chest, but then felt a little unsure of what to do. Christo met her gaze.

"Perhaps, Ma'am, would like to use that on my chest, or my thighs, or my back? I feel I need to be punished for enjoying myself. I am guilty of so many things."

Noosh smiled a quick grateful smile, then smoothed her expression out. She flicked the crop at his thighs. "Tell me the things you are guilty of."

"Of desiring Ma'am's delicious body at every moment."

Flick. "More."

"Of dreaming of Ma'am's sweet cunt wrapped around this cock."

A harder flick. "And?"

"Of wanting to fuck Ma'am so hard that she screams." *Flick.* A red welt appeared across his pecs. "God, yes..."

"Silence."

Christo grinned. "My apologies, Ma'am." His cock was rock-hard, and it was all Noosh could do to keep herself from dropping to her knees and taking it in her mouth. Instead, she teased him, straddling him, letting him notch the end into the entrance of her cunt – then pulling away. Christo groaned.

"Tell me you want me."

"God, I want you, so, so badly..."

She stood close to him. "Lick my pussy, Serf."

Christo obliged, and Noosh sighed as his tongue lashed around her clit. "Do you want to fuck me, Serf?"

"God, yes." His voice was muffled, his enjoyment at eating her out obvious. Noosh smiled.

"If I set you free, will you fuck me until I scream for mercy?"

"Yes, Ma'am."

"You'll have to be punished afterward."

"My pleasure."

She loosened his bindings, and he took her on the floor, thrusting hard into her, his gaze never leaving hers. God, he was the sexiest fucking man she had ever known. She crushed her lips against his then nibbled his ear, whispering, "Switch."

Christo understood immediately, his grin widening. "You want this cock, baby girl?"

"Yes, Master."

He slammed his hips harder, pinning her hands to the floor, taking control. "You're mine, you understand?"

"I do. I'm yours."

"What would you like me to do, baby girl?"

Noosh nipped at his bottom lip. "If Master pleases...he could hurt me."

Christo smiled. He ran his hand down her body. "Hurt this beautiful body?" He dipped his thumb into her navel and pressed down hard, surprising her, but Noosh found her cunt responding to the sharp pain. Christo finger-fucked her belly-button as his cock reamed her cunt so hard that she screamed out. His free hand clamped over her mouth and he nuzzled at her ear. "I'm going to blindfold you, baby, and then your body is my playground, understand?"

He made her come again then lifted her into the chair he had vacated. He wrapped a blindfold around her eyes. "You won't know what's coming, pretty girl."

Noosh shivered in anticipation as he trailed a crop over her skin then gasped as he brought it down hard across her belly. The sweet pain made her cunt quiver, her legs tremble.

"Good," Christo said approvingly, "good. Tell me who you belong to, pretty girl."

"You, Master, always you."

Crack! The crop came down on her inner thigh, and she moaned.

"Spread those sensational legs for me, woman. Wider. Wider. Until your hips burn."

Noosh complied, lost in the moment, in the role-play. She felt something push into her cunt – a dildo? His lips met hers, and he kissed her deeply, his tongue delving deep inside her mouth as he fucked her with the dildo. "Are you wishing that was my cock?" He asked, murmuring to her as he kissed her.

Noosh nodded. "But I am yours to do with as you will, Master."

He pinched her nipples. "That's right..."

She felt his tongue sweep over her nipples, and then he began to suck as he pushed the dildo in and out of her. Noosh felt her climax building and building until she groaned and shivered and felt her cunt flood with her arousal.

"That's it, pretty girl, get nice and wet for me. In a moment, I will release you, and you will straddle me and ride me hard, understand?"

"Yes, Master."

Eventually, he released her and she straddled him and

guided him inside her. Christo's eyes were shining. "Equals?" He asked, as a way of finishing the role play.

Noosh grinned down at him, her breasts bouncing against her chest as she thrust harder onto his cock. "Equals."

"I love you, pretty girl."

"I love you too, handsome. How did I do for my first time?"

Christo laughed. "Wonderfully. Thank you for indulging me."

"It was honestly my pleasure. Damn, that was intense."

They finished making love and lay for a few minutes. Noosh grinned over at her lover. "I'm actually exhausted."

Christo laughed. "Always a sign of a good night. Shall we go home, baby?"

Noosh rolled onto her side and snuggled into his chest. "Pizza first?" She said hopefully, and he laughed.

"You got it, sweetheart."

DESTRY WATCHED them sit in the pizza place, sharing pizza slices and laughing together. When his guy had called him and told him they were at a BDSM club, he could hardly believe it.

He hadn't believed it until he saw them leaving, disheveled and obviously post-coital. So the little slut was into pleasure and pain, huh?

Whore.

Jealousy twisted in Destry's gut and he fingered the gun he always carried with him – not the one he'd shot Noosh with, of course – that one was hidden far, far away from here. He could hunt them down now, shoot them both dead. But it would be disastrous for his long-term plans.

No, he would kill Noosh soon enough, but he would do it how he wanted to. Slowly, agonizingly…and now he knew what he would do with the Montecito kid. God, that little shit had been the bane of his life for too long, and now he had his hands on Destry's property?

He would force him to watch Noosh's murder before putting a bullet in that stupidly good-looking head of his. He would make Montecito watch Noosh scream as he gutted her slowly, as she bled out in front of him.

Destry rolled up the window and drove away, smiling.

CHAPTER EIGHTEEN

Noosh felt her face burning as Allison read through the new story she had written, and when Allison gave a hoot of approval, she could have died from embarrassment. Allison took her spectacles off. "Noosh...do you know how good this is?"

Noosh chuckled. "I hope so. It was...well researched."

Allison laughed, looking at her with new respect. "I'll say. Lucky girl. With that gorgeous man? I'm very happy for you, Noosh. And this..." she waved the story in her hand. "This is perfect for your debut story. I take it Christo's okay with you telling this story?"

"He is. He supports me one hundred percent." Noosh couldn't help smiling at the thought of Christo.

"Good. Then work on your soundbites, get them processed and you can head into the editing suite once we're done with the senator's interview. Sure you don't want to stick around for him?"

Noosh's smile had faded at the mention of Destry. "Definitely not. I don't mean to let you down, but I can't be around the man."

Ally nodded. "One day, you'll tell me the real story, but for now, I respect your wishes." She handed the story back to Noosh and smiled at her. "Great job though, Noosh. Congrats."

"Thanks, boss."

HAVING MADE appointments for future interviews, Noosh was on her way out of the building when Liam stopped her to talk. "Nice diamonds," he said, nodding approvingly at her dragonfly necklace. "Looks like Tiffany's. Custom-made?"

Noosh flushed and nodded. "It was a gift from Christo."

Liam smiled. "That man is crazy-go-nuts for you, Nooshy."

"And I, him. How's your love life?"

"Hectic and complicated, but that's nothing new. You know, we haven't been out for drinks for weeks."

Noosh looked ashamed. "I know, and I am sorry, Li. Look, how about a double date? Me and Christo, you and whichever man you choose. Friday?"

"Friday is good. *La Forge*?"

"*La Forge*."

"Making plans without me?"

Noosh froze. Behind her, Destry and his entourage were piling through the doors. Destry wore a supercilious smile that made Noosh want to punch it right off his smug face. He had the nerve to put a hand on the small of her back as he greeted Liam. Noosh moved away, not caring if she looked rude.

"Oh, are you leaving us, Miss Marsh?"

Fuck off, creep. "They're waiting upstairs for you, Senator."

"I wonder," Destry looked around, bestowing his best politician smile on the others, "would you mind giving me and Miss Marsh a moment? I'd like to ask her about her story, and I think we'd better do that in private."

God, no, please. But everyone nodded and drifted away, even Liam, although he shot a strange look towards Destry.

As soon as they were alone, Destry's smile vanished. "I had hoped that by now, Anoushka, you would realize that avoiding me isn't an option. You are mine, remember?"

"Shove it, arsehole," she shot back, "you don't frighten me."

"I should. I *really* should." He prodded his finger hard into her belly, and she winced. "Those three bullets I put in you will be nothing to what's coming, Anoushka. And who knows? Maybe it won't be only your life that is forfeit."

Noosh froze. "What?"

Destry's smile was chilly, his eyes cold and dead. "Break up with Montecito or find out exactly what. You have a week, Anoushka, and then I expect you to deliver yourself to my hotel room, ready to be at my side as I reach the highest office in this country."

Noosh felt sick. "And then what?"

"Then, just as reelection looms, a tragedy. You will be found stabbed to death, and my approval ratings will go through the roof out of sympathy, and I'll be returned for a second term. So, you have a choice, Anoushka. You die soon, along with your family, your friends, your lover...or I give you two years to live. Don't think I'm serious? Watch me."

He walked away, leaving Noosh frozen and terrified. So...her destiny was to die at his hand, was it?

No. Fuck you, Destry.

She knew exactly what to do.

In the cab she called her interviewees and rearranged her schedule, then sat back in the cab, running through what she would say, how she would approach the meeting she was about to have.

As she pulled up to the mansion, she felt a wave of nervousness. When he walked out of the house and down the steps to meet her, she wondered if she was doing the right thing.

She stepped out of the cab, and Fogliano Montecito smiled at her. "My dear, what a pleasure."

She shook his hand. "Mr. Montecito, thank you for agreeing to meet with me."

He was studying her closely with that same intense stare his son had. "What is it, Noosh? What is troubling you, my dear?"

Noosh felt close to tears. "Mr. Montecito, I need your help. I think Christo and I might be in terrible danger and I don't know what to do.

CHAPTER NINETEEN

Christo tried to call Telly again, but it kept going to voicemail. He hissed in frustration. Bertie glanced over at him. "Nothing?"

Christo shook his head. "I hope she's okay. Papps's spies are everywhere."

"Well, so are ours. Word is Papps is at the radio station being interviewed as we speak. Is Noosh there?"

"No, thank god. She's out doing interviews for her story. Listen, Bert...we need to stop Papps from terrorizing her, and with any luck, the whole country by becoming president."

"Does she know you know?"

"No, and I want it to stay like that. I don't want her to think I'm snooping on her, or sully our time together with his bullshit. God, what am I talking about – bullshit? He fucking shot her, for chrissakes." He felt sick.

Bertie sat down next to his friend. "We don't know that for sure, Christo. I mean, yes, probably based on what we know, but we can't go all in on him without proof. We'll lose credibility, and it could put Noosh more at risk."

The friends sat silently in Bertie's palatial penthouse over-looking Central Park. Christo stared out at the people below. "Some days," he said, "I just want to take her and get away from all of this. Go find our little piece of heaven where no one knows us." He looked back and saw the concerned look on Bertie's face and smiled sadly. "Oh, I know, running away would be a bad idea. We need to make sure Noosh is safe. She's still young, still has her career, her whole life in front of her. And I never want to be one of those men who shut their love up in an ivory tower."

"No, you don't. We both know that's just another type of abuse." Bertie was quiet for a moment, considering. "There is someone we could go to for help."

Christo was confused for a moment, then his expression cleared. "No. No way. Bringing my father into this would be disastrous, Bert, and you know it."

"Would it, though?"

Christo turned away from his friend, not wanting Bertie to see the desperation in his eyes. Because he too had wondered if his father could do something about Destry Papps. He certainly had the connections. Christo sighed. *No*. It would mean going back on everything he had ever fought for, all his autonomy, his independence from Fogliano and his business. No, he, Christo, would figure this out. He and he alone would bring down Papps and give Noosh her life back.

He turned to Bertie. "No, Bert. This stays between you and me. Understood?"

Bertie nodded but looked unhappy. "What are you going to do, Christo?"

Christo shook his head, his eyes full of misery. "I don't know, Bert. I have no fucking clue what to do. How the hell am I going to save her?"

FOGLIANO SAT WITH NOOSH, holding her hands as she explained

everything about Destry Papps's threats. His eyes were full of sympathy, and Noosh began to feel better as she described her predicament.

"And my son knows nothing of this."

Noosh shook her head. "I'm scared that if I tell him, he'll do something brave and stupid, and it'll cost him everything." She searched Fogliano's eyes. "Can you help me? I wouldn't ask if I wasn't desperate."

Fogliano got up and paced around the room for a few moments before sitting down again. "My dear."

A thrill of hope ran through her. "Yes?"

"I cannot help you."

The weight of disappointment and grief came crashing down on her. "I understand."

He smiled a little. "I know it's not what you wanted to hear, but hear me out. I cannot help you while Christo remains in the dark about this situation. I won't lie to him anymore. Lies and secrets have already cost me his love." He reached over and patted her hand. "What I will do is provide discreet protection for you."

Noosh felt hopeless. "But you can't protect everyone all the time. My parents, my colleagues…no. It's okay, I'll figure this out. Thanks for your time."

Fogliano studied her. "You are a very brave woman, except for one thing. You need to trust that Christo will do the right thing by you. Even seeing you together for that short time the night I came to his apartment, I could see it. You belong together. He loves you with the same kind of intensity that I loved his mother. And I know you feel the same way."

"If it were just my life, I would never have bothered you," Noosh said quietly. "But the thought of anything happening to Christo…"

"Tell him, sweet girl. Tell him, and we'll figure this out together."

Noosh half-smiled. "You want him back."

"I do. In that way, I think we can help each other. In the meantime, stay safe."

"I'll try."

IN THE CAB on the way back into the city, she reflected. She knew what Fogliano was doing – he was using the situation she was in to try and get his son's love back. Did she blame him?

No. In the meantime, he was right. She needed to tell Christo everything. If they were to have any kind of future together, she needed to learn how to trust. It was just…she knew how passionate Christo was – he would fight his way through fields of Secret Service agents to get to Destry if he knew she was in danger – and get himself killed in the process.

Damn it. She touched the little dragonfly at her throat, her chest pounding with sadness. Why couldn't the universe give her this happiness? Why was it always tempered with fear or upset?

Noosh leaned her hot forehead against the window and prayed the cab driver didn't see her silent tears fall.

WHEN SHE GOT BACK to the radio station, Liam was uncharacteristically quiet. She frowned at him. "What's up?"

"Shit's hit the fan," he said, then pulled her aside. "The interview did not go well. Ally asked him about the stuff that's been going on in Washington, about the sex scandals, and he went crazy. Absolutely freaked out on her. Walked out. Ally's in shock, Seth is fuming."

"Oh, god. What on earth did she say to him?"

"Not sure. Maybe you should go up. Ally probably needs to see a friendly face at the moment."

Noosh nodded. "Are you okay?"

"Yeah, just... What a prick."

You have no idea. She hugged him. "Come up in a while when things have settled."

"Laters."

SHE RODE the elevator up to the studio, dumping her bag on her desk. It was too quiet. She went to find Ally. Her boss was in her office, her face pale, but Noosh could see the anger still in her eyes. She knocked tentatively at the door, and Ally waved her in.

"I want to congratulate you," Ally began, making adrenaline spike through Noosh's system. Was she in trouble? "On your incredible judgment of character. Destry Papps is an asshole."

Noosh breathed a sigh of relief. "Yes, he is. What the hell happened?"

Ally tapped her pencil on the desk in annoyance. "I asked him a question that hadn't been cleared. I always do that – the people who come on my show expect the difficult questions. And the question I asked...Noosh, it wasn't even personally directed at him. I asked the other candidates the same question."

"The sexual harassment question? That's pretty standard nowadays, isn't it? Colbert, John Oliver, those late-night guys are asking the same thing."

"Right? And Papps went ballistic. I just don't get it."

I do. Ask a rapist, on the record, about sexual harassment when he's running for the highest office in the land? Of course he's going to flip out. "He was arrogant enough to believe you wouldn't dare ask the great Destry Papps about it. Arsehole."

"You told me he was a nightmare, and I didn't realize how

right you were." Ally studied her for a minute then got up and shut the office door. "Noosh...there's more to your hatred of Destry Papps than just instinct, isn't there?" She sat down on the corner of her desk, and Noosh met her gaze without saying anything.

A strange expression crossed her boss's face, and she drew in a shaky breath as she looked at her young friend. "My god, Noosh...what the hell did he do to you?"

CHAPTER TWENTY

Christo was already waiting in reception at five p.m., and suddenly Noosh felt shy. She had gone to see his father without telling him. Would Fogliano have told him?

By the sweet smile on Christo's face when he saw, Noosh guessed not.

"Hey, lovers, have a good night." Liam waved at them as he made his way out of the reception area.

"Bye, mate."

"Night, Liam."

"Don't forget *La Forge*!"

Christo looked at her, a question in his eyes. Noosh kissed him, smiling. "We have a double date on Friday."

Christo grinned. "Cool. How are you, my darling?"

Terrified. But she kept the smile on her face. "Better now that you're here. Ally had a difficult day, so I spent most of the afternoon trying to cheer her up."

"Good friend."

"And as such, I think you should feed me." She dragged him out towards the car. "I am starving."

"When aren't you?" Christo rolled his eyes, and she backed up and kissed him, then put her mouth to his ear.

"When your huge cock is nailing me to the bed or the floor or against a window. Then all I'm hungry for is you...only you."

She reached down, squeezing his cock through his jeans, and he groaned. "Such a tease. Now I have to go eat with a hard-on."

Noosh grinned at him. "Not necessarily."

"Oh?"

"Get in the car and drive, Montecito."

SHE WENT DOWN on him in the car, sucking and teasing his cock until he came, swallowing his seed down. Christo somehow managed to keep control of the car, and then as he pulled into the parking lot of the restaurant, he got out of the car and took her hand.

"My turn," he said and led her into a dark alleyway at the rear of the restaurant. He pushed up her dress and ripped her panties from her. Lifting her up, he fucked her against the wall, clamping a hand over her mouth to muffle her cries. Noosh let her hair fall over both of them as she kissed him. God, would she ever get tired of this? Ever?

"God, I love you so much," she whispered then came, shivering and shuddering as Christo pumped his seed deep into her belly.

Giggling, they went to eat, then went home and made love again. Noosh pushed every other thought away and just memorized every moment with this incredible man.

They fell asleep just after midnight, but were woken at three o'clock by a call from a sobbing, hysterical Allison, calling them to tell them Liam was dead.

. . .

Outside, the pre-dawn New York sky was a sickly shade of yellow, but Noosh stared at it unseeing. She felt numb and cold, even Christo's arms around her didn't help.

Liam had been mugged, or so the police said, on his way home from work. He'd tried to fight them off and they had stabbed him to death. Liam, her buddy, her pal, was gone – and in her bones, Noosh knew this was Destry sending her a warning sign. It was too coincidental.

For fuck's sake, she berated herself, *not everything is about you, woman.* It wasn't unheard of, after all, for people to be mugged in this city. *Jesus.*

She told herself that a few times before the message pinged on her phone, and with a sinking heart, she realized she had been right.

One down, six to go. Days that is…you know what to do.

Bastard. She wanted to scream, but she knew he had her. His meaning was clear. *Break it off with the man you love and be mine… or I'll kill them all.* Another message came soon after.

Make an excuse and meet me in the alleyway next to the hospital in ten minutes. Be even a second late, and I'll give the order for your mother to be killed.

All the air was pushed from her lungs, and reigning in all the panic she felt, she turned to Christo. "I need a minute. I need some air."

"It's not safe out there alone."

She tried to smile at him. "It'll just be for a minute."

Reluctantly he let her go. Like an automaton, Noosh walked down the stairs and to the alleyway behind the hospital.

"Good. You're early."

Noosh walked straight up to him. "Kill me. Now. This minute. Because I would rather die than spend a moment longer being hunted by you."

Destry smiled. "You're under the impression you're in charge here. In case you still think that..." He handed her his phone. On it, a video was playing, a live stream. Two people tied to chairs, beaten and bloody. Noosh almost passed out. Her parents.

"*No...no...please...let them go.*"

"My pleasure. You just have to do one thing. Break up with your boyfriend. But here's the rub, Noosh. You'll be wearing a wire because I want to hear it. I want to hear you break his heart. I want to hear you tell him you don't love him, that you never did."

Noosh gasped. "You really are a psychopath. Did you have Liam killed or are you just using a tragedy for your own purposes?"

"You know the answer to that, Anoushka." Destry touched her face, and she winced away from him. He looked over her shoulder. "Do it."

Noosh turned to see one of Destry's goons behind her. Helpless, she let him wire her. This was really happening, and there was nothing she could do to stop it. *Oh god...*

Destry's expression was hard as stone. "When you go home, tell your boyfriend you're leaving. I'll send Gerry to pick you up. You know what to do." He grabbed her face, pinching it hard between his fingers. "I'll be listening. When I think you've done a good enough job, I'll release your father. When you're at my apartment, I'll give the order to release your mother."

"How do I know you're not lying?"

Destry gave her a wintry smile. "You don't."

He turned and got back into the blacked-out sedan, leaving Noosh to stare in horror after him.

CHRISTO WAS GETTING antsy waiting for her, so when Noosh reappeared, he breathed a sigh of relief. He smiled at her, but her face was drawn and pale. "Are you okay?"

Noosh didn't answer and wouldn't meet his eye. Instead, she went to Allison, who was sitting, mute with shock, and put her arms around her. "I think you need to go home now, Ally. There's nothing more we can do here. Liam's family will be here soon."

Allison shook her head. "I want to wait for them. You and Christo should go. Seth is on his way too."

Allison wouldn't take any argument, so ten minutes later they were back in Christo's car, heading for the apartment. Noosh said nothing, just stared out of the window. Christo took her hand with his free one, but she didn't wrap her fingers around his like she normally did. Christo felt a ribbon of unease curl in his stomach, and when they were back in his apartment, he took her in his arms.

"I know this must be diffi –"

"Christofalo, we need to talk." Her voice, normally so warm with a current of humor in it, was cold and dead. Christo nodded, his heart beginning to beat uncomfortably against his ribs.

"Okay."

Noosh stepped away from the circle of his arms. "Christofalo...I don't want this anymore."

He was confused. "Want what?"

She met his gaze. "This. *Us.*"

It took a moment for her words to sink it. "What the hell are you talking about?"

"It's over. It's done."

Christo shook his head as if to shake her words from his brain. "Noosh, you're upset. Please, let's just calm down, regroup."

"I don't love you, Christofalo."

It was like a sledgehammer to the heart. Christo stared at her in disbelief. "What?"

"I don't love you. I don't think I ever did. This was a fantasy. I don't belong in your world. I thought I did, but you see...I was only ever interested in your money."

"Bullshit. That's not you. Why are you doing this?" He cursed the fact that his voice broke, and he stepped towards her.

"I went to see your father."

That floored him. "*Why?*"

Noosh gave him a wan smile. "I told him that unless he gave me what I wanted, I would be gone. He didn't give me what I wanted, so I'm gone."

Christo ran his hands through his hair, staring at the women he thought he knew, and didn't recognize her. "Who are you?"

For the first time, her voice shook. "To you, I am the past now, Christofalo. Forget me."

Christo stepped towards her, but Noosh stepped back and held her hands up. "Please," she whispered. "Please, don't."

"I love you, goddammit, and I know you love me. Whatever this is...it's bullshit. You and me forever, remember? You said that!"

"I lied."

"No."

Noosh turned away from him. "I'll get my things. You never have to see me again."

Christo grabbed her arm. "Don't walk away from me! This is... I mean, what the *fuck*, Noosh? Was that not you and me fucking in the alleyway tonight? Laughing, kissing, making love? Jesus Christ, I *know* you love me."

Noosh snatched her arm away from him. "Forget me, Christofalo. Forget me."

"Noosh…"

She suddenly stepped towards him and pressed her lips to his. She grabbed his hand and drew something on his palm, an outline of something – a cross? What the hell? He could feel her tears on her cheeks as she rested her cheek against his for a second. "Don't follow me."

Christo closed his eyes for a long moment, and when he opened them, she was gone.

CHAPTER TWENTY-ONE

ne month later...

DESTRY PAPPS, his face triumphant, spoke to his campaign team as they all raised their glasses. "Friends, we're way ahead in the exit polls. When the nation goes to the vote in a month's time, I have no doubt we will soon be having this meeting in the White House. Tomorrow, we begin a week of campaigning in the key states, and I am very excited to introduce the world to my partner in this. Ladies and gentlemen, my fiancée, Miss Sarah Marsh."

The room erupted in applause as Destry took Noosh by the hand. She didn't smile or react – how could she? Destry had her pumped so full of sedatives that she could barely function. Underneath the beautiful Elie Saab dress she wore, her body was black and blue from his beatings. It had almost become a routine. Jacked up from campaigning, he would return to their hotel and use her as a punching bag. Thankfully, so far, he hadn't raped her, but Noosh knew it wouldn't be long before he grew tired of waiting for her to agree to have sex with him.

He'd lied, of course. He hadn't released her parents, but at least the beatings had stopped, and they were being cared for, albeit as hostages. "They're being kept in a facility where they will be very comfortable."

"For how long? You can't keep them prisoner forever."

"Can't I?" Destry laughed, then his smile faded. "Just until you're dead, Noosh. So, if you're good, two years." He leaned in and kissed her cheek, nuzzling her ear. "Or until I can't wait any longer to slide that knife into your belly. I must admit, it excites me almost as much as fucking you would."

"You're a sick *fuck*." She'd slapped his face, and he'd gone to town on her, punching her to the floor (careful not to bruise her face, of course) and kicked her viciously in the stomach.

That had been last night, and now he was expecting her to play nice with his cronies. He'd obviously expected her to act up, so he had his personal physician prescribe her sedatives. Now she felt as if she were in a different world.

The only faint glimmer of hope was Gerry Noll. When Destry had introduced her to his executive team, Gerry had looked surprised to see her – astonished, actually. Destry had known to keep them apart, however, but Noosh had seen the questions in Gerry's eyes. She longed for the day when she could talk to Gerry alone. Maybe he would help her.

Because she felt utterly hopeless. On the few occasions when Destry left her alone, she thought only of Christo, how heartbroken he had been. She would never forget that beautiful face broken with grief. *Oh, how I love you. I love you,* she thought, *I'm so sorry.* She had tried to give him as many clues that something wasn't right during that last conversation – using his full name and drawing on his hand. She hadn't dared write anything down – she didn't know if Destry had cameras in their apartment, but she wouldn't put it past the bastard to do so.

But she guessed Christo hadn't picked up on her clues. If only she could get a message to him. She figured Gerry was her best shot, but she would have to be entirely sure.

Destry was guiding her around the room, introducing her to various people who she barely registered. She shook their hands, unsmiling, and kept quiet as Destry had instructed her to. The silent candidate for First Lady.

First Lady... how ridiculous that sounded to her, but Noosh couldn't comprehend that Destry would actually *win* the presidency. But stranger things had happened. *And it's not as if I have anything better to do.* Destry had made her quit her job at the radio station and wouldn't even allow her to speak directly to any of her former coworkers.

In the morning, they would hold their first photo call as a 'couple.' Noosh felt sick at the thought of it, knowing Christo, Ally, all her friends would see her at Destry's side and condemn her. Destry might control her outward behavior, the way she was to dress, what she said, but he couldn't control the misery in her eyes, and she intended to let them do her talking for her.

Please, Christo, my love, my heart, watch my eyes – in them, you'll find everything you need to know.

Please...

THE NEXT MORNING, Christo sat in his farmhouse, where he had retreated after Noosh had left, and watched the morning news, torturing himself by watching every story on Papps and Noosh. Christo could barely stand to look at her; so beautiful, so cowed by her abuser. What the hell was wrong that she would go back to him?

"He shot you, for chrissakes, Noosh. I *know* you hate him as much as I do..."

"I might have some news on that front."

Christo jumped as Bertie's voice came from behind him, then he got up to hug his friend. Bertie had been his rock for the last month, the only reason he hadn't fallen off the wagon or offed himself. Bertie had been the one to calm his pain, his anger, and had been unwavering in his belief that Noosh had not left Christo voluntarily. "That girl loves you with all her heart, Christo. There's more to this than we know."

And now he gave Christo a folder. "What we've found out so far. Her parents have been missing for six weeks, and what do you know, powerful people within the Met have sidelined the inquiry into their disappearance."

"God." Christo looked through the papers. "So, Papps had them snatched?"

"Looks like, and if he threatened them..."

Christo nodded. "But it doesn't make sense that Noosh wouldn't come to me. And why the hell did she go see my father behind my back?"

Bertie held his hands up. "That you're going to ask him yourself, buddy. He won't talk to me." He gave a small grin. "Fog and I have never gotten along."

"Because you don't take his crap," Christo said darkly, and then sighed. "But if Noosh went to him asking for money..."

"She said that?"

"Well, no, but the inference was there."

Bertie's mouth set in a grim line. "What were her exact words?"

"That she went to my father and asked him to give her what she wanted or she, and I remember this, she said she was 'gone,' and that he didn't give her what she asked for."

Bertie was quiet for a long moment. "Well, it certainly

doesn't sound good, but Christo, we need to know what she asked for. I'd bet my life it isn't what we think."

"So...I'm going to have to see my father."

"If you want your lovely girl back, yes."

It was Christo's turn to be quiet. "I just have this feeling... Papps will kill her, Bertie. It's what he wants. He wants to control her life, and then he wants to kill her. We have to do *something*."

Another story flashed up about Destry and Noosh, closeups of them. Bertie and Christo watched, and then Bertie gave a small laugh. "Look what she's doing, Christo."

Noosh, pale and drawn, had her fingers at her throat, playing with her necklace as the cameras zoomed in. She was tapping the dragonfly pendent, subtly but repeatedly. Christo thought back to when he had given it to her, then the terrible day she'd left him.

"Shit."

"What?"

Christo turned to his friend, life coming back into his eyes. "She was telling me, even then, that what she was saying wasn't real. Shit, I never got it."

Bertie looked confused and even more so when Christo grabbed his hand and traced a pattern on his palm. "What the hell?"

"What was that? What shape?"

"I don't know, dude, a cross?"

Christo smiled for the first time in weeks. "No, man, it's a dragonfly. It's our safe word. She was trying to let me know she was in danger." He nodded at the television. "And that's what she's doing there. She's asking for my help." He got up, grabbing his coat and heading for the door.

Bertie, still a little bemused, trailed him. "Where are we going?"

Christo, his eyes alive with anger and hope, smiled grimly at him. "We're going to see my father."

CHAPTER TWENTY-TWO

"You did well today," Destry said in the car back to the hotel. "Everyone was very impressed."

"By what?" The sedatives were wearing off now, and Noosh felt cantankerous, wanted to goad him. "The dead-eyed half smiles, the look of disgust every time your filthy hands touched me?"

Destry gave a half-smile. "It's almost like you're asking me to punish you. But then again, that's what you and the criminal were into, wasn't it? Tell me, did he spank you?"

"Go fuck yourself."

Destry laughed. "Well, speaking of fucking, I think tonight I'll be staying in your room."

Noosh froze. "No."

"It wasn't a question. And if you know what's good for you, Anoushka, you'll at least pretend to enjoy it."

Noosh turned to stare at him for a long moment. "What happened to you, Destry? What made you like this?"

Destry didn't answer, and Noosh gave him a cruel smile. "Did Mommy not *wuv wittle* Destry enough?"

His fist connected with her face so hard that her head

bounced into the window and cracked it. Noosh felt as if her cheekbone had shattered. Destry was on her then, unhitching his seat belt and dragging her to the floor of the limousine.

It took less than five minutes, but Noosh felt like dying the whole time. Concussed, she had no way to fight him off, and as Destry came inside her, she closed her eyes and wanted death. When she felt the steel against her skin, she opened her eyes.

"Do it. Kill me, you bastard." She grabbed the knife in his hand and tried to stab herself. "I'd rather be dead than have you ever touch me again."

Destry, calming from his rage now, pulled the knife away and dragged her back to the seat. "Don't ever talk to me like that again, bitch. Here, clean yourself up." He threw a pack of tissues at her.

Her head hurt so bad, but Noosh didn't care. She shrank away from him and curled up on the seat, pressing a tissue to the cuts on her head. *Fucker.* Her anger soon gave way to shock by the time they reached the hotel and were spirited up to their suite, not through the foyer, but via the goods elevator. *A practiced maneuver*, Noosh thought. She swayed a little, her head spinning, but Destry made no move to steady her. Noosh stumbled out into the penthouse as the elevator reached Destry's suite.

To her surprise, Gerry was there, and he looked up with a smile that faded when he saw her battered face, the blood on her clothes. Noosh turned her head so he could see the damaged to the right side of her face.

"What the hell?"

"Anoushka, go to your room. I'll send Dr. Jacobs in to help you. Gerry, shut your mouth, you look like a goldfish."

When Noosh didn't move, Destry sighed in exasperation and grabbed her upper arm, dragging her to her room and practically throwing her in.

Noosh slammed the door behind him and pushed her dresser across the doorway. Destry wouldn't be getting in here this night. Why would he want to? He'd taken what he wanted in the car.

Noosh went to her en-suite and cranked on the faucet on the tap. A second later, she turned it off. Evidence. She should collect as much evidence as she could of what he had done to her, but how? She didn't have a phone or a camera to take pictures of her injuries. She sat down on the cool tile floor, tugging off her shoes, ripping her way out of the dress she had worn for the photo calls and interviews. Ha, interviews. She barely spoke, and when she did, she made sure it was in a cold, dead voice. Still, she had done what she had done from the start of this charade. *Dragonfly. Dragonfly.* Every time she was on camera she touched it repeatedly, hoping against hope that Christo would see it, understand.

Help me. Save me. I love you.

Noosh began to cry softly. She didn't understand how the hell she was going to deal with what little life she had left. She was going to die, that was clear, but Destry wouldn't hurt anyone else if she could help it.

There was a gentle tapping at her bedroom door, and she sighed. "Go away, Destry. You've already taken enough from me."

"It's Gerry, Noosh."

She hesitated for a moment then pushed her dresser aside and let him in. He held up a first aid kit. "His majesty changed his mind about calling the doctor. So here I am." He touched her face. "Jesus, Noosh, what happened?"

"You know what happened," she said roughly. She walked back into her room, glancing at the first aid box he held. "Got a rape kit in there?"

Gerry's face paled. "No," he said quietly, "no, I haven't. God, really? Christ."

Noosh's smile was unfriendly, her eyes narrowed. "You knew. You knew what he was like, what he did to me. What he did to Telly. Don't plead ignorance now, Gerry. You were complicit."

Gerry set the first aid box down on the bed. "Come sit, let me deal with that."

Noosh was unwilling, but she knew her wounds needed dressing. Her *wounds. Jesus. H. Christ, who lived like this?* She let Gerry clean the cuts, press butterfly stiches onto them. "I wonder what lie he'll tell the public about this."

Gerry sighed. "He's already put out a press statement. A car wreck."

"Let me guess: As Senator Papps and his companion were driving back to their hotel, their car was hit by a hit-and-run driver. Both Senator Papps and his companion – I don't merit an actual name – were slightly injured, although, miraculously, Senator Papps doesn't have a scratch on him, and his whore looks like she's gone five rounds with Floyd Mayweather."

Gerry gave her a smile. "At least you still have your sense of humor."

Noosh shot him a glare, "You think rape is funny too? Murder? Kidnapping my parents?"

"I'm sorry. Noosh," he lowered his voice, "do you think you're the only one he's manipulated?"

Noosh studied him. "No, but I'm probably the only one he's personally put three bullets into. He probably gets his goons to do everyone else."

Gerry had gone very still. "What?"

Noosh smiled coldly. "He shot me, Gerry. In cold blood, at point-blank range."

She saw Gerry blanch, and she gasped. "You really didn't know?"

He shook his head. "God, no, I...never thought him capable of that."

Noosh made a disgusted sound. "Either you're lying, or you're naïve." She studied him. "He's going to kill me, you know. He told me to my face. When the mid-terms come up, I'll be mysteriously murdered. Sympathy for the candidate means he wins in a landslide. My life means nothing now, Gerry."

Gerry closed his eyes. "What can I do?"

"Help me."

"How?"

Noosh sighed. "I don't know."

"Hey." They both jumped as one of Destry's bodyguards appeared in the doorway. "The Senator asked that you both join him in the living room. There's some breaking news."

Noosh and Gerry looked at each other, but both obediently followed the bodyguard into the main room of the suite. Destry gave Noosh a cruel smile. "Come sit with me, Anoushka."

Sighing, she did as she was told. No use antagonizing him now. If Gerry was going to help her, it paid to keep Destry as sweet as possible, so he didn't suspect anything.

On the television, the news anchor was talking about a car being found by the Brooklyn Bridge.

"The vehicle was identified as belonging to Telly Wyatt, New York socialite and the former wife of presidential candidate Destry Papps. Police indicate that, sadly, they believe Ms. Wyatt jumped from the bridge to her death. A source close to the Wyatt family told AP that Ms. Wyatt has experienced depression since her divorce and that lately, she had seemed secretive and withdrawn."

Noosh felt shock travel through her – she glanced at Gerry, who looked as if he might pass out. Of course. She'd forgotten that Gerry had loved Telly.

"Well, that's going to save me a shit ton of money every month." Destry sat back, grinning. Some of his security chuckled uneasily, but both Noosh and Gerry stayed silent. Destry looked at them. "Come on, that's a little funny, at least."

"Destry..." Gerry looked sick. He got up and went to pour himself a glass of scotch, not asking permission. Destry watched him with a smile.

"What's the matter, Gerry? Disappointed you missed your opportunity to fuck my ex?"

Gerry downed his whiskey. "My friend just died. Have some compassion."

Noosh was astonished. Gerry never, ever talked back to Destry. *Ever.* She tensed, waiting for Destry to explode. But Destry merely shrugged and ran a hand down Noosh's back. "Don't be sad. All this talk of ex-wives has given me an idea, something that will please our base and the more conservative members of the party. A wedding. Nothing flashy, nothing that looks like we spent campaign money on it. City Hall. Plenty of press. This week."

"No." Noosh shook her head, and Destry smirked.

"You really don't have too much choice in the matter, Anoushka. Set it up," he barked at Gerry, and then got up, pulling Noosh to her feet. "I'll be in my fiancée's bed until further notice."

As she was dragged across the suite, Noosh turned to look desperately at Gerry. He gazed back – and gave an almost imperceptible nod. It could have meant anything, but a rush of adrenaline and relief flooded through Noosh's body.

He was going to help her.

CHAPTER TWENTY-THREE

Christo shifted uncomfortably in the chair in his father's study. He shot an impatient look at Bertie. "So, this is his game now? Keeping us waiting?"

"Dude, chill. We're here for your girl. If Fog wants to play games, let him, if it makes him feel superior, let him. Noosh's life is at stake, not your pride. Suck it up."

Christo's eyebrows shot up, and he smiled for the first time in weeks. "Wow. Tough love time."

Bertie nodded. "You betcha."

Christo chuckled. "Well, alright then." His phone beeped with a message, and he flicked through it. His smile faded. "No. No...oh god."

"What?"

Christo dropped his head into his hands. "Telly. Telly's dead."

"What the hell?"

"Suicide. Oh fuck, oh fuck...I got her killed."

"Yeah, *not* so much."

Both men jumped and turned to see the very-much-alive Telly walk into the room, flanked by Fogliano and his lawyer.

Christo gaped at her, and she laughed, coming to him and hugging the stunned man. Bertie smirked and looked at Fogliano.

"You behind this?"

Fogliano inclined his head gracefully. "It's just the first move, my friend." As Telly released Christo, he looked at his son. "Hello, Christofalo."

Christo steeled himself. "Hi, Dad."

The two men stared at each other for a long moment, then Fogliano put his hand on his son's arm. "Why don't we all sit and discuss how we can get your girl back?"

"I WENT to Fogliano because I didn't know who else to turn to. Destry has people in his pocket in government, law enforcement and so many other places that you wouldn't believe." Telly looked at Bertie and Christo. "I think, and correct me if I'm wrong, that Noosh had the same idea."

"She did."

Christo looked at his father. "Dad, I have to ask you something. Noosh, when she left me, she told me she'd been to see you, that she'd asked you for something, and that if you didn't give it to her, she would be gone." He drew in a deep breath. "Dad, please tell me. Did she ask you for money?"

Fogliano smiled at his son. "No, Christofalo, she didn't come to me for money. She came to me for protection...for you."

Christo didn't expect the rush of relief to hit him quite so hard, and he bent double, dragging breath into his lungs. Telly rubbed his back, and for a moment they all sat in silence.

"But you turned her down?" Bertie, this time, asking the question he knew Christo wanted to ask.

"I did," Fogliano said carefully. "My experience told me that if Noosh were to believe I was handling it, she would become less...careful. As it turns out, I should have told her I had every intention of helping the both of you. Christofalo...Christo...I have done many things in my life, many things I regret, but none more so than the times I have brought pain to my family. You, your mother. I know you blame me for her death, and I blame myself too. I did not see how sick she was."

He looked away from his son for a long moment. "When we met...the love, Christo, the love we had for each other. I saw it in your Noosh's eyes. She adores you, loves you, would die for you."

"And I for her," Christo said quietly, and Fogliano nodded.

"I know that, son. So, quietly, I began to reach out to my contacts, to see how we could bring Papps down and set Noosh free from his influence. I asked around, especially after she left you, supposedly for him."

"And what did you find out?"

Fogliano hesitated. "We found where her parents are being held, a small holding on the Scottish borders. My men are watching, waiting for my cue to intervene."

Christo looked at him sharply. "Why haven't you got them out?"

"Because, Christo, if Papps thinks he no longer has leverage over Noosh, he'll kill her. Calm down." Bertie's voice was hard.

Christo sighed. "Of course, I'm sorry." He looked at Telly. "How do you come into this...and why fake the suicide?"

Telly smiled at him. "After you and I spoke at the Bethesda Terrace, Fogliano approached me."

"I had you and Noosh watched – merely for protection's sake, of course," Fogliano added. "I knew that if we were to bring Papps down, then Telly would be our way in. She could testify against him, ruin his chances in the election. Therefore, her life was in danger, so we cooked up the fake suicide. We'll drop her on him at the most crucial moment."

"How?"

"A press conference," Telly said. "I'm going to tell the total truth about Destry Papps."

"They'll paint you as a bitter ex-wife looking for revenge."

Telly nodded. "Quite possibly, but I have another ace up my sleeve."

"What?"

She smiled. "Gerry Noll. Destry is convinced he is loyal to him, and he is – except for one weakness."

"What?"

"Me. Gerry and I have been seeing each other for a year or so. I credit him with my staying alive all this time. Destry trusts him – or rather, is arrogant enough to believe Gerry won't turn. If I go public, I guarantee Gerry will back me up."

Christo shook his head. "That's too flimsy for me. I need assurances."

"There are none, son," Fogliano said. "We're dealing with a psychopath with immense power and reach. To him, women are objects, to own, to possess, to kill. Up until he met Noosh, he was very careful to cover his tracks, as was the case with your friend, Jasmine. But his obsession with her…"

"Is his weakness." Christo sat up, fire raging in his eyes, and Fogliano nodded.

"And yours."

"No," Christo shook his head. "She is my *strength*."

Fogliano smiled at his son. "For whatever has passed between us in the past, I have never been prouder of you than I am at this moment. We will fight for your love, Christo. Even if it costs us everything."

Bertie's phone beeped, interrupting the moment, and they looked at him as he held his phone up, grim-faced. "Looks like we've got a date to aim for. The Senator has just announced he's getting married."

24

CHAPTER TWENTY-FOUR

Noosh lay under Destry's heavy, sweating body as he pumped away at her. She tuned out everything, wishing she could just decide to die and that would be that. He raped her every night now, and she had forced herself not to fight him. Keeping Destry sweet was one thing; however, pretending to enjoy his 'lovemaking' was another.

After he'd finished, he rolled off of her and got up. Thankfully, he always used a condom, and now as he went into the en-suite bathroom, he gave a long sigh.

"Anoushka, when we are married, I expect you to be a willing partner. I expect you to be present."

No chance. Married. Fuck, no. She sat up, waiting for him to leave the bathroom before she could bathe his stink off of her. He came back but grabbed her arm as she got up and pulled her back down on the bed. He ran a finger down her belly, tracing the scars there and smirking.

"In two years' time, I will drive you to a private cabin I have on Long Island. There, I will take your life. I will stab you so many times that the medical examiner won't bother to count the wounds. Your body will be discovered and I, devastated by my beautiful wife's death, will order a full investigation...and Christofalo will be arrested and tried for your murder. He will be found guilty, the knife that killed you hidden in the home that you shared. He will go to prison...and be found dead soon after – shanked in the showers by some of his father's enemies. He will get it in the gut, like you, Anoushka. That must some comfort, knowing you and your criminal will die the same way."

Destry said this all in a sing-song voice, but his words had the opposite effect than what he wanted, to frighten her. Instead, Noosh started to laugh. Destry's face creased in rage, but she kept on chuckling.

"You really are batshit crazy, aren't you?" Noosh pushed him off her. She got up and went to the drawer of the bathroom, pulling out a pair of scissors. She handed them to him. "Do it now. Kill me. Stick those in my belly. Come on, you coward, what are you waiting for?"

She grabbed the hand with the scissors and pressed the sharp tip into her navel. "Push it in. Gut me. Fucking slaughter me, Destry, because I swear to god, tonight is the last night you'll ever touch me."

"Don't test me, little girl."

"No, I think I *will*. This is it, Destry, this is the limit to my patience. Just who the fuck do you think you are? Go on, kill me, kill my parents, Christo, everyone I care about. Because I swear to you, you won't get away with it, you vile disgrace of a human."

Destry grabbed her neck and forced her against the wall, choking her. Noosh felt the scissors press hard into her skin. *"You fucking little whore!"*

Noosh kneed him hard in the groin. She didn't care now, she *wanted* him to hurt her – badly – so badly that he couldn't write it off as an accident, that it would be obvious to the world what a monster he was.

He let her go, buckling as he rode out the pain in his balls.

Noosh slid down the wall, panting hard, her throat sore. Finally, Destry stood up, looking down at her with undisguised hatred. "You will pay for that, Anoushka. But not until we are married. Our honeymoon will be nothing but unimaginable pain for you. Remember that."

He left her alone, and Noosh curled up. What had she achieved? Not much. Too late, she saw that he had taken the scissors with him – why the fuck hadn't she waited until he was asleep and used them on him?

Because he had her parents. If Destry turned up dead, they would be killed immediately. God, he really had her, didn't he?

Noosh couldn't cry – she had no tears left. She dragged her robe on and curled up in the corner, not wanting to lie in the bed where she was raped. She fell into an uneasy sleep, only to wake suddenly when a hand touched her.

Gerry put his finger to his lips. "He's asleep, I only have a few moments."

Noosh stared at him for a moment. "You'll help?"

He nodded. Noosh considered, then took her necklace off and dropped it into his hand. "Take this to Christo. Tell him all you can. Tell him…I'm sorry and that…I love him. I will always love him no matter what. Make sure he gets my parents out safely. They must be his priority."

Gerry nodded and got up to go. She grabbed his hand. "Thank you."

He nodded. "For Telly."

"For Telly."

CHRISTO WAS STILL AWAKE. He was back in his old bedroom at his father's mansion, which felt weird and yet…after Bertie and Telly had retired, Christo and Fogliano had talked properly for the first time since…forever. They spoke about Ornella, his father's pain at her sickness, her passing, his guilt. He apologized over and over for beating Christo.

"I cannot pretend to be a good man," he said. "But I can try to be a better father."

It was almost dawn before his father retired. He tentatively hugged his son, a little awkwardly, but Christo returned the embrace. Fogliano studied his son. "Trust in her love. Trust in your love. Dream about her, son. Dream about your future, the family you will make together. *Believe.*"

Christo closed his eyes and imagined he and Noosh were back in their little Italian villa. He remembered how she would love to stand naked looking out over the ocean. He dreamed that he was with her now, sliding his arms around her waist, pressing his lips down on her shoulders, breathing in her skin, the scent of fresh air and clean linen.

"I love you," he murmured, and she turned in his arms, pressing her breasts against his bare chest, her dark brown eyes soft with love as she cupped his face in her hands.

"I love you too, Christo, so, so much."

His mouth found hers, hungry for his kiss, and they embraced until they were breathless. Christo slid his hands between her legs and smiled.

"You're wet."

"For you, always, baby." She slid her hands into the waistband of his light cotton pants and stroked his cock. It quivered and stiffened in her hands, and as it hardened, she pulled on the drawstring of his pants, and they fell to the ground.

The scene shifted. They were in the bedroom, Noosh was on the bed, and as Christo watched, she slowly spread her legs, smiling at him. He gazed at the beautiful sight of her cunt – pink, swollen with arousal, glistening, damp. He gave a groan and covered her body with his, sliding his engorged cock deep inside her velvety cunt. The gasp she gave spurred him on as he moved in and out of her. She clung to him, rubbing her hard nipples against his chest, kissing him deeply, her fingernails digging into his buttocks, urging him deeper, harder, faster.

Her cry as she came was like music to him, and when he too reached his climax, pumping his seed deep into her belly, she whispered over and over how much she loved him.

The scene changed again, and this time she was barefoot, wearing the lightest white cotton dress, her belly swollen with his child. Before he knew it, there was a child, a dark-haired, caramel-skinned child with his green eyes running in the fields behind the house, he and Noosh chasing her as she giggled and screamed with joy.

Another change. A hospital bed, a new-born child, a boy with his father's dark curls. An exhausted but elated Noosh kissing his tiny head, then pressing her lips to Christo's.

Finally, as Christo gave into sleep, Noosh, beautiful in white, tiny flowers in her hair, walking towards him, towards the altar where he stood. "Finally," Christo said to her just as the image dissolved and sleep took him.

When he woke in the morning, Christo knew that even if he had to kill to do it, he would make that future come true.

CHAPTER TWENTY-FIVE

Noosh woke on the day of her wedding, wishing she was dead. Gerry had gone AWOL with her necklace and nothing had happened. *Nothing.* She felt betrayed, depressed, her last hope gone. Had Gerry changed his mind? Or had Destry discovered his lieutenant's duplicity and killed her only ally?

It didn't matter. In a few hours, she would be Destry's wife – and the thought made her gag – and it would be all over. She would kill herself if it weren't for the fact that Destry would have no reason to release her parents. She was utterly trapped.

A minion of Destry's had brought her a dress to wear. Ivory, clinging to her every curve, but still respectable – for the photos, of course. The one thing he couldn't make her do was smile. *Fuck him.*

She dressed slowly, deliberately not brushing her hair, but Destry had thought of that, of course, and sent in an army of make-up artists and hairdressers and by the time she was led – at gunpoint – to the waiting limousine, she looked nothing like herself. God, let this be over with.

. . .

At City Hall, Destry had a fleet of journalists clamoring for the first look at his new bride. Unsmiling, Noosh stepped from the limousine to flashing light bulbs. Shaking, her fingers went instinctively to her throat but found it bare. Not even her dragonfly to keep her from going insane. Destry had his hand wrapped around her upper arm as he flashed his thousand-watt smile at the reporters, answering their questions, laughing with them.

"Hey, guys, I'd love to stay and talk, but I gotta get inside and make this little beauty Mrs. Papps."

His smile disappeared as soon as they were inside, and Noosh noticed his security team had cleared the hallways. Destry marched them towards the courtroom. Noosh balked as he opened the door, and she stopped, panic setting in.

"I can't do this." She looked at Destry with pleading eyes. "Please...don't make me do this."

Destry smirked and dragged her into the room. The court bailiff looked startled.

"Is everything okay?"

Destry gave her a sincere smile. "Oh, just being playful. That's what we do, we joke around. Don't we, darling?"

He looked at Noosh, and all she could see in his eyes was murder. She nodded dumbly.

The bailiff looked unsure. "Well, okay. The judge will be with you shortly."

For a moment they were alone, and Destry grabbed Noosh's face. "Don't forget, slut, that it's only due to my goodwill that you're still alive. That I'm willing to give you two years. So make this good. Play your part. Or Mommy and Daddy might suffer the consequences."

He let her go as the courtroom doors opened and the judge came in, along with two of Destry's security team. Their witnesses. Noosh didn't even know their names.

The judge ran through the procedure then began. Destry had apparently paid him to be more flowery than usual for a courtroom marriage. As they got to the "Does anyone object?" part, Noosh felt the desperate urge to scream out "Yes! Yes! I object!" but Destry was standing too close, was gazing down at her, tension rolling off of him, daring her to speak. So, she stayed silent and closed her eyes.

"I object."

For a second, Noosh thought she had conjured his voice from her dreams. She didn't want to open her eyes in case it wasn't true, but something made her look towards the sound.

Christo.

He stepped towards the couple, his eyes never leaving Noosh's face. "I object, your honor."

"On what grounds, Mr. Montecito?"

The judge knew Christo? Noosh was confused. Christo smiled at her, and her heart soared. He was really here for her. "On the grounds, your honor, that the bride is in love with me. On the grounds that I love her more than my own life." He paused and looked at Destry. "And on the grounds that this man is coercing the bride to marry him on threat of death. That over the last few years he has tortured, kidnapped, stalked, raped, and shot the bride because of his obsession with her. That he intends to kill her."

Destry, stunned into silence by Christo's arrival, now exploded. "Get him out of here. Judge, he's a crazy man, the son of a criminal."

Behind Christo the door opened, and a fleet of police officers moved into the room. With them, a pale-faced Gerry. Destry's face drained of blood. "What the fuck is this?"

Christo cleared his throat. "Judge, in two minutes, there will be a press conference that you will want to see. The police here will escort us all to your chambers to watch it. I promise you,

Judge, I mean no disrespect to your courtroom, I'm just asking, please indulge me."

"Judge! Order these men out, for goodness sake!"

But the judge was studying Christo, sizing him up, and then he nodded. "I'll allow it, Mr. Montecito, but I must warn you. Should this be merely a ploy on your behalf to stop this wedding, I will hold you in contempt."

"Of course, your honor. Shall we?"

DESTRY HAD no choice but to join them all in the judge's chambers. He gripped Noosh's elbow painfully. "Don't even think about going to your criminal," he murmured to her. "You'll be dead the second he touches you."

But Noosh couldn't take her eyes off Christo. *I love you,* she mouthed, and he nodded, a small smile playing around his lips. Noosh couldn't help but feel hope for the first time in weeks.

He came for me...

But her parents were still in Destry's custody, and there was no way she could risk doing anything until she knew what Christo's plan was.

The judge turned on the flat screen in his office. He glanced at Noosh. "Ms. Taylor, would you like to sit?"

She smiled at him. "I'm fine, thank you, your honor."

He nodded and gave her a sly wink when Destry wasn't looking. *He's on my side,* she thought incredulously. *There are good people in this world...I'd forgotten.*

She felt someone move behind her and knew it was Christo. Discreetly she reached a hand behind her and felt him squeeze her fingers. It gave her strength.

The TV flashed on a podium set up in front of a bank of photographers. It was with a gasp of shock that everyone in the room saw Telly Wyatt, very much alive, step in front of the cameras. Noosh shot a look at Gerry, who was gazing at Telly with undisguised adoration and relief that she was okay.

Destry was still, his eyes narrowing as he watched his ex-wife begin to speak. Telly's voice was clear, and she didn't look nervous at all.

"Obviously, contrary to recent reports, I am still here, still alive. I apologize to those I hurt by faking my suicide, but as you will see, the ruse was necessary to protect me from my ex-husband. Your presidential nominee, the Senator from New York, my ex-husband Destry Tollhunt Papps is a *monster*, ladies, and gentlemen. He is a domestic abuser, a stalker, and will stoop to nothing less than cold-blooded murder to get what he wants. During our marriage, he frequently beat and raped me. I finally was able to escape when he became obsessed with a young English woman named Anoushka Taylor, his current fiancée. You might know her as Sarah Marsh. That's the name Noosh picked so that she could hide from Destry, but it didn't work. He hunted her down, and eight months ago, he shot and almost killed her."

Telly paused and blew out her cheeks. "Now, I can see the skepticism on some of your faces – am I just the bitter ex-wife? Sure you could think that, I wouldn't blame you. So, I ask Ms. Taylor to come forward and tell her story. Except...she can't. She is currently at City Hall, being forced to marry Destry against her will. Destry's people, the kind of people you don't see on the campaign trail, abducted her parents. They murdered her friend and co-worker. Noosh, if you're able to see this, I swear to you, this will not go unpunished."

"Destry, if you're watching...time's up, and not a moment too soon." Telly stepped from the podium, ignoring the barrage of questions coming her way.

A man who identified himself as the head of the FBI New York field office stepped up in Telly's place. "I can confirm that a warrant for the arrest of Senator Destry Papps has been issued, concerning some documents handed over to us by Gervais Noll, Mr. Papps's assistant. In these documents, we have found evidence of not just coercion of government officials, but of multiple attempts to stalk, harass, and murder Miss. Anoushka Taylor, alias Sarah Marsh."

The room was frozen for a moment then Destry was up. "This is outrageous!"

"Destry Papps, I'm arresting you for the abduction, assault, rape, and attempted murder of Anoushka Taylor." One of the police officers, a fierce looking woman, stepped forward. "We found the gun, Mr. Papps. Or rather...we were led to it."

He glanced at Gerry who was staring at Destry with undisguised hatred. "You bastard," Destry said, "you sniveling little creep."

Christo, seeing Destry was about to blow, reached out his hand to Noosh. She grasped at it – but Destry was quicker. He pulled her back against him, drawing yet another gun from his waistband and pressing it against her throat. His eyes never left Christo's. "I'll kill her without even thinking about it, Montecito."

"My parents..." Noosh, ignoring the pistol pressed to her neck, looked at Christo in desperation, not concerned for her own life now.

"They're safe," Christo was edging closer to them now, his eyes locked on the gun. "My father's men found them and released them. Papps, it's over, give it up."

Destry laughed. "It's not over, scumbag, until I say it is. Do you honestly think anyone will come after me while I have *her*?" He glanced over at the police officers. "I swear I will kill her unless you clear a path out of here."

Christo lunged for the gun, and Destry again was too quick. He shot Christo as Noosh screamed *"No!"* and struggled to get away from him, to go to the injured Christo who lay bleeding on the floor. Destry dragged Noosh out of the room, shooting his way out, helped by his security team as the police officers pursued them.

Noosh was still struggling when Destry, cussing, growled in her ear. "He's dead, bitch. He's gone. Don't worry, you'll soon be joining him." As she cried out, Destry brought the gun down hard on her head, and everything went black.

CHAPTER TWENTY-SIX

Bedlam. The judge and Gerry went to help Christo, who was trying to get to his feet to chase after Noosh. "Hey, hey, hey, slow down."

The judge pushed Christo to the ground. "Careful now, son, that's a nasty wound."

"I have to get to her," Christo said, struggling against the hands that were trying to stem the flow of blood. The bullet had smashed through his clavicle on his left side and was bleeding like crazy, but all Christo could think of was Noosh. Destry had nothing now except his bloodlust for her. If they didn't get to her in time...

Christo's adrenaline was pumping, and he managed to push his way up from the floor. Gerry steadied him, his face pale. Christo turned to him. "Please. You know him better than anyone. Where would he take her?"

Gerry wrapped his arm under Christo's shoulder. "I'll tell you on one condition – I'm coming with you. The second we get Noosh back, you're going to the hospital."

"Not without me." Bertie was there then, and Christo felt relief as he was followed in by Telly and Fogliano. Fogliano took one look at his son and turned to speak to his men. "Find the Senator and kill him. Bring my future daughter-in-law back unharmed."

"No," Christo gasped. "I need to do this. Dad, please…"

Fogliano sighed, knowing Christo would not be told otherwise. "Judge, do you have someone here who can travel with my son, to keep him alive while he looks for Noosh?"

IN FIVE MINUTES, on Gerry's advice, several cars left New York City in different directions. Christo, his arm and shoulder heavily bandaged, was being driven by Gerry towards Westchester. "He has a small place that he thinks no one knows about. Details are buried deep in the documents I handed over to the FBI… If he's going anywhere, it's there, but it's a good idea to have people go to all his places."

Gerry looked over at Christo. "You doing okay?"

Christo nodded. "Why didn't I get between them? God dammit, I thought we'd won. I thought…"

"Hey, all hope is not lost. Noosh knows you love her – I saw it in her eyes, she had hope again. She's survived him once – she'll fight like crazy to get back to you, I know it."

Christo looked at him gratefully. "Gerry, I still can't figure out how you stayed with him so long."

"Would you believe me if I told you that in the beginning, he was a good man?"

"Nope."

Gerry laughed. "Well, he was. He had vision, intelligence, and compassion. Ironic, that last one, considering what he's become. There was no indication, you see, none. I've asked myself over and over what happened to change him, but I can't figure it out. Hell, I never saw it coming. I was like one of those frogs in hot water."

"Huh?"

"You put a frog in boiling water, it jumps out right away, right? But put a frog in cold water and gradually heat it up...it doesn't know it's cooking to death."

"Gotcha." Christo sighed. "Hell, I'm not judging you, man. How could I, being the son of Fogliano Montecito? I knew what my father did for a living, I knew most of what his organization was involved in. Did I technically do anything illegal? No, but I was complicit."

"Yup, that about sums it up." Gerry sighed. "By the time I realized what Destry was...I was in love with Telly. I needed to stay to keep her safe – I at least had influence in that way." He looked over at Christo, his expression guilty. "I should have protected Noosh better. I'm sorry."

"Hey, you gave me her necklace, and you put your own neck on the line by going to the FBI. They give you a rough time?"

Gerry laughed. "You could say that. At first, at least, but when I rolled over on Destry, they got sweet real quick. I gave them everything. The man deserves to be in prison, Christo."

"Hey, you don't have to tell me that."

They drove in silence for a while before Christo's phone began to buzz. It was Bertie. "Hey, you're about ten minutes behind them."

Christo sat up. "How do you know?"

"The FBI traced them to the road you're on – we're all turning around, but you're the closest. The FBI is sending out helicopters now."

"Thanks, Bert." Christo relayed the news to Gerry, who hit the gas.

"Let's go. Let's go get your girl."

Noosh came around as Destry drove over the county line into

Westchester. He had the radio on and Noosh heard the announcers talking about the car chase. She sighed – they were coming after them. In a way, she felt glad that this was happening – one way or another, it would be over tonight. She might die, probably *would* die, but so would Destry. If he was arrested...would she ever feel safe? Would Christo ever be safe?

"What are you smiling about, bitch?" Destry had dropped all pretension of class now, reverting to the animal he was. He looked desperate, deranged.

"Just that you're fucked, Destry. Your chickens have finally come home to roost."

He was sweating profusely, his eyes darting to the rear-view mirrors. Above them, a helicopter could be heard, tracking them. "Fuck!"

He spun the car off the road and into a wooded area. Noosh was thrown about in her seat – only the fact that her arms were tied behind the seat kept her from flying through the windshield, especially when the car slammed into a tree.

Destry was raging. "They might catch me, but they won't take this moment away from me, Anoushka." He leaned over and rummaged around in the glove compartment, drawing out a lethal looking knife. He grinned then as her eyes widened. "Yes, Anoushka. They might catch me, might throw me in prison... but you'll still be dead."

It was over. Noosh drew in a deep breath as he raised the knife. Suddenly his face, contorted with bloodlust, was highlighted as car headlights glared behind them. Noosh gasped as she heard Christo screaming for her.

"Christo!" Her call was cut off as Destry drove the knife into her belly. *God, no...please...not now...not so close....*

Destry stabbed her again and again, merciless, and Noosh felt herself dying. "Please stop," she said weakly, "I'm already dead."

It had taken seconds to tear her open, but Destry's maniacal grin was ripped from his face when Christo hauled him away from Noosh with every last bit of strength he had left. Noosh's door opened, and Gerry was there, freeing her hands and pressing down on her wounds.

He lifted her out and began to carry her to the car. Noosh, barely conscious, moaned. "No...Christo..."

"He's taking care of Destry, honey. We have to get you to a hospital. The Feds are right behind us."

Noosh opened her eyes and looked around wildly for her lover. She saw him struggling with Destry, bleeding heavily as Destry pummeled him. With only one arm in operation, even Christo's rage and grief couldn't compete. Destry kicked Christo in the head, knocking him back, then he lunged for his gun.

Noosh's eyes widened as Destry turned towards them and pulled the trigger. Gerry stumbled, bleeding from the hole in his chest, and Noosh screamed. Gerry's eyes filled with pain. "Tell her I loved her," he choked out before he tumbled to the forest floor, dropping Noosh.

Pain wracked her body, and she moaned, clutching at her torn belly. Destry staggered over, aiming the gun at her head. "It's all over now, Anoushka."

Noosh closed her eyes, but then heard a yell as Christo threw himself at Destry, forcing him to drop the gun. As Christo tumbled Destry away from her, Noosh summoned up every last bit of her strength and reached for the gun. She staggered to her feet, her free hand pressed to the stab wounds in her abdomen, and stumbled over to where the men were fighting. Christo was weakening, she could see that, and her resolve strengthened.

When she was immediately behind Destry, she aimed the gun. "Destry, look at me, you son of a bitch."

Destry whirled around, and Noosh shot him between the eyes without hesitation. He stared at her incredulously for a moment before dropping. Noosh, feeling herself weakening from blood loss, gave him a humorless smile. "I'm glad you saw it coming, scumbag."

Destry slumped to the ground, eyes staring blankly. Noosh bent down and pressed the gun to his skull and emptied the rest of the gun into his head. She didn't realize she was sobbing until she felt Christo's arms around her, pulling her away from her dead tormenter.

Christo, his face wracked in pain, wrapped his good arm around her, his lips against her forehead. "Hang on, baby, please. I can't lose you now."

Noosh gazed up at him, her eyes no longer full of fear or pain, but soft with love. "You came for me. After those terrible things he made me say to you…"

"Don't think of that now."

She heard cars approaching – help on its way – and knew she had to try to hang on. "We get our happy ending, Christo."

He smiled down at her through his tears. "Yes, we do, baby. Yes we do."

CHAPTER TWENTY-SEVEN

"Anoushka Taylor, would you please stop getting yourself into these situations? I just repaired you once already."

Beth grinned at her patient as Noosh was wheeled out of surgery, dopey from the anesthesia, but still managing to smile at her friend. Beth checked her vitals and swept a hand over her forehead. "You, young lady, are a very lucky girl. The knife missed your vital organs and your arteries. The scar tissue from your shooting actually deflected the blade on some of the wounds."

"Christo...how is he? Is he okay?"

Beth smiled. "He's fine, sweetheart, apart from being worried about you. His surgery went well, and he's back in his room." She chuckled. "Damn, girl, you know how to pick them."

"Are my mum and dad here?"

Beth's smile faded. "They are. They've been worried as hell about you. Your boss is here too."

"I don't have a boss anymore," Noosh said weakly, but Beth smiled.

"That's not what *she* says. Anyway, for now, just rest. You'll see all of them real soon."

Noosh closed her eyes, the remnants of the anesthesia coursing through her veins, and sank thankfully into the darkness.

SHE FELT his lips against hers and opened her eyes. It was nighttime, the hospital quiet, but Noosh saw his face in the soft light and thought he looked like an angel.

"Hey, beautiful."

"Hey, gorgeous." She reached up and stroked his face. "How are you feeling?"

"Shouldn't I be asking you that?"

"I'm okay, more than okay. Is your shoulder broken?"

"My clavicle is fractured, but apart from that, I'm dandy."

She giggled at his mischievous smile. "Why are you so cheerful?"

Christo pulled his chair closer so he could lay his head next to hers on the pillow. "Because, against all the odds, we made it."

Noosh smiled. "We did?" Her smile faded. "Gerry?"

Christo shook his head. "Telly's pretty cut up."

"Oh, god, I'm so sorry. Without him helping me…" Her voice trembled and her eyes filled with tears. "Poor Gerry. Poor Telly."

Christo smoothed his hand over her forehead. "I will be forever grateful. And speaking of which…"

He reached into his robe pocket and brought out her necklace. Noosh smiled, holding her head up so he could fasten it around her neck. She touched the dragonfly. "Did you ever see –"

"You signaling me? Not at first, but when I did…god, Noosh, at that moment, I knew you loved me. I knew you needed my help."

"Our safe word worked." Noosh pressed her lips to his, lingering over the kiss. "Hey," she said, her eyes hopeful, "when do you think they'll let us out of here?"

Christo chuckled. "Baby. You need to recover before we even think about sexy times. Don't rush it, we have the rest of our lives to get down and dirty. You are going to marry me, right?"

"Christofalo Montecito, are you really proposing like that?" Noosh faked her outrage, making him laugh and giggling herself, wincing when her stomach muscles protested.

"Yes and no. Believe me, when we both are out of here and healthy, I'm going to propose properly in our villa in Italia, when my cock is buried deep in your beautiful cunt, I'll ask again."

Noosh groaned, "Dude, you're making me so horny."

Christo grinned and slid his hand under the blanket, and Noosh sighed as his fingers made contact with her clit. "Let me help you out with that," he murmured, his lips against hers, and he stroked her into the most mellow orgasm.

Endorphins flooded her system, and Noosh gazed up at her lover with shining eyes. "I love you so much."

"I love you too, my sweet darling. Rest now, baby, soon we'll be in Italy....so very soon."

CHAPTER TWENTY-EIGHT

It was the way he had imagined it all those months ago when she was gone. Christo stood in the doorway of their villa and watched Noosh as she stood at the cliff edge, looking out to sea. The Mediterranean sun had turned her already caramel skin a deep russet, and her hair, long, thick and lustrous, hung in a dark curtain almost to her waist.

It had been a year and a half since Destry Papps had died, and every day since then, Christo had fallen even more in love with Noosh. Her bravery, her resilience, her huge heart. She had returned to work at the radio station and told her true story, knowing that people wanted to know. To Christo's amusement, she had interviewed his father, and become his father's buddy, always giggling together whenever the family was gathered.

Christo and his father had become closer than Christo ever believed they could be, and he credited Noosh entirely for that. Fogliano had all but turned into a legitimate businessman, cutting ties with some of the seedier contacts and turning towards more charitable pursuits.

Christo pushed away from the stone doorway and went to

her, sliding his arms around her waist. Noosh leaned back into him, turning her head for a kiss. "Hey, gorgeous. Our last day."

"Ha," he nibbled at her earlobe. "Don't put it like that. Say the final day before the wedding and we're inundated with family and friends. Say it's the last time we can call ourselves single people. Say it's the last day that we have to wait to call each other Mr. and Mrs."

Noosh giggled. "Mr. and Mrs. Montecito. I like the sound of it."

Christo pressed his lips to her temple. "You know, I could take your name."

Noosh smiled. "You are sweet, but I will be proud to be a Montecito."

Christo was unbelievably touched, and he gave a bemused laugh. "I never thought I would hear anyone say that."

Noosh turned in his arms and gazed up at him. "There's a lot to be proud of, Christo, especially these last two years. I hope...I hope so much that you realize that."

"If there were a way to tell you just how much I love you, Noosh, I would say it, but there are no words." He kissed her tenderly then grinned. "Hey, kiddo, how about marrying me?"

She laughed. "What about tomorrow?"

"Done."

Christo grinned widely and swept her up into his arms. "Did you know, in this part of Italy, it's traditional for the bride and groom to make love for the whole day the day before their wedding?"

Noosh giggled, her arms locked around his neck. "Are you making that up?"

"Oh yes, but it's still going to be true today." Christo grinned down at her.

. . .

IN THEIR BEDROOM, a warm breeze was blowing through the sheer white drapes, billowing at the windows. Outside, they could hear the crashing of the waves on the rocks on the shore. They kissed softly as Christo unbuttoned her dress, sliding his hands inside to cup her breasts, to stroke her stomach as Noosh pushed his shirt aside. They took their time, undressing each other slowly, until – naked – they tumbled to the bed.

Christo covered her body with his, hitching her legs around his waist, his huge cock nudging against her sex. "I'm sorry, baby, I can't wait."

Noosh grinned as he slid into her, sighing happily. "Never apologize for that, baby. God, that feels so good. Deeper, baby, deeper."

She rocked her hips up to meet his, allowing his cock to plunge deep inside her. Christo's eyes never left her face as they moved together. "I've never seen a more beautiful sight than your face when we make love," he murmured, trailing his lips along her jawline and thrusting harder.

Noosh tangled her fingers in his hair, crushing her lips against his as they made love, his cock growing even harder inside her as they fucked, letting themselves go, their animal need for each other feral and uninhibited.

She felt him come, sending thick streams of creamy white semen deep inside her. Noosh felt her entire body vibrating with ecstasy, that incredible feeling of being somewhere between life and death, utterly lost in the man she loved. "*Ti amo, ti amo*," she whispered in his native tongue, and Christo smiled down at her.

"*Bella* Anoushka, my love, my heart."

NOOSH WOKE on the morning of her wedding day and felt one hundred percent different to her first wedding day. She felt alive, vital, and almost sick with excitement. There would be no hurried City Hall wedding for her and her beloved Christo. She turned on her side and watched him sleep – they'd had no time for the old custom of not seeing each other on their wedding day. He was almost forty now, only a few weeks away, but he looked no older than his late twenties. She cupped his face with her palm, tracing her thumb over his cheek, marveling at his physical beauty. It was only made more appealing by his kind heart. She barely recognized the man who had taken her and then thrown her out of that club in New York all those months ago.

"We've been through so much, baby," she whispered it, so as to not wake him, but he opened those brilliant green eyes of his and smiled at her.

"I can't wait to begin the rest of our lives together, my darling Noosh. Good morning, beautiful." He leaned over and kissed her, gathering her to him. His cock was already hard, and she grinned as she pushed him onto his back and straddled him.

"Happy wedding day, gorgeous," she said, guiding him inside her.

They made love quietly, drinking each other in until they both looked at the clock regretfully. Their wedding planners would be here in less than an hour.

CHRISTO WAITED until Noosh's mother, Preeti, had borne her daughter off to get ready for the wedding before he got Bertie. Bertie was leaning against the outside wall, watching Noosh's father, Bernard, and Fogliano chuckling with each other over a bottle of very expensive scotch. Bertie nodded at them as Christo joined him.

"I hope Noosh knows she might have to support her own

dad while he staggers up the aisle. Those two are already three sheets."

Christo grinned. Noosh's father was a quiet and staid man, but he had hit it off immediately with Fogliano, much to everyone's surprise. Their friendship had eased the potential difficulties of being unable to pay for his daughter's wedding himself – something Christo and Noosh had worried about. Fogliano had taken Bernard aside after their engagement party.

"My dear Bernard, there is something I must ask you, from a father to a father. Noosh tells me that you have always provided for her, no matter how strained things became, that she never wanted for anything. I see it in her personality, her warmth, her love. She credits you and Preeti for it. I wish I could have been that person for my son, especially after my wife died. But I was not, and I will spend the rest of my life trying to make up for it. Which is why I ask you now for a favor. Please, Bernard, let me pay for the wedding. It is such a small thing for me, but it would mean the world."

Bernard Taylor had known the other reason for Fogliano to say this to him, but he was grateful that Fogliano went out of his way to make it seem as if Bernard were doing him a favor.

Now, Christo took Bertie aside. "So, the farmhouse?"

Bertie grinned. "The new buildings will be finished by the time you and Noosh get back from India. The contractors we chose are superb, I'm glad to say. Leave the rest to me, buddy."

"Thanks, man." Christo smiled with relief. "She's going to love it."

Bertie laughed aloud. "You and Noosh both. Now, let's get you ready."

PREETI HELPED her daughter into a beautiful white sari, a nod to

Preeti's heritage that Noosh had insisted on. "I know you'd love me to have a traditional Indian wedding, Mum, but I think this is a good compromise, isn't it?"

Preeti kissed her daughter's cheek. Noosh was almost her mother's mini-me – same warm beauty, soulful brown eyes, and caramel skin. "Darling, after the few years you have had – we have had – I wouldn't care if you were married in a trash bag."

Noosh laughed, then studied herself in the mirror. The sari, delicately decorated with dark gold beads, fit her body perfectly and made her dusky skin glow. "A fusion wedding," she grinned, and Preeti laughed.

"Well, your grandmother is already in the kitchen with the caterers – god help them if they mess up the curry dishes."

Noosh giggled and hugged her mother. Preeti had been remarkably resilient, even in the face of her own abduction and torture. Noosh had confided in her about killing Destry, how odd and distressing it had felt to take another person's life. She told Preeti while she didn't regret killing that monster, she didn't want her mother to think any less of her for being a killer.

Preeti had held her daughter in her arms and whispered in a fierce voice, "Nothing, nothing could ever change my feelings for you, my precious one. You did what you had to do. You saved us all, my darling."

Noosh remembered that now as Preeti wound her hair up into a loose bun at the nape of her neck, then fastened the wedding jewels in her hair. "I love you, Mum."

Preeti looked close to tears. "I love you too, Anoushka. I've never been as proud as I am of you today."

Noosh blinked back her own tears. "Mustn't ruin your great make-up work." She grinned at her mother with shining eyes.

Preeti touched her cheek. "You never needed much. Your beauty shines from inside you."

A tear did escape then. "I get it from my mum and dad," Noosh said softly.

The moment was ruined by the alarm clock making them both jump, then laugh. Noosh looked at Preeti and gave a shaky sigh. "It's time."

"It's time."

CHAPTER TWENTY-NINE

Christo's world became all about the beautiful woman walking towards him down the aisle. For a moment, it was as if every moment of their relationship flashed past his eyes – that first meeting at the club, their fraught parting, seeing her at the radio station and feeling utter shock and overwhelming delight as he saw her face again. The anticipation of their lovemaking as she recovered from the shooting, the miracle of their love. The horror of her stabbing, of feeling her life slip away as he held her in his arms.

They had made it. And now, in a few short minutes, they would be bound together forever.

Bernard placed Noosh's hand in Christo's, and Christo shot his almost-father-in-law a grateful smile before turning his attention to the women before him. Noosh smiled up at him, her face radiant with joy and love.

"God you're beautiful," he whispered and without thinking, pressed his lips to hers. A ripple of low laughter went through the gathered company, and Noosh giggled.

"I think we're supposed to wait to do that part," she said in a stage whisper, and Christo laughed.

"Oops."

Laughing, they turned to the priest and in no time at all, the vows were spoken, rings were exchanged, and they were married.

"*Now* you can kiss her," the priest laughed, and they needed no encouragement as their friends and family burst into cheers and applause.

"W E. A RE. *M ARRIED*." Noosh said it again, still not believing it as they settled onto the private jet ready to take them on their honeymoon to India. She grinned over at her husband. "How very grown up."

"Really quite spiffy," he said, teasing her, and she stuck her tongue out at him and giggled. Christo leaned over to kiss her. "Wifey."

"Hubby. Listen, how long do we have to stay belted in?"

"Just until we take off. Why?" But he was grinning – he knew exactly why.

"I had planned on today being one of the days where we slip away for a quickie, but it didn't turn out like that."

Christo laughed. "We almost got lucky...until your mother found us."

"The look on her face was priceless – and a little admiring." Noosh sniggered at the memory of her mother catching Christo with his pants around his ankles. "I don't think she bought our explanation that you were just, um, rearranging your underwear."

"Good god, I will never be able to look her in the eye again."

"She only saw your perfect bubble-butt – and she is still a woman. I swear, she looked at me with new respect." Noosh was enjoying his discomfort.

"Just for that, I'm going to do things to you that she definitely wouldn't approve of."

Noosh wriggled impatiently as the plane began to taxi along the runway. "Well, you'd better. What did you have in mind?"

"Oh, no." He shook his head. "Show, not tell, today, Mrs. Montecito." He let his fingertips drift up and down the inside of her thigh until she moaned, wanting him to touch her sex, but he merely grinned and wouldn't. "Have patience."

As the plane took off, they gazed at each other, then the moment the seatbelt light pinged off, Christo released his belt. "Stay where you are," he said in a low voice as he moved onto his knees, spreading her legs and settling between them. He tugged at the belt of her ruby-red dress.

"I remember this dress. You were wearing it the first time I saw you. God, when I saw you, so innocent, so vulnerable in that seedy club, I wanted you so badly."

Noosh smiled down at him, her eyes full of desire. "I never dreamed I would do something like that, but the sadness in your eyes...not to mention your gorgeous face," she giggled, "and I could not have resisted for a moment. I still feel like that...except now the pain has gone."

"For both of us." He pushed aside the fabric, revealing her underwear, her soft skin. He pressed his lips to each of her scars – her war wounds, she called them – then looked up at her. "You blow my mind, Anoushka Montecito. My life began when I met you."

"As did mine," she said. Christo kissed from her belly to her breasts, then caught her lips with his.

"Noosh, every inch of your body is golden, heaven, and made for fucking."

Noosh colored but smiled at the compliment. "Then fuck me, husband."

Christo smiled wickedly. "All in good time...for now, I want to taste your delicious cunt." With one movement, he ripped her panties from her, making her gasp at the quick pain, and lifted her buttocks. He smiled one last time before burying his face in her sex.

Noosh gasped as his tongue lashed mercilessly around her clit, and he slid two fingers into her sodden cunt. He brought her to an almost unbearable climax, leaving her shivering and trembling. He swept her up into his arms and to the bedroom at the back of the plane.

Noosh tore at his clothes, ripping open his shirt and taking his nipple into her mouth, nibbling and flickering her tongue around it until she felt it harden. She trailed her lips down his flat stomach and took his already tumescent cock into her mouth. Hollowing out her cheeks as she sucked him, drinking his seed down as he bucked and jerked beneath her.

Christo flipped her roughly onto her back and pinned her hands above her head. Noosh's breath quickened as she saw the dangerous desire in his eyes. He pushed her knees up to her chest and launched his cock into the red and swollen cunt. Their eyes locked as they fucked, not two beings now, but one, completely united in their love.

They fucked until they were exhausted, then fell asleep in each other's arms. When they awoke, the plane was flying over the subcontinent. They landed, and once they were through customs, Noosh grinned at Christo. "Now," she said, "time to introduce you to my heritage."

THE HONEYMOON WAS as full of love, laughter, and exploration as they had planned, but the day Christo would never forget was the day they traveled to Agra to see the Taj Mahal. Christo hadn't been prepared for the majesty, the beauty of the tomb, and he knew Noosh was watching him for his reaction. He looked down at her. "There are no words."

Noosh smiled. "I know."

"Have you been here before?"

She nodded. "When I was a kid. I didn't get it then. I mean, it's beautiful, and I knew the story of Shah Jahan and his love for Mumtaz Mahal…but I couldn't imagine a love like that." She took his hand. "I do now."

Christo was too moved to speak, and so Noosh led him around the mausoleum, telling him the love story between the Shah and his wife. "It's a full moon tonight. They allow night viewing…want to stay?"

CHRISTO WRAPPED his arms around her as they watched the moon soar in the night sky and give the Taj an otherworldly glow. Noosh snuggled into his embrace. "Happy?"

"Like you wouldn't believe, baby."

"Good. Christo?"

He smiled down at her. "Yes, baby?"

Noosh smiled at him, her eyes shining. "You're going to be a daddy."

Christo blinked, then gaped, then laughed. "What?"

Noosh giggled. "I found out three days ago, just before the wedding, and I was going to tell you straight away, but then I remembered we were coming here. I thought it was the perfect place to tell you that we're going to have a baby."

Christo was speechless for a moment then whooped loudly, hugging her tightly. They laughed together, and he apologized to some other tourists who he'd startled. "Sorry, sorry…we're having a baby!"

His joy infected all around them, and they had to field many congratulations before they were able to be alone again.

"I can't believe it. The doctor said..."

"The doctor said it would be difficult for me to conceive, but not impossible." Her smile faded a little. "Papps couldn't take that away from us, after all."

Christo swept a hand through her hair. "I know you've been thinking about him lately, I mean, I could tell it was backing up on you. He's dead, Noosh, he can't ever hurt us again. Never, ever again."

And finally, she believed him.

CHAPTER THIRTY

"Mumtaz Montecito."

"No. *No way.*" Noosh giggled as they drove back to the farmhouse from the airport. She stroked his cheek as he drove. The Indian sun had turned his olive skin a deep gold – it made his bright green eyes and his almost-black hair even more affecting and desirable. He grinned at her.

"Careful. Last time you looked at me like that, I done gone and got you good and knocked up."

Noosh laughed. Their Indian honeymoon had been perfect, and now they were returning home to begin their lives together and await the birth of their first child. They had figured out – roughly – that Noosh must not be more than a couple of months pregnant.

"Which leaves seven months for us to get the farmhouse childproofed. Your workshop, for example, had better be locked. Can you imagine a baby in there, crawling around?" She shuddered.

"If it's a boy, I'll get to teach him wood-turning."

"Dinosaur. What if our *daughter* wants to be a carpenter?"

"Her too," Christo said hurriedly. "Sorry, that *was* bad."

"You're forgiven...this time. And besides, our daughter will be too busy curing cancer and winning Oscars to be carving wood."

"That's an eclectic career path you've chosen for her."

They continued to rib each other, joking around until Christo pulled into the long driveway to their farmhouse. As they approached, Noosh exclaimed in surprise. "What on earth?"

There were two new buildings on the site – one next to Christo's workshop, and one built onto the farm, next to their bedroom. Noosh looked at Christo questioningly. He grinned.

"My wedding present to you. Let's get settled and I'll show you around."

THE BRICK BUILDING NEXT to Christo's workshop turned out to be a recording studio – small but with state of the art equipment. Noosh couldn't believe her eyes. Christo grinned at her. "I know you want to start doing independent documentaries for the station and for yourself. I thought this would help."

Noosh put her hand to her mouth, so utterly shocked that she couldn't speak for a moment. "My god, Christo...this is... incredible. Thank you, thank you."

She threw herself into his arms, any fatigue from the journey forgotten, and kissed him madly.

"You like?"

"God, yes...can I play?"

Christo laughed. "Of course...but hold that thought. Let me show you the other room...I think you might enjoy that one even more."

Noosh gave him a quizzical look and then began to smile. "Lead on, hubby."

She was right, the room did lead off of their bedroom, and when Christo opened the door, Noosh saw why, and started to laugh. "Oh, you naughty, *naughty boy,* Mr. Montecito..."

The room featured a bed, swathed in pure white mosquito netting, but it was the only innocent-looking thing in the room. Along the walls, stocks, handcuffs hanging from the walls and racks of riding crops and whips. A white cadenza stocked with dildos, vibrators, gags, leather belts, and straps. On the nightstand next to the bed, lube, massage oil, feathers. Noosh went around the room, touching everything, a slow smile spreading across her face.

Christo waited for her reaction. Noosh went to him and stood in front of him. Slowly, she unbuttoned her dress and let it fall to the floor. Underneath, she was naked, not having bothered to put underwear on for the jet – they'd fucked their way back over India, Europe, and the Atlantic Ocean.

"You like?" Christo asked as he slid his arms around her waist, and Noosh nodded, her eyes locked on his.

"Oh, I like, Mr. Montecito... I like very much. Promise me this...even when we're responsible parents, we'll still make time for this."

Christo grinned down at her. "I thought we said no promises?"

Noosh pressed her lips against his. "That was another lifetime, baby, another lifetime." And they began to make love, knowing this was only the beginning of their beautiful story.

THE END.

SIGN UP TO RECEIVE FREE BOOKS

Sign Up to Receive Free E-Books and Audiobook Codes.

Would you like to read **The Unexpected Nanny, Dirty Little Virgin** and **other romance books** for **free**?

You can sign up to receive these free e-books and audiobooks by typing this link into your browser:

https://www.steamyromance.info/free-books-and-audiobooks-hot-and-steamy/

Or this one:

https://www.steamyromance.info/the-unexpected-nanny-free/

PREVIEW OF PLEASE ME

DESIRED BY THE BILLIONAIRE (LOVER BOYS ROMANCE)

By Michelle Love

Blurb

He's the most exciting man I've met in a long time—and the most dangerous. His reputation precedes him, and I have a job to do—keep my client out of trouble and out of Stone Vanderberg's newspaper column.
But, God, no one told me he was this magnetic, this sensual, with his machismo such a turn on.
Every time he is near me, my body betrays my own promise not to let him near me.
I crave him...
I don't know how much longer I'll be able to resist him...
... or even if I want to.
I'm supposed to be working but all I think of is what Stone Vanderberg wants to do to me.
And what I am desperate to do with him...

Following a story to Cannes in the south of France, renowned journalist and billionaire playboy, Stone Vanderburg, is enchanted when he meets a beautiful young woman, Nanouk Songbird. The attraction between them is immediate and undeniable, and they have a sensual, thrilling affair.

Stone Vanderberg. That's the name that causes excitement amongst the Hollywood types flocking to the south of France—and with good reason. Am I cocky and arrogant? Sure. But I don't believe in false modesty, and I know I'm a good-looking guy, I know my body is rock-hard, and my cock has legendary status.

I use that name to get what I want—and what I want is *her*... Nanouk Songbird may not be like the flashy actress types that I usually get into my bed—but then again, she's just a human, too. She won't be able to resist me, I know it. Oh yeah, she'll be in my bed before the end of the week, moaning and crying out my name over and over as I f*ck her into submission...

Yeah, she won't be able to resist me...won't she?

CHAPTER ONE

Cannes, France...

Stone Vanderberg wondered, as he did every year, why he came to this film festival. It wasn't as if his long and successful journalistic career had focused on moviemaking, or even celebrity, but he had a fascination with the self-congratulatory ways of the movie stars, directors, and producers who flooded the south of France every May.

One year, almost twelve years ago, he'd written a sarcastic, cynical piece for The New Yorker which had proved wildly popular, and ever since, it became one of the most anticipated stories to come out of the festival every year.

Even the stars and studio bigwigs loved being roasted by Stone Vanderberg—all publicity is *good* publicity, after all—and, for Stone, there were always the perks. He stayed at the *InterContinental Carlton* on the seafront in the Sean Connery suite every year—paid for by the magazine, of course—and there was no shortage of beautiful women eager to bed the handsome writer.

Stone Vanderberg was the eldest son of a Long Island billionaire—the Vanderbergs were old money going generations back who rivalled the Gettys and Rockefellers in terms of prestige and money. Stone and his younger brother Ted, a movie agent, might be heirs to billions, but they stood on their own two feet in the world due to their well-earned international reputations as hard-working, hard-playing lotharios.

Now, Stone sat on his hotel balcony, watching the hordes of tourists and movie people mill around on *La Croisette Boulevard* below him. It was hot already at seven a.m. He'd spend the day watching and listening to the actors and actresses who were out in force to promote their movies. Stone would be invited multiple times to dinner or for drinks, or as he had found out, asked outright to have sex with them—by both the actress *and* the actors.

He had that kind of magnetism. Stone stood six-feet-six, with a broad-shouldered, ripped body from working out at four A.M. every day. At forty, with his dark-brown hair flecked with grey, his dark navy-blue eyes intense, Stone used his machismo, his power, to get what he wanted, and he made no apology for it. He liked hard work and fucking—*especially* fucking. He'd never married because, as he told interviewers, why would he want to settle for just one woman when he could have many? He knew he was arrogant, but he justified it with his charm.

Stone, contrary to his confident demeanor, actually believed in getting more bees with honey, than by jackbooting around. He made sure his conquests were clear that it was just for a night, and he always treated them well in the morning. His colleagues, especially his subordinates, adored him—he was a fair, inclusive employer who paid above the odds and nurtured his staff and their dreams. His personal assistant, Shanae, a gorgeous blonde from Charleston who dressed like someone from Dallas or Dynasty back in the Eighties, all shoulder pads and power suits, was a firecracker who mocked Stone mercilessly and hilariously to his face but was as fiercely loyal as a bulldog. Shanae and Stone shared a sibling-like relationship—despite Stone's man-whoring ways, Shanae had made it clear when she took the job that sex wasn't on the cards.

"I don't shit where I eat," she had said to him during the interview. "I know about men like you, Stone Vanderberg, and that monster in your pants is never going to get near my good girl."

Stone had given her the job on the spot. Now, checking the time back in New York, he debated calling her, knowing she would still be awake, playing retro videos games and eating peanut butter cookies.

Maybe not. She wouldn't thank him for the interruption. Instead, he went back into his room and into the bedroom of the suite. Last night's conquest was just waking up. He smiled at her.

"Hey, Holly."

Holly was a fun redhead who grinned back at him. "Hey, dude. Listen, I'll get out of your hair in a sec, but I need to shower. I have a meeting at ten, and my hotel is way out of town."

"Sure thing, honey. Come join me?"

Holly laughed. "If I do that, we'll end up fucking and I'll be late. Can I just hop in quick?"

"Of course."

She kissed him as she passed him and reached down to squeeze his cock. "Great night, babe."

"Right back at you."

Stone heard the shower running and sighed, content. This was what he liked—great sex followed by a friendly chat in the morning and no expectations. Holly had been an exceptional fuck, too—athletic, uninhibited, and good-humored. Gorgeous, too: punky, tattooed, different from his usual choice.

He thought about that now. *What is my 'usual' choice?* He smirked to himself. Beautiful. Sexy. With any luck, *not* skin and bones. With all the actresses being coerced into sample sizes by designers for this shindig, finding Holly who wasn't a size zero had been a miracle. But, Stone considered, that was probably why she wasn't doing as well in her career as some of the skeletons in designer duds haunting the festival.

"Hey, Hols? When you get back to the States, call me. We'll set up a profile piece for you. Get your name out there."

Holly stuck her head out of the bathroom door. "Is this a *thank you for sex* thing?"

Stone grinned. "No, it's a *good things should happen to a great woman like you* thing."

Holly flushed with pleasure. "Don't worry, I won't tell the world the great Stone Vanderberg is a teddy bear." She kissed him. "Thanks for an amazing fuck, Stone. You're the best."

"Oh, I know."

Holly rolled her eyes, laughing. "Later, babe."

THE ROOM RANG with silence after she'd gone. Stone considered that he wouldn't mind running into Holly again one day—she was a breath of fresh air. He grabbed his notepad—he was an old-school kind of writer—and headed out to wander through the crowds. Snagging his accreditation from the appropriate festival tent, he headed to the International Village, a series of pavilions where movie people networked and promoted their films.

In the Italian tent, he saw Cosimo DeLuca chatting to a group of producers. Stone waited until the other man was free before greeting his old friend. "Cos, you look ten years younger."

Cosimo grinned. "That would be Biba."

"How is she?"

"Pregnant again. Planned, I should add. We can't wait. Now that this latest movie is in the can, and after this thing, I can go home to Italy and forget about the movies for a few months." He looked around. "I've been trying to grab Eliso—I'd like him to consider a role, but I keep missing him."

Eliso Patini was perhaps Italy's most famous actor, but he was notoriously private. He was also Stone's best friend. Stone shrugged. "You know if you call him, he'll always call *you* back, Cos. I think you're on the list of five people he *will* return a call for."

They both laughed. "You doing your yearly article?"

Stone nodded. "It's been disappointingly drama free this year."

"I might have a tip. Apart from the fact that Stella is here and looking to upstage Jennifer Lawrence... *again*," Cosimo laughed, "I hear Sheila Maffey is here and very unhappy."

"About representation?"

"Yup. She has a point. Not one of the judges this year is either a woman or a minority. It's all looking very white." Cosimo shook his head. "In this day and age, it's a disgrace."

"No arguments here, although two middle-aged white men probably shouldn't be the champions for it," Stone said with a sigh.

"We can be allies. Anyway, the studio sent along a lawyer with Sheila for her press interviews. The poor kid. She looks like she would blow away in a breeze, but she seems to be fending off the worst and keeping Sheila in line."

"They sent a woman to silence a woman?"

"No, actually, the lawyer seems to be completely on Sheila's side, so that's good. Kid just clarifies language. You know Sheila though, it won't be too long before she blows up."

Stone nodded his head, thinking. "Thanks for the tip, man. Might be worth a look."

"Listen, let's do dinner before the end of this thing. I have to get to my next suck-up meeting." Cosimo slapped Stone's shoulder. "I'm just so relieved I'm not in competition this year. Later, my brother."

"Later, buddy."

As Cosimo walked away, he turned back and called out. "The Maffey thing is at *La Salon des Independents*, down on *Rue Louis Perrissol*. Sheila's on a roll. You should still catch them there."

"Thanks, man."

STONE WALKED the few blocks to the café. Years of pounding Cannes' side streets had made him an expert at the layout, and he had been to that bar before. The maître d' greeted him and asked him if he wanted a table.

"Miss Maffey's here?" Stone's voice was even, but he slipped a fifty-euro note to the woman. She smiled.

"Yes, sir. I believe there is a table nearby."

"Good girl." He winked at her, turning on his patented charm and she simpered at him. She led him to a table across from Sheila, who, as Cosimo predicted, was making her case to an unfortunate journalist.

Stone sat down and glanced over casually. At first, he just registered Sheila, magnificent in white, her dark hair piled up on her head, her elegance complimented by discreet but priceless jewels. From Stone's practiced eye, he estimated Sheila was wearing at least two million dollars-worth of gems. He hid a smile. Sheila was class and elegance but for a *breakfast* meeting? She was savvy; she knew how to make an impression, Stone had to give her that.

Then his attention was caught by the young woman sitting next to her, and his stomach felt like someone had driven a sledgehammer into it.

She was caramel-skinned, and her long dark hair was pulled into a messy bun at the nape of her neck. Huge, dark, soulful eyes, a rose-pink mouth, the last vestiges of puppy face making her face look younger than he supposed she was, but Stone felt as if his breath was hitching and failing. She was achingly beautiful but not in an obvious way like the actresses he knew—indeed, her face was make-up free—but in a soft, natural way. She was also the saddest person he had ever seen.

Stone caught himself staring, and when she looked up and met his gaze, a frisson crackled in the air between them. He watched as her cheeks blushed a rosy color, and she looked away. *Gotcha,* he thought, then felt bad. She wasn't someone to catch in a trap.

The young woman glanced back at him, and he saw recognition dawn in her eyes. She glanced at Sheila who was in mid-rant, and then suddenly stood. "This interview is ending. Right now."

Both Sheila and the interviewer look startled, but Stone grinned, unrepentant. His girl had recognized who he was and what he was doing, and she was doing her job, protecting her client. He watched her speak quietly to Sheila, who glanced over at him and rolled her eyes. Stone gave her a wave, and Sheila laughed, shaking her head.

"Well, Goddamn, Stone Vanderberg. I might have known."

To Stone's chagrin, her companion was making her way out of the bar with the journalist, and as Sheila was clearly set on talking to him, he had missed his shot at finding out who the beautiful stranger was. Sheila, her glossy black skin clear and glowing, sized him up. They'd had a thing years ago, but Sheila was even more of a commitment-phobe than he was.

Stone kissed her cheek. "Sheila, always good to see you."

"Wish I could say the same. You going to eviscerate me in

your piece? I mean, I don't mind, but what I'm ranting about this time actually means something."

"Nope, just wanted to say hi. Cosimo told me you were here. And for what it's worth, I'm with you on representation."

Her expression softened. "Good."

Stone nodded after her companion. "Studio sending you a muzzle?"

Sheila looked surprised. "Nan? Nope, quite the opposite. She's an entertainment lawyer, but she wants to move into human rights. She figures supporting me with this campaign gets her on the map. Kid's young, but she's tenacious."

"Nan?"

Sheila smiled. "Nanouk, and you leave her alone, Vanderberg. She's way too good for you, you slut."

Stone laughed, not offended in the least. "They always are, Sheila. Come on, I'll buy you lunch."

NANOUK SONGBIRD DUMPED her laptop on the desk in her tiny hotel room and flopped onto the bed. She hated being in Cannes and dealing with so many people around. Living in New York, she told herself that she should be used to crowds, but here, with so many people packed into the small coastal city all wanting to see the same thing, she felt claustrophobic.

And then there was the added irritant of Stone Vanderberg. She knew all about him, of course: the billionaire journalist from the powerful Vanderberg family. They were New York, and more specifically, Oyster Bay, Long Island. She'd grown up across town from their compound, in a tiny wood-frame house with her sister, Etta, who raised Nan after their parents were killed in a car wreck when Etta was eighteen and Nan was twelve. Etta raised the bewildered Nan all by herself, and Nan adored her older sister, and they were happy.

Then, one night, Etta was raped as she walked home from her job at the local library. She was unable to bear the trauma, and a few weeks later, when then-eighteen-year-old Nan came home from school, she found her sister dead from an overdose of sleeping tablets. She left a note.

I'm so sorry, baby bird, but I can't go on. Fly free with all my love, little one.

Nan was left alone and numb. On autopilot, she went through the motions of graduating from high school with a 4.0 GPA and applying to colleges. She got into Harvard Law on a scholarship. There, she met her best friend, Raoul—an easy-going Jewish boy from old money who adored her on sight. Raoul was openly gay, and Nan felt safe with him. The trauma of Etta's rape stayed with her, and although she made friends, she avoided dating, to the chagrin of the college boys who were drawn to her honey-skinned beauty. Nan's heritage—a father from Punjab, India, and a Shinnecock Indian mother—made her beauty exotic and alluring, but she consistently played down her looks, not wanting to be judged by them.

It was a habit she kept up even now. She got up and stripped out of her elegant work suit, hanging it up carefully. She was a jeans and T-shirt girl, and only now could she feel herself relaxing as she undid her hair from its bun and let it fall around her. Thick and lustrous, she knew she should get it cut into a more professional style—it was always messy—but it was her security blanket.

She made herself some herbal tea and pushed open the small door to the tiny balcony outside. The hotel was further into town but if she craned her neck around the side of the building, she could just make out the ocean. No matter. She sat in one of the chairs and sipped her tea. It was quieter here than on the seafront, and she reveled in the peace.

Now, away from Sheila, Nan could think about Stone

Vanderberg. She hadn't expected him to be quite so... magnetic. *Yup, that's the word.* He was tall, at least a foot taller than her, and his broad, obviously worked-out body was the stuff of magazine covers—even the way his casual sweater and jeans hung on his body was like an Abercrombie and Fitch commercial.

His dark blue eyes had met hers, and Nan had felt a thrill go through her. A pulse had begun to beat between her legs, astonishing her. Was this what they called the lightning bolt moment? Or, more likely, she grinned to herself, it was just a primal lust instinct. She wondered what it would be like to be fucked by him. She could imagine he always insisted on being dominant—and to be honest, she wouldn't mind that. His machismo, the slight air of danger in him...

Stop. She was getting turned on, and Stone Vanderberg was way, *way* out her league.

There was a knock at her door. Sighing, Nan got up. Her heart sank when she opened the door. Duggan Smollett, the studio's representative in Cannes this year, smiled at her. Nan's skin prickled. Since her arrival, he had hit on her virtually every time they had met, and he gave her the creeps. His small, silver eyes darted around, and his face was bloated from drink and coke. By the looks of it, he was high now—the sniffling and nose wiping a dead giveaway.

"Hey. Nannynook."

Ugh. "Hello, Duggan, how can I help you?" She deliberately kept her voice even—and her body rigid, preventing him from coming in. He smiled at her.

"Gonna let me in?"

"I'm taking some private time, Duggan." She didn't care if she had to be rude; he wasn't getting in. She didn't work for him.

"Oh, okay. Well, look, I was just checking in. How did the interview with Sheila and *Time Out* go?"

"Fine, nothing to report. I sent you the e-mail a little while ago." *Which you saw and then decided to come to my room to intimidate me. Asshole.*

Duggan smiled nastily. "Didn't see it. Well, okay. The premier's tonight, and I was wondering if you'd like to have dinner with me afterward."

Not a chance in hell. "I'm sorry, Duggan, Sheila's invited me to dine with her."

"Maybe some other night."

Nan didn't answer him. "Is there anything else?"

"No, no, just checking in. Well… bye for now."

"Goodbye, Duggan." There was a little satisfaction in closing the door in his face, but she double-locked it to be sure. Duggan was a predator and a coked-up one at that. Not worth the risk.

Nan found Sheila had sent her a message.

Warning, Sneaky Smollett is looking for you. Sorry, kiddo. Still on for tonight? S x

Nan smiled. Sheila was the best part of her job at the moment. She loved the actress' passion for her art, for her causes. Sheila wasn't a woman who sat down and shut up. She spoke out no matter who tried to put her down.

She was also one of the kindest people Nan had ever met, and they had bonded almost immediately upon acquaintance. Nan had to admit to herself that Sheila reminded her of Etta so much that she had almost morphed the two women in her mind. *Don't get too attached,* she told herself, *Sheila might be a friend, but this is still a job.*

Nan checked her watch. She had a few hours before the premiere. Jet lag was catching up with her, and she eagerly crawled under the comforter and curled up to grab a couple of hours sleep.

THE DREAM BEGAN PLEASANTLY ENOUGH. She was walking a red

carpet alone with the cool breeze blowing off the ocean. No one else was around, and the peace was incredible. Then she saw him—Stone Vanderberg. He held his hand out to her, and she took it. He drew her into his arms and kissed her, his mouth sweet, his lips passionate against hers.

Then smiling, he turned her around and locked his arms around her. Nan saw Duggan walking towards her, smirking nastily. She began to panic, but Stone put his lips to her ear. "It's alright, darling. It'll only hurt for a moment…"

She began to scream as Duggan drove a knife deep into her over and over…

Nan awoke, shaking and terrified.

CHAPTER TWO

Eliso Patini, movie star, grinned up at his girlfriend as she lay on top of him, breathless and sweating from fucking. He bunched a thick swath of her honey-gold hair around his fist. "God, I love you, Beulah Tegan."

Beulah smiled. "Glad to hear it. Now, come on, old man! Let's go again."

Eliso laughed. As Beulah stroked his cock back into full erection, he ran his hands gently down her curvaceous body. They had been together a little over a year, and in that time, Eliso had found himself a changed man. Yeah, it was a cliché: a movie star with a *Sports Illustrated* model, but Beulah Tegan—a cockney from London—was so much more than a beautiful face and a stop-the-traffic body. She was funny, erudite, and above all, kind, and Eliso had fallen for her as soon as they had met.

Eliso himself was a one of a kind, an actor who didn't sleep around, who didn't cheat when he was in a relationship, despite the fact he regularly ranked in the top ten 'Most Gorgeous Men in the World' lists. His easy-going manner belied a towering acting talent which could make an audience laugh one moment, then leave them weeping inconsolably the next.

His shaggy dark curls and large expressive green eyes were magnets to women, as well as his storied prowess in bed, but Eliso had always longed for a partner rather than just a quick lay. As fate would have it, when the year before he'd been seated next to Beulah at a fashion show and found her to be as bored as he was by the fashion and the vapid people, he knew he'd found a kindred spirit.

Beulah straddled him now and impaled herself onto his cock with a shuddering moan. "God, you're huge," she said, "I swear your cock gets bigger every day. Fuck, that's good."

She was riding him, taking him deeper. He stroked her flat belly, cupped her full breasts, and gazed up at her. Her tawny hair tumbled around her, and Eliso wondered if he'd ever seen such a beautiful sight. Beulah grinned down at him. "You have mushy in your eyes."

"Wanna get married?"

Beulah laughed. "How come you always ask me that when we're fucking?"

"Because I mean it. Marry me."

Beulah shook her head. "Not yet, sexy boy. We both have too much to do in our careers yet."

"Screw my career."

"I'd rather screw your monster cock. Besides, I couldn't take you away from your adoring fans—and, seriously, Eli, you're right on the cusp of something huge. Unlike me," she giggled then, "I'm *actually* on something huge."

She began to move faster, tightening her cunt around his cock, and Eliso groaned as she began to milk him, his cock pumping thick creamy cum deep into her belly. Beulah gave a long groan of ecstasy as she came. As both tried to catch their breath, Beulah detached herself and lay down next to him, stroking his face. "I love you, Eli, so, *so* much. But before we do the whole domesticated thing, we need to finish what we started. Then we can build a family with no regrets."

"Smart girl."

"You know it."

Eliso glanced at the clock. "What time did we say we're meeting Stone?"

"At the premiere. Don't make that face, we have to go to the premiere—you promised your agent. If you're a good boy and pose nicely, I'll blow you in the restrooms."

Eliso broke out laughing—that comment was just like Beulah. She had no time for airs and graces. "Deal."

FLASHBULBS IN THEIR FACES, Eliso and Beulah did their job, smiling for the cameras and even kissing when they were asked. During the entire time, they kept up a softly spoken private conversation, mocking the paparazzi, and talking dirty to each other.

Finally, inside the *Palais des Festivals et des Congrès,* Beulah made good on her promise, sucking his cock in one of the stalls of the restrooms, both of them giggling and laughing, then Eliso fucked her against the cool tile, kissing her passionately.

Eventually they made their way to the auditorium. Eliso saw Stone and made his way over to him with Beulah on his arm. The two men hugged. "Hey dude." Stone grinned at his friend, and Eliso introduced him to Beulah, who sized him up.

"Yep, you'll do," she said in her cockney accent and Stone laughed.

"Glad I come up to scratch. Listen, how come I've only just been introduced?"

Eliso looked sheepish. "Sorry, man, I know it's been too long. Time got away from me."

Stone grinned. "Come on, let's watch this thing, then we can start drinking."

"Yeah," Beulah said to Eliso, "I like this one."

They laughed and went to find their seats.

Stone sat down next to his friends and chatted with them until the lights went down. The director had just walked out onto the stage to introduce the movie when a commotion was heard at the door, and Sheila Maffey walked in, smiling, calling her apologies to the director who took the interruption in good grace.

Sheila waved and found her seat, and behind her, Stone saw a very red-faced Nan, trying to disappear into the floor. She looked up before she sat and met his gaze. Her color deepened, and she quickly sat down, out of his eye-line. Stone smiled to himself. He knew Sheila would be at the party after the movie and hoped her lovely companion would join her there. He would make sure to introduce himself properly this time.

That was easier said than done. Nan was clever enough to stay out of all limelight at the party. Frustrated, Stone searched the crowd for her, but couldn't see her anywhere. Beulah excused herself to use the restroom, and Stone looked on as Eliso gazed after her. He grinned at his friend. "You are in love."

Eliso nodded. "I don't deny it, man. I'm done, she's the one." He laughed, then studied his friend. "What about you?"

Stone shrugged. "There's a very beginning of something... I think. I don't know. I've never spoken one word to the girl I'm interested in."

Eliso's eyebrows shot up. "What's this? Stone Vanderberg has a crush?"

Stone snorted. "I wouldn't call it that—just an interest."

"Is she here?"

"Somewhere. She's with Sheila, a lawyer from the studio."

Eliso nodded. "Oh, the girl who looked like she was about to die from embarrassment?"

"That's the one."

Eliso nodded approvingly. "She's beautiful. Go for it, man. About time you found your Beulah."

Stone chuckled. "Yeah, I don't think it'll be quite that magical, but I like your optimism."

"It happens, man. 'The one.' It's a real thing."

"If you say so."

He finally spotted her just before midnight. Her long hair was down, and she'd kicked off her heels and was sitting outside on the balcony, hidden away behind a palm. Her eyes were closed, and she was leaning back against the cool stone. The night was much cooler now with a breeze picking up from the ocean. Stone tried not to notice how her nipples were hard and showing against her dark burgundy dress.

"Hi."

Her eyes flew open, and there was that beautiful blush again. "Hi."

Stone held his hand out. "Stone Vanderberg."

A slight smile. "I know who you are, Mr. Vanderberg." She stood up and shook his hand. God, she was tiny. "Nanouk Songbird."

"Hi, Nanouk. Beautiful name."

She nodded—she's obviously heard that before, and he cursed himself silently for his unoriginality. "I guess you knew who I was when you shut down Sheila's interview. Let me put your mind at rest. Off the record. All of it."

"Thank you, I appreciate that. Although, I'm sure if you were to write something supporting Sheila's campaign, she wouldn't mind."

Stone smiled. "And the studio?"

Nan didn't answer, only smirked, and Stone decided he liked this woman very much. She had a rebellious streak. "Are you enjoying the party?"

"To be honest, I've never enjoyed this part. Too many people."

"Where are you from?"

She laughed, and it lit up her face. "New York."

Stone looked bemused. "Too many people... here?"

"I know, I know, the irony. But at least in New York, they ignore you. Here, everyone is after something." She shuddered and for a moment, Stone saw the sadness return to her eyes. Nan cleared her throat and shook her head to dismiss whatever she was feeling. She studied him. "Actually, we have something in common."

"We do?"

"Oyster Bay."

Stone was entirely taken by surprise, and for some reason, he was delighted. "You're from there?"

Nan nodded. "I still live there."

Stone smiled. "I don't get back as much as I would like to. Maybe I should," he said, idly and waited for her reaction.

"Nan?"

Damn. Damn. Damn. Stone looked around to see Sheila bearing down on them. Was it his imagination or did Nan look a little annoyed at the interruption, too? In a flash, her expression was smoothed out into a friendly smile. "Hey, Sheila. Did you need something?"

"No, darling, I just wanted to say goodnight." Sheila eyed Stone. "Didn't I warn you away, Vanderberg?" She laughed aloud and kissed Nan's cheek. "Still, the night is young. Enjoy, both of you." She winked at Stone as she disappeared back into the party.

Nan's phone bleeped, and she sighed, checking it. "God, what now?" She mumbled and groaned. "Damn it." She looked at Stone, and he saw a little regret in her eyes. "Mr. Vanderberg, I'm sorry, you'll have to excuse me. It's still mid-afternoon in Los Angeles, and my boss wants to talk to me. It was nice to meet you."

"And you. And it's Stone, for the future."

She shook his hand, and he held onto her hand a beat too long. "...and you can call me Nan. Goodbye... Stone."

"Bye, Nan."

Her perfume, jasmine, wafted over him as she grabbed her shoes and passed him. He wanted to grab her hand, pull her into his arms, and kiss that beautiful mouth. Yup. He was enchanted. Nan Songbird was someone he wanted to get to know better, and he knew he wouldn't be satisfied until she was naked in his arms, in his bed, and crying out his name as he fucked her into paradise.

NAN WASN'T PAYING attention as she walked along the corridor to her hotel room. She was checking her text messages but hadn't read a single one properly. She was thinking of Stone Vanderberg's hand in hers, the feel of his skin on hers. The way he looked at her made her think dirty, dirty thoughts, and it taken all of her self-control not to press her body up to his masculine frame. God, the man was gorgeous.

She fumbled the key card, and as she bent to pick it up, she felt arms ago around her waist. "Yeah, baby, that's more like it."

Duggan. She struggled against his arms, but he held her

close, grabbing the key card and opening the door. He threw her in before slamming it closed behind him.

Survival instinct kicked in, and Nan scrambled across the room. Duggan was twice her size. "Get out!" she said firmly, but of course, he ignored her and came for her, hands clamping down onto her arms and dragging her toward the bedroom. As he yanked roughly at her dress, Nan felt the fabric rip. *No. This was not going to happen.*

With all her strength, she jammed her thumbs into Duggan's eyes, clamping her fingers around his head, digging her nails in as hard as she could. Duggan gave a roar of pain and tried to shake her hands off, but Nan, her face grim, locked them harder around him.

"Unless you want me to blind you, motherfucker, you will let me go! Right. Now."

Duggan's hands dropped. Pushing hard, Nan walked him backwards towards her door, not letting go. "Open the door, Duggan."

"I can't fucking see, bitch."

"Feel your way," she snarled, "You seem to be very handsy. *Feel* for the door handle, asshole."

Duggan got the door open, and Nan forced him into the hallway. As she released his head, he managed to punch her hard in the stomach. As she doubled over with a grunt and he lunged for her again, she heard shouting, and two huge jocks came bearing down and dragged Duggan away down the hall. A woman, apparently with the jocks, came to help her up. "Are you okay?" American.

Nan shook her head. "This asshole just tried to rape me."

Duggan was struggling, but even in his coked-up condition, he was no match for his captors. The other woman took Nan into her room and called down for the manager of the hotel.

After Duggan was taken away, and the hotel manager

finished apologizing profusely, Nan called her boss in Los Angeles and told him what had happened. He was appalled. "Nan, I cannot tell you how sorry I am." There was a pause. "Do you want to press charges?"

Nan sighed. She knew full well what Clive was asking. The studio would rather not have a scandal on its hands when its films were in competition. "No. But I want assurances Duggan will be dealt with, and I want to change hotels. I don't feel safe here."

Relieved, Clive told her he'd call her back, and within an hour, she was being moved to the Carlton and into the Grace Kelly suite. Nan was a little overwhelmed, but the hotel manager assured her all was well. "Miss Bellucci checked out of the suite this morning, Miss Songbird."

Nan wondered how much the studio had to lay down to get her this room and which A-lister got bumped. But she didn't care. Yes, they paid for her silence, but she was safe and far away from Duggan. Clive told her the man had been fired. "We take sexual assault very seriously, Nan. Anything else you need—just say the word."

Nan was happy just to be out of Duggan's reach. The Carlton had security out the wazoo because of the fleet of A-listers staying there. Her suite was incredible—more luxurious than Nan had ever experienced, but all she cared about was the freedom. She stepped out onto the balcony; at this hotel, the view was panoramic. She looked at her watch; it was almost four A.M. now, and she had to be up by seven to meet Sheila.

Nan felt utterly wrecked by exhaustion. She quickly showered, got her clothes ready for the morning, set an alarm, and then fell into bed and an uneasy sleep.

CHAPTER THREE

Stone couldn't get Nan Songbird out of his head. Damn Sheila for interrupting, and damn that phone call from her boss. They had been connecting, for Chrissakes, and without the interruptions, he would be waking up in this bed with a beautiful woman, instead of alone.

He told himself Nan was no different from the rest of the women he bedded. He couldn't get involved—not now.

But Nan was haunting him. Stone was determined he would have her before he left Cannes... it was just... he didn't know if he could forget her once he left. *Damn it, she's just another girl,* he told himself. He got out of bed and went to work out, pounding the treadmill hard, trying to get the excess tension out of him. His piece was coming together; he knew he could finish up today, then kickback for the last few days of the festival.

He met Eliso and Beulah for lunch downstairs in the Grand Salon and learned they were leaving the next day. "Eli's been at me to visit Italy with him...meet the parents. Scary." Beulah didn't look at all scared, and Eliso grinned at her.

"They're going to love you."

Stone smiled at the pair of lovebirds, but for a strange

moment, he felt lonely. He had avoided all attachments for so long that seeing his brother-in-arms, his wingman Eliso, so in love and deliriously happy, was a stark reminder than he, Stone, didn't have that. Had *never* had that.

He looked up as a movement caught his eye and saw Nan Songbird walk into the restaurant and look around with nervous uncertainty. Stone saw her hesitate, obviously trying to decide whether to stay or cut and run.

"Excuse me a moment." He got up and went over to her. He was gratified by the relief he saw in her eyes that she knew someone. "Hey, Nan, are you okay?"

She smiled at him. God, she was lovely. "I am, thank you. I've just... I've never been in this restaurant before."

"Well, would you like to join us?" He nodded back at the table where Eliso and Beulah were sitting. Beulah grinned at Nan, and Eliso put his hand up in greeting. Nan colored but smiled back at them.

"You're very kind, but no, I'm actually meeting a friend... and there he is. Late as usual." Nan smiled at Stone apologetically. "Thank you, though. It was good to see you again."

Stone touched her cheek with a fingertip. "You, too."

Nan smiled and colored slightly, before stepping away from him somewhat awkwardly.

He watched her walk over to a friendly looking man in a grey suit and hug him. Stone registered that a part of him felt a pang of jealousy even though he had no right, but he soon realized that, judging by the body language between Nan and her lunch companion, there was nothing to be envious of.

Stone went back to his table and to the questions from his friends. "That's your crush?" Beulah said, obviously enjoying Stone's discomfort. "She's gorgeous, mate, and she likes you, I can tell."

"You can tell from twenty feet away?" Eliso sneered at his girlfriend.

Beulah stuck her tongue out at him. "A *woman* can tell." She studied Stone, who was smiling to himself. "You like her."

"I don't know her, but, yeah," he admitted to Eliso's shocked expression and Beulah's victorious cackle, "She intrigues me."

"Yeah, I bet you'll end up 'intriguing' her, too—all day and night."

Stone grinned. "I adore you," he said to Beulah, "Run away with me."

"Just let me get rid of this old man."

Eliso shrugged good-naturedly. "I'll just say that Stone is older than me by fifteen days and leave it at that."

Beulah sighed dramatically. "Guess it'll have to come down to cock size then. Whip 'em out, boys."

Stone and Eliso both pretended to unzip, making Beulah break into raucous laughter. Nearby diners looked around in irritation, but when they saw the gorgeous woman laughing, they soon forgave the noisy table.

NAN SAT down with Raoul in the sunshine, grinning at him. "God, I missed you, Owl. All these damn actors and actresses... I need someone boring and dull like you."

"Oh, ha ha, you little bitch," Raoul grinned at his friend, knowing she was teasing him. "What's up with you? You've aged fifty years! Look at those crow's feet. And your bolt-ons have sagged bad, girl," he nodded at her perfectly perky and entirely natural breasts.

Nan giggled. She adored this man. She had met Raoul when they were in law school, and they quickly become inseparable. Raoul was her best friend, her confidante, her brother. He came from a long line of wealthy New York lawyers, and growing up, he hadn't even questioned his career path. In court, he was a ruthless defense lawyer, grilling witnesses until he broke them. Out of court, however, he was funny and kind. Always searching for Mr. Right, he despaired over Nan's 'tragic' love life. "If only I was straight, Nook."

"If only."

Now, though, he was grilling her about Stone. "So, you like him?"

Nan rolled her eyes. "Dude, I've spoken about six words to the man."

"Nook, don't lie to me. You have *horny* in your eyes. I haven't seen that look since we did that Keanu Reeves marathon at the Majestic back in college."

"That doesn't count," Nan said, deflecting his question. "There isn't a human alive that could resist Keanu."

"True story, but back to Wonderdong Vanderberg. I have heard he is *packing*, girl, so when in Cannes…"

"You are such a pimp. You ever thought about going into the sex trade?"

Raoul grinned. "If it meant you getting laid…" His smile disappeared. "Nook?"

Nan was pale, and she started to tremble. Raoul looked in the direction she was staring. A man was gazing at her, and his expression was anything but friendly. As they watched, he narrowed his eyes at her before turning on his heel and walking off.

"Who the hell was that?"

Nan smiled a brittle grimace. "Duggan Smollett. He's from the studio." She looked down at her hands. "He tried to rape me last night."

"What the fuck?" Instantly, Raoul was furious and halfway out of his chair before Nan dragged him back down.

"I dealt with it, Owl. Sit down. People are staring."

Raoul didn't look happy. "So that explains the Grace Kelly suite. The studio?"

"Yep. Look, it's okay with me. Dealing with the police will just create more of a nuisance, and I can do without that."

Raoul sighed. "God, Nan..."

"I know. Let's change the subject, huh? How's your dad?"

"He's good. In fact, I'm here as a double agent."

Nan grinned at him. "And here I was thinking you were just here to stalk Chris Hemsworth."

"Oh, well, that too, *obviously*," Raoul laughed. He leaned forward, eyes shining. "But even better... Sarah Lund is retiring from Dad's firm in the next six months. He has an opening for a junior partner."

"And Sarah Lund is a..."

"Criminal lawyer. Defense. Interested?"

Nan was elated. "Are you kidding? Of course! Jeez, Raoul... is your dad sure? I mean, I have very little experience in criminal law, but hell, that's what I've wanted to do since I graduated."

"I know, and so does he. He'll have you work side-by-side with him at first to get the experience you need, or as he says, mostly for your own confidence. He believes in you, Nook. We both do."

Nan felt close to tears. Alan Elizondo was one of New York's most successful and well-regarded defense attorneys. He ran a tight ship with a close cohort of hand-picked attorneys and very few chances for young lawyers to break in. That he wanted *her*...

"God, Raoul, I don't know what to say."

Raoul grinned. "Yeah, you do. Say yes. This is what you've wanted. Out of the entertainment business and into criminal law. Congrats, Nook, you deserve it."

NAN WAS STILL on a high later as she met up with Sheila and

went through her schedule for the next few days. Sheila noticed the younger woman's good mood and asked her about it. Nan explained about the job.

"Well, I'll miss you, but I know this is what you wanted, Nan. I'm very happy for you." She hugged Nan. "Just promise we'll stay friends."

"Always," Nan told her with a smile. She stayed for tea with Sheila, and when Sheila went to her next appointment, Nan returned to the Carlton and headed to the elevator. A couple of hours sleep, then maybe a light supper and walk along the waterfront? If she milled in with the crowds, she would feel safer. It was her night off, and she was determined that the thought of Duggan Smollett wouldn't ruin it.

She had just pressed the button for her floor when the elevator door opened again and Stone Vanderberg stepped in. Her heart began to thump hard against her chest. "Hey."

"Hello again. We keep running into each other." God, even his voice made her sex pulse with desire.

"We do. Thank you for your invitation earlier—it was very kind."

"My pleasure." His eyes were intense fixed on hers. "Did you have a good lunch?"

"Very, thanks."

The tension was unbearable. Nan's breath began to quicken. They gazed at each other, and then Stone stepped closer to her and bent his head down toward hers. His mouth was only an inch from hers when the elevator doors opened again and a raft of people, chatting and talking, poured in. The press of the crowd herded Nan and Stone against the back wall of the elevator. With his body pressed against hers and his navy-blue eyes locked on her, Nan couldn't look away. He could have done anything to her, but what he did do made her heart skip a beat.

He took her hand. Linking his fingers in hers, he didn't try to do anything else. He didn't press his groin against hers and any of countless things many other men would have tried—and *had* tried with Nan in an enclosed space. Stone Vanderberg took her hand and *held* it and Nan was lost.

It seemed impossible that, when the elevator stopped on the seventh floor, they wouldn't end up in the same suite. The elevator emptied out and, still holding her hand, Stone led her down the hallway. Nan walked as if in a dream, a dream broken only seconds later by a voice calling her name.

No. No, go away... "Miss Songbird? Miss Songbird? I have an urgent message for you from Miss Maffey."

Nan and Stone stopped, and Nan could have screamed. Stone didn't look happy either as the bellhop handed her a message and left. Nan read the note and sighed. She looked up at Stone. "Sheila got nabbed for an impromptu interview by Jay McInerney. She wants me there. I'm so sorry."

Stone smiled down at her... *God, his smile...* and he cupped her cheek in his hand. "No problem. Dinner, later?"

Nan nodded. "How about I meet you at this restaurant?" She showed him the note.

"The *Rue du Suquet*? Perfect." He stroked her cheek, seeming to hesitate. "I want to kiss you so badly, Nan Songbird, but I think if I do, I won't be able to stop myself from... and I don't want to get you fired."

Nan laughed softly. "Anticipation, Stone Vanderberg."

"Anticipation. Ten P.M?"

"Until then."

SHE WAS STILL SMILING, and her body seemed to burn with excitement as she took a cab to the *Rue du Suquet*. She walked into the restaurant and asked for Sheila. The maître d' looked confused. "Is Ms. Maffey here? Please wait a moment, Mademoiselle."

He returned a moment later. "I'm sorry, Mademoiselle. Ms. Maffey isn't here."

Nan frowned and pulled the note from her purse, checking it again. She looked apologetically at the man. "I'm sorry, maybe the booking is under Mr. McInerney? Jay McInerney?"

The man looked embarrassed. "No, I'm sorry."

Nan nodded, her face burning. *What the hell?* "No matter. I'm sorry to bother you. Listen... while I'm here, do you have a reservation for ten P.M. available?"

The maître d' looked uncertain, and Nan, feeling guilty, decided to use the only tool at her disposal. "It's for Mr. Vanderberg. Stone Vanderberg."

The maître d's expression cleared, and he smiled. "Of course, an old friend. Table for?"

"Two, please. A private booth if one is available." If she was going to name drop, she was going to go all the way.

"Of course." The maître d' was looking at her with more respect now, and Nan smothered a laugh. Oh, the life of a billionaire. She didn't think Stone would mind.

Nan checked her watch. It was almost nine P.M. Mentally cursing herself for not taking Stone's cell phone number, she went across the street to another bar and called Sheila. Voicemail. She shook her head. *What the hell was going on?*

Nan sighed. Well, she had time for a drink and to relax before her date with Stone. She ordered a martini and sat down.

STONE WAS STILL SMILING to himself as he went down to the bar in the Carlton. As he sat at the bar, he recognized Nan's lunch date already seated there and introduced himself. Raoul Elizondo smiled at him.

"Good to meet you, Mr. Vanderberg."

"Stone, please, and likewise. We have a friend in common."

Raoul nodded, his merry eyes dancing. "Ah."

Stone grinned. "Is it that obvious?"

"That you like our Nanouk? Yes, but I think it may be mutual."

"Sorry if I seem presumptuous."

"You don't, and I'm all for it. Nan and myself have been friends since college, and this is the first time I've noticed that particular gleam in her eye. Sorry," Raoul laughed when Stone's eyebrows shot up, "I'm not one for beating around the bush, so to speak. You like her, she likes you—a done deal. Just don't hurt her, blah, blah."

Stone decided he liked this man very much. "Nan has good taste in friends."

Raoul raised his glass. "Thank you." His smile faltered a little. "I'm just thankful that, well, someone will look out for her. I have to leave in the morning, and with that Smollett guy still hanging around..."

Stone's heart gave a lurch. "Who?"

Raoul hesitated. "She'll probably kill me for telling you this..." He told Stone about Smollett's attempted rape of Nan. "He was fired by the studio, and I'm worried he'll take it out on her."

Jesus. "She didn't mention it, but then, really, we just met. But I'll look out for her, don't worry."

"Sorry to dump."

"Seriously, man, I'm glad you told me. I..." Stone trailed off as he saw Sheila Maffey walk into the bar. For a second, he waited for Nan to follow her, and as Sheila saw him and walked over, his heart began to beat a little faster. Unease crept over him. "Hey, Sheila... did Nan catch up with you?"

Sheila blinked. "Nan? No. Why?"

Realization crashed into Stone's mind, and he cursed out loud, standing up. His reaction unnerved Raoul, who realized something was wrong. "What is it?"

"Nan was told to come meet you at a restaurant at *Rue du Suquet*. I think she's being set up."

"Oh, no! By Smollett?"

"He wants to get her on her own."

"Jesus… let's go."

CHAPTER FOUR

Nan didn't notice the text messages blinking on her phone until she walked back out on the street. As she walked past the entrance to an alleyway, strong arms reached out and grabbed her, a hand clamping over her mouth. "Say one word or scream and I'll gut you right here, bitch."

Oh God no... Duggan. He dragged her backwards down the darkened alleyway, stopping behind a dumpster and slamming her against the wall. Terrified, Nan's body shut down, and she couldn't breathe. She could feel something pressing against her belly—a weapon? Duggan's face was red with anger. "You got me fired."

Nan swallowed hard. "*You* got you fired, Duggan. You're lucky I didn't call the police."

He laughed in her face. "Hard to testify when you're dead, pretty girl."

Now she felt the sharp tip of the knife he was pressing against her. "You kill me, you go to jail forever. Plenty of people know what you did to me, Duggan."

"Like they're going to think this isn't just a thrill kill. Beautiful girl on her own, found raped, robbed and stabbed to death?

There's one a week, baby girl, and they won't even bother to look into your murder."

"You really going to kill me, Duggan? You want that to be your legacy?" The knife was really cutting into her skin now, tearing through the fabric of her white dress. He would only have to apply a little more pressure and it would sink deep into her soft, vulnerable flesh.

For a long moment, time stopped, and then he smiled. "Yes, I really do. Bye bye, beautiful."

Nan closed her eyes and waited to die.

Then she gasped as the knife was ripped away from her, and she opened her eyes to see Stone Vanderberg pick Duggan up and smash him to the ground, pummeling the man. Sheila and Raoul were close behind him, Sheila going to Nan and wrapping her arms around her. Raoul helped Stone drag Duggan toward the street as a couple of gendarmes came running.

AFTER NAN WAS QUESTIONED for hours, they finally allowed her to go get checked out at a hospital. She objected but Stone, Sheila, and Raoul all insisted. Duggan was arrested. "He doesn't see the light of day," Stone had sternly ordered the police sergeant.

Eventually, as dawn broke, all four went back to the Carlton. Word had spread about the attempted murder, and Nan found the stares of the hotel staff intrusive and upsetting. Sheila kissed her cheek. "Baby girl, rest. Call me when you're ready. I'm so, so sorry."

Nan saw Stone and Raoul exchange a loaded glance, and Raoul came to hug her. "My flight is in a couple of hours, but I can cancel."

"No, please, I'm fine," she said but hugged him hard. She heard him give a little sob.

"I'm so sorry, Nook."

She knew he was devastated about what happened. He had known how Etta's rape and suicide had scarred her, and now that this had happened, Nan knew Raoul would dwell on it. "Owl, I'm okay, I promise."

He studied her, then nodded at Stone. "Don't be too much of a feminist to not let Mr. Vanderberg look out after you."

Nan chuckled. "Still matchmaking."

"Always. I love you, Nook."

"Love you, too, Owl."

FINALLY, alone in her suite, they sat together on the couch. Nan smiled at Stone. "This was a really strange way of getting to know each other."

Stone grinned. "I'm just glad you're okay." He looked down at her dress, and his smile faded. There was a patch of blood that had seeped from the tiny cut Duggan's knife made. "My God."

Nan flushed and covered the spot with her hand. "I'm okay."

Stone gazed at her in silence for a long moment, then he slowly leaned in and pressed his lips to hers. The kiss was soft and brief, but it left her lips tingling. "Stone?"

"Yes, baby?"

She stroked his face. "How about we take this dress off and throw it in the trash?"

His smile was wide. "I like that idea." He got up and offered her his hand, which she took, standing up to meet him. He drew her into his arms and kissed her, his fingers gently drawing the zipper on the back of her dress down, tantalizingly slow, until she was desperate for him to rip the dress from her.

But he knew what he was doing—that was clear enough. Slowly, he slipped the dress from her shoulders, trailing his lips along her throat to her shoulder, then as he drew the dress down lower, he freed her breast from the lacy cup of her bra and took her nipple in his mouth. Nan gasped and caught her bottom lip in her teeth as his tongue flicked around the small nub. His hands were on her waist, stroking the soft skin, before his fingers tightened firmly onto her flesh as he pulled her closer, his desire becoming animal.

Nan could have screamed when his mouth left her nipple, but, grinning, Stone swept her up into his arms and carried her to the bedroom. "God, you're a beautiful woman," he murmured as he pulled her dress off and laid her down. His fingers snagged the sides of her panties as he swiftly drew them down her legs, and then he was hitching her legs over his shoulders. The second his tongue lashed around her clit, Nan knew that this was going to be the most erotic night of her life. Stone teased and flicked his tongue so expertly, that when he finally plunged his tongue deep into her cunt, Nan cried out and came almost immediately, shivering and trembling, all control lost.

Stone's lips found her mouth as she was tearing at his shirt, desperate to run her hands over his hard body. The thickly muscled arms and shoulders she revealed were powerful and rock hard.

Nan took his nipple into her mouth and worked her tongue around it, pleased when she heard his groan of arousal. Stone expertly kicked off his pants and underwear, and Nan stroked his huge, thick cock against her belly. His eyes were soft. "I've been thinking about this for so long..."

"I want you inside me," Nan whispered, her shyness overwhelmed by her desire for him, and he nodded. He reached down to his pants, pulling a condom out of his back pocket. Nan grinned.

"Why do I think you're always prepared?"

Stone chuckled, and she was glad he was good-humored during sex—there was nothing worse than a po-faced lover.

But Stone was anything but stone-faced. He smiled down at her, brushing his lips over hers. "Nanouk...." He thrust into her, and she gave a sharp intake of breath as he filled her entirely.

She moaned with pleasure, and Stone gathered her to him as they moved together. "Wrap your legs around me, beautiful. Let me in deeper."

She obeyed him, tilting her hips up to meet his, squeezing her thighs around his waist as they fucked. Stone kissed her, pouring every bit of desire he felt into his kiss. The way his eyes held hers made Nan feel like the most beautiful thing in the world at that moment.

Their bodies fit together perfectly, despite the difference in height. Her belly pressed against his; her breasts crushed against his rock-hard chest. His cock, thick, long and powerful reamed into her swollen, sensitive cunt, and Nan cried out as her orgasm hit, arching her back. Stone groaned and came, too, his lips against her throat, his cock pumping hard.

They collapsed back on the bed together, and Stone quickly and gently excused himself to deal with the used condom. Nan tried to catch her breath, her body feeling strange as if it wasn't hers. Stone returned and lay down beside her, drawing her close. Nan nuzzled close to his immense size and warmth. In his arms, she felt safe, she realized—something she hadn't felt for a long time.

"Are you okay?" Stone asked, his voice tender, and she smiled up at him.

"More than okay... that was incredible."

He chuckled. "Yes, it was..." They gazed at each other for a long time, then Stone pressed his lips to hers. "Nan Songbird... do you get into Manhattan often? For reasons other than work, I mean."

Nan smiled. "You don't have to do that, Stone. I know the

rules men like you play by, and it's okay. I'm not asking for anything from you than this moment here."

Stone blinked. "I meant what I said... I'd like to see you again."

She studied his expression—he seemed genuine, and a flush of pleasure ran through her. "Really?"

His chuckle was soft. "Really. I know my reputation, Nan, and believe me, I've more than lived up to it. But... this feels different. Don't you feel that, too?"

Slowly she nodded. "I do... but then I don't have a great deal to compare it with."

Stone looked confused. "What do you mean?"

Nan said nothing but held his gaze, watching understanding —and then shock—creep into his expression.

"No *way*," he said softly.

It was her turn to laugh. "Yes, *way*. I was a virgin."

"Holy fuck."

Her mouth hitched up in a grin. "Well, it was kind of biblical, yes." Stone laughed, but his eyes still registered confusion.

"No, seriously, Nan. You were a virgin?"

"I know, in this day and age, it's crazy. But I never felt the urge to make love to anyone before now. I guess that's kind of fucked up—I'm twenty-eight years old, but things happened when I was younger. My sister was raped. It had an effect." Nan had no idea why she was telling this man all of this, but she wanted him to understand her: why she had held back on losing her virginity and why she had finally chosen the person to give it to. She felt anxiety for the first time as she waited for his reply.

"Sweet Nan... my God, you're just... unique," Stone shook his head, and she felt his arms tighten around her. "Thank you for the honor... God, that sounds weird, but I mean it."

She smiled at him. "But it doesn't mean you owe me anything. That's what I'm getting at. I know the way the world works, and how someone powerful and desirable works. I'm not a little girl."

"Nanouk Songbird, can I get a word in?" Stone was laughing now, and she had to giggle at his expression.

"Sure, sorry."

"For one thing, stop apologizing. For another... can we just see where this goes? For once in my life, I have a woman in my arms who, for want of a better word, isn't interested in *Stone Vanderberg*—his money, position, society, or any of that bullshit. I knew that about you the first time I saw you, and you shut down Sheila's interview. You had my number, and I cannot tell you how thrilling that is to me. You're a challenge, and God knows, I need that in my life. For years, I admit—I've screwed my way around the globe and had a fantastic time doing it. Beautiful women are two-a-penny, Nan, although they pale in comparison to you."

Nan flushed at the compliment. "But?"

"But none of them have had the potential to be more than a fuck-buddy," he said, honestly. "But with you... there's a possibility I've found something extra, something I didn't know I was looking for until now."

Nan's emotions were in turmoil. "What? What are you looking for?"

Stone's handsome face was soft. "A best friend," he said simply, and Nan's eyes filled with tears.

"Really?"

Stone nodded, drawing her closer and kissing her. "Really." And they began to make love again.

CHAPTER FIVE

A week later and the film festival was coming to a close. Sheila Maffey had taken home the Best Actress award and was throwing a party for her fellow cast and crew. She had insisted on Nan inviting Stone and Nan being off duty for the night.

"Have a relaxing time, darling. You've been my rock here—you really have." Sheila nodded toward Stone who was talking to some of the crew. "And Stone Vanderberg is crazy about you, that's obvious."

Nan had flushed, but she had to admit—it really did seem like Stone was happy. He looked up now; his gaze going directly over to her and leaving her with a wink. He was so tall that he towered over most of the other guests. *My lover, my friend.* The past week had passed in a delirious whirl of love-making and talking and laughing, and now she couldn't imagine a time when she hadn't known this man.

Tomorrow, after the Festival closed, Stone intended to take her to his private villa in Antibes. He had persuaded Nan to take a week's vacation. "Just so we can really have some time to ourselves before we get back to our real lives—we can figure out how to make this work."

Nan had said yes without hesitating. As the party drew to a close, Stone appeared back by her side and took her hand. "Shall we?"

HER HEART WAS POUNDING as they drove through the night, the top of Stone's rented Mercedes down. Nan let her long hair fly free, and Stone grinned at her as she tried to control it. Nan gave up in the end, and by the time Stone parked the car outside the villa, her hair was a mess of tangled waves. "Shot," Nan said, trying to tame it. "How come in the movies that's supposed to be sexy and yet in real life, I just end up looking like a Wookie?"

Stone burst out laughing. "Yeah, but, *sexy* Wookie."

Nan grinned. She had discovered that Stone shared the same goofy sense of humor as her—something she would never have expected. His outward appearance was so together, sometime even severe in his masculinity, that Nan was surprised when he could be as kid-like and silly as she was. There was a twelve-year age gap, but she never felt it once.

Now, he took her hand as they entered the warmly lit villa. "Are there other people here?"

Stone shook his head. "I asked the staff to prepare the house but other than that... it's just the two of us." His voice had dropped to a sensual purr and Nan shivered with anticipation.

"So, you have me all alone for a week."

"What *shall* we do?" Stone grinned as he drew her into his arms. Nan pressed her body against his.

"I can think of a few things..."

With a growl, he swept her up into his arms and carried her as she giggled furiously into the villa. They didn't make it as far as the bedroom before they were ripping each other's clothes off.

They made love on the cool tile floor, ignoring the hard ground as they fucked with abandon.

THE NEXT MORNING, Nan slowly woke, laying on her stomach, feeling Stone's fingertips drawing up and down her spine. She opened her eyes and smiled at him. His delicious navy eyes were soft with adoration. "Waking up with you, Nan Songbird, is the perfect way to begin a day."

"Right back at you, handsome." Nan couldn't believe how comfortable she was with this man—this man whose family and status were so far above her own humble background.

But here, in this Mediterranean paradise, she could pretend that they were just two people enjoying a passionate, fun affair, and that the outside world or their lives had no bearing on it.

The sex was incredible. Stone was a tender but masterful lover, and he made Nan curious to be more adventurous. When she told him that, Stone smiled. "We can be as adventurous as you like, baby."

After dinner one night in the old town, Stone led her down the old stone streets of the city, and he fucked her against a stone wall down a dark side alley as people passed by the street end, his hand over her mouth to stifle her cries of pleasure. The thrill of almost being caught infected her, and Nan knew she would be open to trying anything with this man. She didn't want to think about going back to the States and have the real world intrude into her little bubble.

It wasn't just the sex either. They talked about their families. Stone told her about his brother Ted, who managed Eliso's career as well as other major movie stars and his parents who were loving but kept themselves to themselves in their Oyster Bay mansion.

"Are you and Ted close?"

Stone nodded. "We are—the best of friends. We had a sister, Janie. She died when she was only five."

"Oh God, how awful, I'm so sorry. Was she sick?"

Stone shook his head. "She drowned in the ocean next to our property. Ted was with her. I don't think he's ever forgiven himself, even though he was only a kid himself."

"Poor thing." Nan sighed. "So much pain."

"You mentioned your sister."

Nan nodded. "Etta was everything to me and when she died..."

"I know." Stone cupped her cheek in his hand. "You're not alone anymore."

Nan swallowed hard and looked away. "Don't promise anything, Stone. I just ask that. Don't promise anything."

THEY TALKED ABOUT THEIR DREAMS. Stone and Nan shared a love for their respective jobs. "When I go back to New York," Nan told him, "I'm finally going to be able to work in the criminal law realm. I'm so excited—I can't even tell you."

Stone grinned at her. "I can tell. What is it about criminal law?"

"I like puzzles, especially when it comes to human motivation," she said, honestly. "I think it stems from my sister's suicide, to be honest...the thought processes behind people's actions."

"But you'll be working for a defense lawyer?"

Nan nodded. "The experience will be invaluable, and Alan is taking a risk taking on someone like me. So, eventually, yeah, I'd like to prosecute and get rapists off the street, but it's always useful to see the other side of it, too."

Stone studied her. "Playing devil's advocate...?"

Nan smiled. "Go on."

"How do you not let Etta's situation color your attitude to the defendants?"

Nan sat up. "That is a very good question, and I've asked myself that over and over. If I ever thought I couldn't put my personal feelings aside, I would recuse myself from the case."

Stone nodded but stayed silent. Nan studied his expression. "You don't think I could do it?"

"I would never say you were incapable of anything. I just can see how passionate you are about things."

Nan grinned and wriggled into his arms. "You're biased."

Stone kissed her, tightening his arms around her. "I admit I am."

"So, you know about my Achilles' heel… what's yours?"

Stone hesitated. "You really want to know?"

"Of course."

He drew in a deep breath. "Kids."

"Kids?"

He nodded. "It's probably why I've gotten to forty and never been married. Kids. I don't want them. Seeing my parent's grief after Janie died… it's that thing that terrifies me—losing something, or someone, I loved again."

Nan was a little shocked. "Stone, we all lose people."

"I know, and I also know it's foolish to try to minimize personal loss. I'm reconciled to the fact that my parents will die and my brother someday. It's the reason I've never gotten close to someone."

Nan nodded but was quiet for a long time after. It hurt to think that yes, this little period of time with Stone was temporary, but they had both known that, hadn't they? It hurt to hear it out loud though.

STONE NOTICED Nan was quieter after their talk and wondered if he had hurt her feelings. At dinner, over Stone's signature pan-seared sirloin and salad on the terrace of the villa, he took her hand. "What I said, Nan... I didn't mean *us*. Although I don't know what 'us' means at this point."

"Let's just enjoy this week," she said, smiling at him. "We said no promises."

"We did. But I would like to see where this goes. I understand if you have reservations. There's a significant age gap between us, after all."

"That's not an issue, but... God, I don't know, Stone. I'm new to all of this. I don't know how to do it." Nan looked away from him, and he was horrified to see tears in her eyes.

"Hey, hey, hey," he said softly, stroking her hair. "Don't cry, baby, it's okay. Let's just enjoy ourselves these last few days."

LATER, as she lay naked in his bed, Stone took her hand and turned it palm-side up, then kissed the inside of her wrist softly. "Nanouk Songbird, you have enchanted me." He trailed his lips up her arm, along her shoulder to her throat. Nan wrapped her legs around his hips, gazing up at him, as his mouth found hers.

His dark eyes crinkled at the edges as he smiled down at her, and his cock plunged deep inside her. Would she ever get enough of this man? His big, powerful body dominated hers so entirely when they were fucking, and she knew, to her regret, that she would never get a better man in her bed. *Oh, damn it, oh damn it.* Nan knew she was falling for him and the thought terrified her. She knew, once they were out of their Antibes bubble, every small difference in their lives would begin to create cracks —and the thought of it made her chest hurt.

No. Focus. Focus on these few days and make them the best days of your life.

So, they swam in the warm ocean, explored the old town, ate

at incredible restaurants, went dancing in sultry nightclubs and made love endlessly. Stone made her laugh constantly. The sight of this huge mountain of a man goofing off like a teenager warmed her heart and made it even harder to contemplate the end of their fling.

IT WAS the eve of their last day, and they had returned from a day trip to Monaco, exhausted and hungry. They grabbed dinner at a small café in the old town, and then walked slowly back to the villa. Both of them were quiet, their fingers entwined, knowing that soon, they would be flying back to New York and their real lives.

In the bedroom Stone left the light off, a full moon casting an ethereal cast into the room. He pulled slowly at the belt of her dress and peeled it from her shoulders, wanting to look at Nan in the moonlight. Her soft beauty killed him: her large chocolaty brown eyes gazing up at him, the soft blush of her caramel skin. "There isn't a more beautiful sight in the world than you, Nan Songbird, at this moment."

She blinked slowly at him, her mouth curving up in a shy smile, but she remained silent. He freed her breasts from her bra and drew her panties down her legs. For such a petite woman, her legs went on for days, shapely and toned. Stone drew his fingers down her belly, splaying his fingers out over the soft curve of it. He dropped to his knees and buried his face in it, his tongue tracing a pattern around her deep navel.

He felt her tremble as his fingers trailed up her inner thigh, stopping before they touched her hot sex. He teased her, stroking every part of her, but never touching her groin. Stone gazed up at her. "Open these beautiful legs for me, my darling."

Nan shivered as she obeyed him, and he grinned. "I have an idea. Do you trust me?"

She nodded, and he stood, scooping her up and carrying her into the kitchen before sitting her down on a wooden chair. "Wait here."

In the bedroom he snagged a couple of his neck ties and took them back to the kitchen. "You want to stop, just say it," he told her as he wound the tie around her eyes, then bound her hands behind her. "This is supposed to be fun, to be exciting, but if you get scared..."

"I won't." Nan grinned and spread her legs slowly and he could see how excited, how wet she was for him. Stone smiled. He knelt down and licked her cunt, making her shiver. "That's just a tiny preview, baby."

Stone grabbed an ice cube, and putting it in his mouth, trailed it from her throat down to her navel. Two fingers on his left hand slid inside her slick cunt as his thumb stroked a rhythm on her clit. With the ice cube on his tongue, he took each of her nipples into his mouth in turn and teased each nubbin until Nan was writhing on the chair, the pleasure clearly almost unbearable. Her sex flooded with moisture, soaking his hand, and Stone felt triumphant. He trailed the ice cube down her stomach again and circled it around her navel, then downward, licking it into her sex as she moaned her excitement.

Her clit reacted to his tongue, hardening and pulsing with desire. The ice cube melted quickly, and he buried his face in her sex, his tongue plunging deep inside in quick, sharp jabs until Nan cried out, coming, her entire body trembling and drenched in sweat.

Stone smiled and moved up to kiss her mouth. "Can you taste yourself on me, beauty? You taste like honey." He kissed her thoroughly, his tongue lashing around hers. "Nan?"

"Yes?" She was breathless, utterly under his control.

"I'm going to fuck you until you weep, pretty girl."

She moaned, and it was such a magical sound to him that he

was desperate to be inside her. He unzipped and freed his cock, straining and throbbing, and quickly releasing her hands, he tumbled her, still blindfolded, to the floor. Nan giggled then gasped as he thrust into her hard, his hands pinning hers to the carpet, his powerful legs spreading hers wide, his thighs heavy on hers. "Tell me you're mine, Nanouk Songbird..."

"I'm yours," she whispered, her voice breaking a little, "I'm yours, Stone..."

Stone slammed his hips harder and harder against hers, making her cunt pulse and convulse around his cock. Their breath mingled, their kisses wet and animalistic, hungry for each other.

Nan could feel an explosive orgasm building, every cell in her body on fire and when it hit her, it felt as if she would die, completely taken out of her own body and soaring into the heavens. Stone was relentless even as she cried out. He tore the blindfold from her eyes, and she gazed into his navy eyes, which seemed black, full of desire and danger.

I could die right here, she thought, *and it would be okay with me.* The passion she felt and the feral desire in his eyes frightened her a little. The force of her feelings for this man scared her.

"You drive me crazy," Stone growled at her as he too came, his cock spasming as it pumped out his cum. Nanouk felt the power of it releasing inside her—did the condom break?

She saw in Stone's eyes that he was thinking the same thing. "It's okay," she said softly, "I'm on birth control."

The relief she saw in his eyes gave her a strange pain that she couldn't understand. He kissed her tenderly now as if she were the most precious woman he had ever held in his arms, and she knew that couldn't be true.

As he gathered her into his warm embrace, her head against his hard chest, Nan suddenly felt tearful. This was all illusion—

a beautiful illusion, yes—but there was no way it would survive outside this week.

Just enjoy it, don't dwell. But she felt as if she could cry and never stop. *Fuck.* Wasn't this feeling what she had run away from all her life? And all in less than a week, she had destroyed her peace of mind for what? She looked up into the eyes of the man she had given herself to and felt a rising panic. *I'm lost,* she thought, and *it's going to hurt like hell to say goodbye.* Stone was watching her, his eyes curious, seeing her turmoil.

"What is it, baby?" His voice was soft, full of love, of compassion, but she just shook her head.

"Nothing. Just hold me, please."

STONE WAITED until Nan had fallen into a fitful sleep, and then slipped from the bed, standing at the end of it for a second to watch her sleep. He didn't want to think about tomorrow, but his life was way too complicated for him to ask her to share it. Nanouk deserved better than a part-time lover, and Stone knew as well, that he too had to step away before he fell too deep.

Because Nanouk would be very easy to fall in love with—very, *very* easy—Stone told himself fiercely that he wasn't in love already, but he knew it to be a lie, and he couldn't handle it. What if he hurt her? She was too good for him—he knew that. She deserved a protector, a champion, an equal, and Stone Vanderberg, for the first time in his life, knew he wasn't enough for her.

God, the thought of not being able to see her, touch her, make love to her after today was killing him, and that's why he knew he had to end things. They had promised each other until tomorrow, and as much as it would hurt, he would keep to that.

He went into the kitchen and grabbed a glass of ice cold

water for his parched throat. Stone closed his eyes. *Don't fall for her, but don't waste a single second that she could be in your arms.*

He went back to bed and gathered her into his arms. Nan opened her dark brown eyes and smiled at him sleepily, and slowly they began to make love, knowing it may be the last time.

In the morning, he woke, and Nan was gone.

If you want to continue reading this story, you can get your copy from your favorite vendor by searching for the title:

Please Me

Desired by the Billionaire (Lover Boys Romance)

You can also find the e-book version by typing this link in your computer's browser:

https://www.hotandsteamyromance.com/products/please-me-desired-by-the-billionaire

OTHER BOOKS BY THIS AUTHOR

Other Books By This Author
Saving Her Rescuer: A Billionaire & A Virgin Romance

I was just trying to get away from my crazy ex for the weekend when I ended up in a giant pileup on the highway up to Gore Mountain.

HTTPS://GENI.US/SAVINGHERRESCUER

∽

Sensual Sounds: A Rockstar Ménage

Lust. Lies. Double lives.

. . .

The rock and roll industry is full of people who are looking out for themselves and willing to do anything to rise to the top.

https://www.hotandsteamyromance.com/collections/frontpage/products/sensual-sounds-a-rockstar-menage

∽

On the Run: A Secret Baby Romance

Murder. Lies. Fraud. Just another day in the lives of billionaires and women on the run.

https://www.hotandsteamyromance.com/collections/frontpage/products/on-the-run-a-secret-baby-romance

∽

The Dirty Doctor's Touch: A Billionaire Doctor Romance

I am a master. An elitist. I am at the top of my field, and I know what I am doing.

https://www.hotandsteamyromance.com/collections/frontpage/products/the-dirty-doctor-s-touch-a-billionaire-doctor-romance

THE HERO SHE NEEDS: A Single Daddy Next Door Romance

HE'S the only man I've ever wanted...

HTTPS://WWW.HOTANDSTEAMYROMANCE.COM/COLLECTIONS/ FRONTPAGE/PRODUCTS/THE-HERO-SHE-NEEDS-A-SINGLE-DADDY- NEXT-DOOR-ROMANCE

YOU CAN FIND all of my books here

HOT AND STEAMY Romance
https://www.hotandsteamyromance.com

ABOUT THE AUTHOR

Mrs. Love writes about smart, sexy women and the hot alpha billionaires who love them. She has found her own happily ever after with her dream husband and adorable 6 and 2 year old kids.
Currently, Michelle is hard at work on the next book in the series, and trying to stay off the Internet.
"Thank you for supporting an indie author. Anything you can do, whether it be writing a review, or even simply telling a fellow reader that you enjoyed this. Thanks

Facebook

facebook.com/HotAndSteamyRomance

COPYRIGHT

©Copyright 2020 by Michelle Love - All rights Reserved

In no way is it legal to reproduce, duplicate, or transmit any part of this document in either electronic means or in printed format. Recording of this publication is strictly prohibited and any storage of this document is not allowed unless with written permission from the publisher. All rights are reserved.

Respective authors own all copyrights not held by the publisher.

www.ingramcontent.com/pod-product-compliance
Lightning Source LLC
LaVergne TN
LVHW021656060526
838200LV00050B/2374